DEKALB
PUBLIC LIBRARY
DE KALB, IL 60115

P9-DEP-906

THE IRISHMAN'S HORSE

ALSO BY MICHAEL COLLINS

Red Rosa
Minnesota Strip
Freak
The Slasher
The Nightrunners
The Blood-Red Dream
Blue Death
The Silent Scream
Shadow of a Tiger
Walk a Black Wind
Night of the Toads
The Brass Rainbow
Act of Fear
Castrato
Chasing Eights

THE IRISHMAN'S HORSE

A NOVEL BY

MICHAEL COLLINS

DONALD I. FINE, INC.
NEW YORK

Library of Congress Cataloging-in-Publication Data

Collins, Michael, 1924–
The Irishman's horse : a novel / by Michael Collins.
p. cm.
ISBN: 1–55611-185-1
I. Title.
PS3562.Y4417 1991
813′.54—dc20 90-55093
CIP

Manufactured in the United States of America

10 9 8 7 6 5 4 3 2 1

Designed by Irving Perkins Associates

For Paul Stone
and the future

THE MAJOR

I don't like human nature, I do like human beings.

—Ellen Glasgow

1

The body lay on the floor of the warehouse, a silent no-man's land in the shadows of the single overhead light between me and the tall man.

He was tall and dark haired. The man I'd been watching all night, not the dead man. The dead man on the floor of the dim warehouse was short. A heavy-set, barrel-chested corpse in a pool of blood. The blood had not yet darkened around the dead man's beige silk jacket, expensive cocoa-brown slacks, tasseled brown shoes on small feet splayed at a grotesque angle. A gold watch on his wrist caught the thin light. An expensive watch.

The tall man's voice was cool. "I don't know who you are, mister, or what you're doing, but hear this loud and hear it clear—forget anything and everything you think you've seen."

His gray chalk-stripe business suit, white shirt and blue regimental tie clashed with the clutter and grime of the warehouse on the outskirts of Santa Barbara. I'd followed him to the warehouse that stood dark and silent among the commercial offices and light industrial buildings back between Hollister Avenue and the Southern Pacific tracks in Goleta. Followed and found him standing over the dead man gun in hand until he somehow sensed me and turned, fired as he turned, the 9-mm slugs whining off the concrete pillars to echo away into the emptiness.

"Who, what, when, where and how. Now and permanently. You hear me, mister?"

My cover was one of the pillars. His was the space between two of the heavy crates. I could see only a gray sleeve and the new official army 9-mm Beretta in the dim light of the single bulb. I knew him only as the Major. He wore the well-tailored suit like a man accustomed to wearing something else. Stiff and uncomfortable. In his way. We were both in his way, the suit and me.

"For the good of your country, mister. That's all I can tell you. You understand?"

I'd picked him up outside the two-story Spanish colonial of Esther Valenzuela's parents on Santa Barbara's upper Eastside. *"I know he's watching me, Mr. Fortune. I don't know why. I mean, I met him a few times at State Department affairs when my husband was still in Washington before we were married, but Paul never told me what he did. He just called him the Major. I'm not sure even Paul knows what he does for State. The Major, I mean. Paul is in the embassy in Guatemala City. We live down there, but I came home to visit my parents. They're getting old, they don't like Paul all that much. Oh, they like him, he just makes them uneasy. He's Latino, they're not used to that yet. But they're proud of him being in the Foreign Service, and I think they're coming around. I've been here two weeks, he suddenly showed up yesterday. The Major, I mean. When I went out to try to talk to him he just disappeared. There may be others. I'm scared, Mr. Fortune. Something's wrong, I know it."*

In my Tempo I'd waited on her quiet residential street most of the day. The Major didn't appear until after five P.M., only minutes behind Esther Valenzuela herself in her forest-green Subaru. Either he'd been tailing her around town all day or knew exactly when she would come home. In a spanking new black Buick he settled outside the house without a glance at my Tempo on the opposite side of the street six cars up. It had been a long day, it became a long night.

All night no one came to the house of Esther Valenzuela's parents, no one left. The cars that passed on the back street grew fewer. The noise of traffic on State Street and the distant freeway fell to little more than a faint drone. At midnight the Buick started up, its lights came on, and the Major drove away to Mission Street and the freeway.

His tense voice echoed in the cavern of the warehouse. "You

want to talk about what you're doing here? I'll put my gun away. Step out where I can see you. It'll go a lot easier on you."

I had followed far enough back across Mission, almost missed his turn onto the freeway, but picked him up again in the light freeway traffic late at night. He hadn't seem worried by any possible tail, drove straight to the darkened warehouse in Goleta doing nothing to hint he'd spotted me or even suspected I was there. The hunter not the hunted, no reason to think he had any enemies in Santa Barbara. I parked in a used car lot a block toward Hollister where my Tempo blended in, walked back to the warehouse. Any light inside was hidden, but the Buick stood alone near a side door.

Outside in the silence of the commercial streets at night, I watched and waited until the two shots reverberated across the night out of the hollow sound chamber of the warehouse. Sudden and shattering and gone. No more shots came. What did come were footsteps. Inside the warehouse, quick and hurried. Out through the side door and past the Buick almost at a run. The rapid walk that turned into a short man who reached the street in front, gave a single imperious wave. A long black limousine emerged from the night. The short man slid quickly into the rear, the limo drove away leaving only the silence.

Silence now in the warehouse except for the hidden voice. "If you're with Madrona you're already up to your ass in shit. Don't make the same stupid mistake and end up the same way. Forget the country, think about yourself. One phone call and you're dead tomorrow."

There had been no more shots in the night. My lone hand on the big old revolver in my pocket, I had gone in. The light had been down at the far end of the warehouse, the Major alone under the single warehouse bulb, the 9-mm Beretta in his hand, the dead man on the floor. He sensed or heard me, came around in a fast turn to fire ricochets off the concrete pillars right and left. Shot and jumped between the heavy crates, his quick eyes looking for me but not finding me.

Now I watched hidden in the empty warehouse as he crouched between the crates. He still searched among the shadows for me, but behind my heavy pillar, my revolver in hand where it always made me uneasy, I knew he was stalling. He talked to scare me, intimidate, but also to hold me there. I didn't know why, but if he wanted me there it was no place to be.

Wary and silent, I moved backwards to the side door and out past the Buick and across the dark into the darker penumbra of a three-story building with windows. Circled the opposite way into the high brush between the warehouse and the railroad tracks, and lay hidden where I could see the side door of the warehouse.

I have never been happy with people who tell me there are things I can't know or do for the good of the country, acts I must overlook, forget, pretend I didn't see. Anyone can claim the good of the country, government employees go wrong. This Major was watching my client for no reason she knew, or said she knew, now stood over a body with a gun, had taken shots at me. I was supposed to forget what I had seen. Take his word, step out where he could get a shot at me. Talk to him while whatever he was waiting for happened.

Five minutes later the car appeared.

It drove in hard from Hollister, parked behind the Buick. Two doors slammed in unison, two dark suits hurried into the warehouse. They would be why the Major had been stalling to keep me there. Probably called up by the man who had gone off in the limousine. The Major came out the side door on the run with the two newcomers behind him. Guns out, they separated to circle the warehouse and the nearby buildings. Looking for me. When they didn't find me near the warehouse, saw no car, they assumed I'd gone, didn't search farther. They had other matters on their minds, returned inside the warehouse, came out again almost at once carrying the body of the victim. They dumped the body into the back of the newcomers' car. They conferred, then climbed into their two vehicles and slammed away into the night like tanks leaving a destroyed town for the next target down the road.

I waited ten minutes before I went in again.

Inside the warehouse the single overhead bulb still burned above the stacks of crates in the pillared emptiness. I searched in slow circles. The sporadic hum of the freeway late at night was faint through the interior gloom that echoed to my solitary footsteps. The crates were empty or held nothing more suspicious than water-saver Swedish toilets. The kind the city gives a rebate on when you install them. The dark office was locked.

The first two empty cartridge cases had rolled into the shadow of a doorway on the far side of the bloody patch. The other three had bounced between the empty crates. They were all new 9-mm U.S. military rounds. I put them into one of the little plastic evidence bags I carry, put the bag into my pocket.

But five 9-mm cartridge cases only told me who had shot the dead man, not why. Or they only told me who had probably shot the man, I hadn't seen the shooting. There were a lot of the new 9-mm service Berettas, and there had been at least two men in the warehouse. Two men I'd seen.

There was nothing else. Only the name: Madrona.

My watch told me it was almost two A.M.

2

An eager young man, Paul Valenzuela takes his work seriously. Accepted by the Foreign Service four years ago, he has as his first overseas post the embassy in Guatemala City. The ambassador, a recent appointee more interested in Mayan artifacts and socializing than in the embassy itself, does not appreciate Paul's zealousness. With the Guatemalan government closely tied to Washington, daily business pretty much takes care of itself. There are few problems, and even Carl Foster, the CIA station chief, finds Paul's eagerness and dedication irritating as well as amusing.

"You're not down here to save the world, Paul," Foster tells him.

"Get out and mix more, Valenzuela," the ambassador says. "We have a role in the social life of the country. That's as much a part of the job as filling out forms."

Paul doesn't agree with Carl Foster or the ambassador, has his own view of what he is there to do. At twenty-seven, after all the years of school, college, university and training, he is finally doing what he dreamed of since he was a teenager in the *barrio* of East Los Angeles. But he has learned to keep his thoughts to himself in the ranks of the State Department.

The years in the *barrio* are years of poverty and skimping for his parents, of endless studying for Paul. But the skimping and study pay off with special minority aid, grants and scholarships that take him from the crowded public high schools of the *barrio* to the elite halls of Stanford University. Bright and quick, Paul both surprises and dazzles his professors at Stanford.

It is at Stanford that his father's plan of Paul becoming a lawyer in the *barrio* to lead the fight for a better neighborhood, and even full equality for Latinos, changes to his own dream of a larger mission. On his last summer, when he returns once more to the *barrio* to work with his father in the union hall, he tells the older man he wants to go into the State Department, bring better conditions for all Spanish-speaking peoples everywhere.

His father is disappointed, and his mother cries because he will be far from Los Angeles, but they both soon see that Paul can do more for Latinos in Washington than in the *barrio*. It is a time when most departments of the government are scrambling to acquire minority employees for the core professional levels. On more grants and scholarships, Paul enters Georgetown Graduate School to prepare for the Foreign Service, is recruited by State immediately upon graduation and assigned to the Latin-American Affairs Department for his training.

He has his first uneasiness about his chosen path. The then-Assistant Secretary for Latin America does not have the same view of what the United States should be doing down there that Paul does. The older career professionals smile, tell Paul that Assistant Secretaries come and go but the department goes on. This does not totally reassure him, the older career people do not seem to have views of Latin America much different from those of the Assistant Secretary. But he works hard, is finally given his posting to Guatemala.

The work is routine, but Paul is excited just to be in Latin America where he can learn what the United States needs to do to help his fellow Latinos in these poor countries. He finds that his duties are dull and not especially demanding in a country where cooperation with the United States is close and longstanding on both government and business levels. He really does have plenty of free time. What he decides to do with this free time is not what the ambassador had in mind.

He buys a motorcycle and rides around the rural villages of the highlands west and north of Guatemala City, the lands of the Maya and Quiche Indians. Short next to most Anglos in the United States, he is tall compared with the Indian villagers, is excited to talk to them even with his Angeleno Spanish that makes most of the villagers laugh or close up and back away.

No one stops Paul from doing this, but it is not exactly encouraged either. Most of the embassy staff seem to associate after hours with the same urban and educated Guatemalans they work with every day, go out to the villages only on market days to buy the colorful masks and weavings they can get so cheaply, or to guide visiting officials and important tourists who want the colorful bargains too.

The most famous market town, Chichicastenango, delights him. To go there he winds on his motorcycle up the steep mountain roads crowded with gaudily painted old buses and masses of people with their loads in baskets strapped around their heads. The market square with its sixteenth-century church of Santo Tomas high on a huge pile of masonry like a Mayan pyramid is still dark as the sellers set up their canvas-covered stalls and start their fires. The sound of hands clapping fills the morning as the women shape breakfast *tortillas*, and the aromas of boiling coffee, frying eggs and simmering black beans hover. Everything is for sale and everyone bargains, as much a festival and Indian town meeting as a market. At night, to the right of the church door, a *chuchkajaues* stands with his dark Indian face outlined by dozens of candles at his feet, half hidden in the smoke of a jar he swings in circles as he prays to the saints and the ancient Mayan gods.

On his early trips around the countryside Paul first notices the soldiers. They are on almost every corner in the mountain villages, roam the countryside in patrols that seem to have no military purpose, often stop him on his bike and are surprised and puzzled to find out who and what he is. He sometimes sees U.S. helicopters and military personnel with the patrols. In a small village not far from Chichicastenango Paul meets an older couple, Rolando and his wife, and their two grown sons. Mayans, they have never talked with an American except in the market at Chichi. They are stiff and wary. Paul continues to visit them, brings medicine for one of the sons, and when they realize he works in Guatemala City for the American government, is not a tourist, they begin to talk to him. Paul asks about all the soldiers. They tell him about General Rios Montt who sent his troops to burn four hundred villages, killed hundreds of Mayans including three of Rolando's brothers, and made thousands flee across the border into Mexico for safety. Rolando and his sons hate the soldiers, but there is a civilian *presidente* now, and they have high hopes for a better life.

"DEA needs help against the opium growers," Carl Foster tells him when he asks why U.S. soldiers are out there in the Guatemalan countryside. "We train and advise their military, you know that. Send them technicians."

On his last visit to Rolando's village he learns from a grim *kaibiles* officer in crisp fatigues and jaunty military beret that both of Rolando's surviving sons have been killed by the elite counter-insurgency soldiers, Rolando and his wife are in Mexico with most of the rest of the subversive villagers. When Paul returns to Guatemala City and his functions, he notices for the first time how the civilian *presidente* is always surrounded by a dozen unsmiling generals in his public appearances. This does not give Paul great belief in the independence of the civilian government Rolando and his sons had such hopes for.

Violetta works in a factory, is Ladino, speaks only Spanish. Paul meets her when his bike breaks down in a village near the city of Quezaltenango and her brother fixes it. She is visiting her family who are small business people and who, she tells Paul, don't like her working in a factory, it is not work for a woman. They are also afraid, Paul realizes but doesn't know why. He gives her a ride back to Guatemala City to her husband, two children and factory, visits her two-room apartment a number of times. When Violetta and her husband are arrested, Paul is at the apartment, is arrested with them. The military interrogator sees his papers. A Colonel appears to question him closely about Violetta and her husband. The Colonel escorts him personally to the embassy where the Colonel talks with Carl Foster and the ambassador himself.

"You have to be careful about becoming involved in local affairs," the ambassador says. "They don't like it and neither does Washington, you understand?"

"They seem to like our becoming involved in their military and technical affairs," Paul says.

"Don't be a smart-ass," Carl Foster says.

"That is a matter of policy and agreement, Valenzuela," the ambassador instructs him. "We stay out of their internal stuff."

"Violetta and her husband are nothing more radical than union members the same as most of our factory workers back home," Paul says.

"Here the unions are all communist," Carl Foster says.

"I'm not so damned happy with the goddamned unions at home," the ambassador says.

After the first year Paul returns to the States to marry the sweetheart he met at Stanford and to bring her back. They move into a house in the upper-middle-class neighborhood where most of the staff live. Esther likes Guatemala, and her schoolbook Spanish brings fewer smiles than his *barrio* accent. As they make more friends among the embassy couples and the upper-class Guatemalans their social engagements grow. Paul finds he has less and less time to ride his motorcycle into the countryside.

That is why, when Esther is back in the States visiting her parents, he is so distracted thinking of the free weekend ahead on his bike that he doesn't realize a key is open on the tape machine he is routinely checking in the message room. A local call comes in on the ambassador's line and he hears a voice that speaks in English. It is good American English without the trace of an accent.

"You tell your fucking CIA cowboys they better lay off or I'll start singing songs nobody wants to hear."

3

"What did you forget to tell me, Mrs. Valenzuela?"

My Tempo had been undisturbed in the used car lot. I didn't care how late it was. Driving alone through a small, sleeping city is a peaceful moment, clean and alone. There was solid tranquility in the night to the two-story Spanish colonial of Esther Valenzuela's parents on Santa Barbara's elite upper East.

"Has . . . has something happened?"

Small-boned and pale blonde, Esther Valenzuela looked up the stairs at the rear of the entry hall as if afraid her parents would appear to scold her for waking them at such an ungodly hour. A slender woman with large eyes and a delicate face. Her bones were too prominent to be pretty, but she was much more than good-looking, had the face and interior power that would last once she found the adult under the woman who was still half a child. She was nervous in the green silk robe a proper girl should wear in the house of her parents.

"What do you know about a man named Madrona?"

She had worn an equally proper gray wool skirt, demure white blouse and navy blazer in my office in the Summerland house this morning. Shy and uneasy in a detective's office, but more uneasy about her husband. *"I called his old boss in Washington. Paul's boss, I mean. He said I must be imagining things, Paul was in Guatemala the way he was supposed to be, nothing was wrong. But when*

I called the embassy I couldn't talk to Paul. They said he was on a trip. To Quetzaltenango. That's the second largest city down there. I talked to Paul a week ago, he never said he had any embassy business in Quetzaltenango. If he was going to be gone a while he would have called me. He would always let me know where he was if he could."

"Madrona?" She held the green silk robe close to her throat in the night house. "I don't think I know anyone named Madrona. I mean, I don't know the name. Is he important? Does he know Paul?"

"He's dead. I don't know if he knew your husband or not, but he seems to have known the Major."

"Dead?"

She said the word as if it had been somewhere in the back of her mind for days. A word that hovered like a shadow behind her eyes when she thought about the Major and her husband. A word, a possibility she did not want to think about but that would not go away. A fear she had to think about, face, as I told her what I'd seen in the warehouse.

"The Major . . . killed this Madrona?"

"I don't know what the Major did. There was another man there. A shorter man who whistled up a limo as if he owned it and he probably did. Who is he?"

The little color in her face faded away. "I . . . don't know him either." She shuddered in the chill of the entry hall, shaken by the real face of sudden death. "Who was this Madrona? Why would the Major or anyone want to . . . kill him?"

"His clothes, jewelry say he was a man with money. Latino, I'd guess. Working with or against the Major I can't say. Why anyone wanted to kill him I can't say. Not yet. What he could have to do with your husband I hoped you could tell me."

"What could he have to do with Paul? I don't know anything about him."

"Tell me what you do know. About your husband. About exactly what you did before and after you saw the Major out there watching this house."

She glanced up the stairs again, nervous, motioned for me to follow her back along the hall past the stairs to a small sitting room of the kind where maiden aunts once read and sewed in the late nineteenth century when the house had been built. She gave me a chair in the light of a table lamp she'd switched on at the door, took one of the high old green velvet wingbacks herself.

"What do you want to know about Paul?"

"Who he is, what he does down there, why he went into the State Department."

She told me how Paul Valenzuela had come from the *barrio* of East Los Angeles, wanted to help Latinos the world over, rode his motorcycle down in Guatemala talking to Indians. She was a young woman who would have been taught to offer guests food and drink, make them comfortable no matter how ungodly the hour or who the guest. Even a hired detective. Automatic, a reflex.

"He loves it down there, Mr. Fortune, the people. He wants to help them."

"I'm sure he does, Mrs. Valenzuela." A reflex that was not operating tonight. Blocked by something stronger that filled all the corners of her mind. "Now tell me what else happened. Why you're really so scared. The part you left out this morning."

A pale doll against the green velvet of the high wingback, she didn't act surprised. Or not surprised. Stared at me from the enormous confusion that filled all the space behind her eyes, sure she was imagining everything that frightened her, equally sure Paul was in some terrible danger she shouldn't talk about to me or to anyone. But had to talk to someone.

"He called me."

"When? From where? What did he say?"

The questions seemed to bounce off her unheard in the silent night room. Her blue eyes saw not me but her husband on the telephone, heard his voice not mine.

"I was up very early, eating breakfast. Two days ago. He said he'd heard something. A telephone call. He was talking so low, so fast, I never did understand exactly what it was. Then he was gone. Cut off. Hung up. I don't know which or why. He said something very fast at the end. He'd call again, he had to go, something."

"What had he heard? What kind of telephone call?"

"A call to the embassy. I don't think he was supposed to have heard it. That wasn't clear. None of it was clear. About 'singing songs nobody wanted to hear.' About CIA cowboys and laying off. Whatever that means."

"Where was he calling from?"

She moved her thin shoulders in the green robe, a helpless movement. "He never said. There wasn't an operator. He seemed so close, but . . ."

These days a call from Guatemala could be direct-dialed, sound as near as the house next door.

"When you called the State Department to ask about the Major, about your husband, exactly what did they say?"

"I only talked to Mr. Cole. He's been there thirty years, he trained Paul. Now I guess he's a Deputy Assistant Secretary in Latin American Affairs." The shoulders once more. Helpless and powerless. "He said I was imagining things. He didn't think the Major was even in the country. Paul was in Guatemala as he was supposed to be. I was paranoid. He'd talked to Paul only that morning. Had I been under stress? When I called Guatemala, Mr. Foster said he never heard of the Major, and if there was such a person he wasn't around the embassy."

"Who's Mr. Foster?"

"Carl Foster. Paul says he's the station chief for the Central Intelligence Agency down there. I'm not sure what his job's supposed to be."

"You talked to him about Paul?"

"And the ambassador. They both said Paul was out on embassy business. Carl Foster said he was in Quetzaltenango. I told him Paul would never go away without calling me. He laughed, said maybe the honeymoon was over. Then he said maybe Paul would call me from Quetzaltenango, and if he did to let him know."

"He asked you to tell him if Paul called? Why?"

"I don't know, Mr. Fortune. I suppose so he could show me I was worried over nothing."

The ring of the doorbell shook the silent house. She was on her feet and out of the room before it stopped. The panic of a proper girl that her parents might be awakened at 3:00 A.M. She was too late. Footsteps and an angry male voice came from the second floor.

"Do you know what time it is, Esther!"

"Are you Mr. Valenzuela?" It was a deep, smooth, yet tense voice. *"I apologize for the hour, Mr. Valenzuela, but—"*

The angry answer came from above. *"The name is Conrad, George Conrad, and what the devil do you—?"*

The deep voice was less soothing. *"I have apologized, Mr. Conrad. I suggest you go back to bed."*

"Who do you think you are—"

"My name is Max Cole, from the State Department."

Esther Valenzuela's voice shook. *"Please, Daddy, I'm sorry we woke you, but Mr. Cole and I have to talk. Please?"*

George Conrad's angry voice muttered from above, but his footsteps retreated. At the doorway of the small rear room I could see both Esther Valenzuela and the newcomer in the hall mirror. Deputy Assistant Secretary of State Max Cole was as small and nervous as his voice was big and confident. Five feet seven on a good day, thin gray hair above a high forehead and pink face with a button nose and tiny mouth. A neat, pale gray three-piece summer suit too light for a Santa Barbara spring night. His blue foulard tie a shade askew, his thin hair a few strands wild. A permanent crease between his eyes from thirty years of frowning, deeper as he scowled at Esther, fixed her with that powerful voice.

"Tell me just exactly what made you call me and the embassy in Guatemala City."

"I was worried." Her voice still shook. "I saw the Major out there—"

The Deputy Assistant Secretary waved an annoyed arm. "If it even was the Major, he could have been watching the house next door, someone up the block! I want the truth, Esther."

"When I went out to talk to him he disappeared. He didn't want to talk to me. Why, Mr. Cole?"

She tried to steady her voice, to stand up to the small man with the heavy scowl. Cole heard it too and didn't like it.

"Stay out of what you don't understand, Esther. You hear me? If you care about your husband's career, that is."

She took a quick step toward him in the dim entrance hall. She wasn't a tall woman, but she met Cole eye to eye. "What's happened to Paul?"

The small man met her eyes. "I can't judge what may have happened to Paul, my dear, until I know exactly what alarmed you so much when you thought you saw the Major out there."

If he had anything to give, he was going to get what he'd come for first. Something had brought him from Washington to California at 3:00 A.M. Esther tried to match his scowl and stare, but she was out of her league. Intimidation, deals, negotiations—this was his territory.

"Paul . . . called me. Something about a telephone call, a conversation. The day before the Major was out there. He was cut off. He—"

"Where did he call from?"

"I don't know. What's happened to Paul, Mr. Cole?"

He had what he wanted, had the grace to look away, soften his face. "He's missing from the embassy down there, Esther. That's all I can tell you."

"But—"

"If he should call or contact you in any way, you must tell me at once. I'll give you a number out here as well as the one you have for Washington. At once, you understand?"

He hadn't said that what he had told her was all he knew, but only that it was all he could tell, and I realized that the only way he could even have made it from Washington at this hour was by a fast ride in a private civilian or military jet. How important was Paul Valenzuela? I got a kind of answer almost at once.

"Do you happen to know a man with one arm, Esther?"

At least she didn't look toward the rear where I stood in the room doorway watching them in the mirror.

"I . . . I . . ."

"Did you hire him? A detective, perhaps? If you did, I strongly suggest you fire him."

It didn't tell me how important Paul Valenzuela might be, but it did tell me how important the Major was. And it told me that Deputy Assistant Secretary of State Max Cole had already been in California when the Major whistled him out of bed to brace Esther Valenzuela at 3:00 A.M. There was no way Cole could have come out even on a military jet in the hour-plus since I'd last seen the Major.

Cole's scowl became a smile, the deep voice soothing once more. "You can best help Paul by remaining near your phone, Esther. We'll find him soon, safe and sound. Trust us."

With a reassuring squeeze of her shoulder in the green robe, Cole had made his exit line. Esther Valenzuela stood in the hall for some time after the outer door had closed. I waited for his car to start and drive away in the night before I came out.

"The Major talked to him after I saw the Major in that warehouse, sent him here, but he was in California already. Probably coming to see you in the morning. Is Paul that important?"

"He never was." She still stared at the door where Deputy Assistant Secretary Max Cole had gone out. "He shouldn't be, Mr. Fortune."

I let that hang in the air between us in the quiet house. The Major and the State Department didn't want me to look for Paul Valenzuela. If Deputy Assistant Secretary Max Cole was speaking for the department. They didn't want Esther to look. Stay at home, trust them. They didn't want us anywhere near whatever was going on with Paul Valenzuela, but they didn't offer to explain why. A matter of national interest, or someone else's interest?

"Could Paul be in anything illegal, Mrs. Valenzuela? Or irregular?"

"No! Paul loves his work, Mr. Fortune. Loves Guatemala. He wants to help Latino people everywhere. He could never do anything wrong."

Her fragile face watched me, pleaded. Paul was good, Paul needed help. Distraught in the silent entry hall of the late-night house. What was she to do?

I said, "It looks like your husband heard something he wasn't supposed to, maybe knows something he isn't supposed to. Cole and the Major are worried about that. Very worried. One man's been shot, and they don't seem to want anyone to know what they're doing. Why?"

She continued to watch me. "They . . . you think they're hiding something, Mr. Fortune?"

"They're hiding, all right, the question is what and why. I get uneasy when people tell me to overlook what I've seen for the good of the country. Forget what I know, trust them."

"But . . . they're the government. They wouldn't—"

"The government isn't the country. Power doesn't make right, and government employees go wrong. All we know is your husband seems to have run from them, and they want to find him. I don't know if it's for the good of the country, or for their good."

"Paul would never do anything against America."

Different people have different ideas of what is for and what is against the country, the national interest. "Your Max Cole, this Major and some others want to cover something that's going on. They could be legitimate. They want you and me to trust them, let them handle it. Do you want to do that?"

"I want to know what's happened to Paul."

"You want me to go on?"

She hesitated only a moment, nodded.

I had her write out a check for my retainer before I drove home on the deserted pre-dawn freeway. Wives don't always know everything about their husbands, and clients can cover things up too.

4

It was in the *News-Press* two days later.

Kay had been in Los Angeles for a week. Kay Michaels, who is tall and slim and auburn-haired and the real reason I am in California after a lifetime in New York. She is the only woman anywhere who could and does stand to live with me in the red tiled-roof house we rent in Summerland. When she is away on her modeling-theatrical agency business, I eat breakfast alone in the sunny kitchen if the fog hasn't rolled in. When I eat breakfast alone, I read the newspaper.

MAN FOUND DEAD IN BIRD REFUGE

Sylvestre Madrona, 45, thought to be a Mexican national, was found dead early yesterday at the Bird Refuge. Police say Madrona, who was in Santa Barbara on business, had been shot twice with a 9-mm pistol. Vice president of Mayan Imports, Los Angeles, Mr. Madrona had been staying at the Biltmore where his assistant, Ms. Dolores Shay, could give no motive for the slaying. Police now suspect robbery and are investigating.

All day yesterday I made telephone calls and waited again outside Esther Valenzuela's house for the Major to show. He never did. The embassy in Guatemala wouldn't even talk to me. My contacts in Washington had no information on a major without a name.

The State Department had no information on Paul Valenzuela, Deputy Assistant Secretary Max Cole was in California but Santa Barbara was not on his itinerary. The warehouse in Goleta was leased to a long-distance trucking company with headquarters in Omaha. I had gotten the license of the new black Buick the Major drove, but not of the limousine. My DMV source had not yet gotten back to me on the Buick.

The body in the newspaper had to be the dead man from the warehouse. I went to the police.

Chavalas said, “What’s your interest in Madrona, Dan?”

The year-plus I’ve lived in Santa Barbara I’ve come to like Sergeant Gus Chavalas, even trust him, but in the America of the end of the twentieth century you don’t give anything away. You negotiate.

“I’m not sure yet I have any interest, Sergeant. I need to know more than was in the newspaper.”

“The paper had enough to bring you here.”

Chavalas could negotiate too.

“I’ve got a case he could be mixed up in. Right now it’s only could be.”

In the sunny office above Figueroa Street, Chavalas looked out his window at a jacaranda tree already flowering in the early Santa Barbara spring. He’s stocky and dark and in Santa Barbara most people think he’s Latino. He’s second-generation Greek, but he doesn’t correct them. In California it’s an advantage in his work to be thought Latino.

“Two early-morning sweethearts found him in the bushes over at the north end of the bird refuge. They hadn’t got all their clothes off yet so they hustled to the East Beach pavilion, gave the alarm, went home. No point hanging around with cops all over.”

He went to his private coffee machine, drew two cups. He was waiting for a comment from me that would tell him more about what I knew and didn’t know. I outwaited him. He handed me the coffee, a wooden stick and paper packets of creamer and sugar.

“Wallet with all the papers but no cash. We contacted the company. Mayan Imports brings in handicrafts, weavings, masks from Mexico and Central America. The president, Mr. Tyrone Earl, says Madrona is a terrible personal loss, he's shocked to his shoes. He's on his way up here to identify the body, take care of Madrona's assistant and help in any way he can. All his exact words. He's quite a talker, Mr. Earl."

"On his way? From Los Angeles? When did you call him? I mean, you found Madrona yesterday morning."

"We got a receptionist in L.A. Earl called back. He was down in Mexico, is flying up today."

"He say what business Madrona had in Santa Barbara?"

"Selling to local stores." He checked the jacaranda outside his window again. "The assistant doesn't have any notion of what Madrona could have been doing at the bird refuge that night or at any time. She's a wild kind of business assistant, Ms. Dolores Shay. She shared the room at the Biltmore, doesn't seem to know much about Madrona's business. Her English is really bad, and she never saw Madrona swim or go near a beach or watch birds." He drank more coffee, looked back at me. "You know that spot at the refuge, Dan. Way over near the railroad embankment. Funny place for a stranger in town to be to get robbed. The body could have been there weeks if the hot lovers hadn't decided on a quickie in the weeds. By then the water, wind and time would have wiped most of what we need to tell for sure when or where he was shot."

I tried innocence. "He wasn't shot on the beach?"

Chavalas studied his jacaranda. "We know that, and you know that, Dan. You know where he was shot or you wouldn't be here."

In negotiations you have to give to get. To get more you have to give more. I told him all of it.

"The good of the country? What the hell was Madrona? A Mexican spy?"

"You tell me. Paul Valenzuela works for the State Department. So does Deputy Assistant Secretary Max Cole and maybe the Major."

"And everyone lied about the husband being missing, what this Major was doing and where, until Madrona was killed. You have a name for the Major?"

"No."

"You think he shot Madrona?"

"I think, but I don't know."

"You don't know where to find him? Or this deputy assistant whatever?"

"No." I took the plastic bag from my pocket, tore a sheet out of my notebook. "These are the cartridge cases from the warehouse, and that's the number of the Buick."

He's a street cop, said nothing about withholding evidence. "We'll run 'em, we'll run the warehouse and we'll check into your Major."

The telephone booth was at a Union 76 station on Coast Village Road and Olive Mill. I phoned in, got the message that was on my answering machine. *"You son of a bitch you damn near put my ass in one permanent sling. What the hell are you playing with this time? Don't call on me again for a year, you got that? I had to do a fast and furious song and dance to explain why I was even asking about your fucking Buick. For what it's worth, the thing is registered to good old Uncle Sammy, no names, no agency, no nothing. No contact with me for a goddamned year."*

Once there was a wooden pier that jutted out from the concrete esplanade and narrow beach below where the rich guests left their yachts while they wined, dined, slept and caroused. They still did all those things at the Biltmore, but now if they had a yacht they had to leave it at the harbor marina or anchor offshore and row or swim in.

The hotel itself—sold, resold and renovated some years ago—still looks much the same as it did in Santa Barbara's heyday when the town was the retreat of the old-money rich from back East, the glamorous from a real Hollywood, the truly famous and powerful from everywhere. A rambling two-story stone building with a darkened red-tile roof, it was almost lost behind dense semitropical vines and vegetation across a sloping green lawn. The short drive curved from the beachfront road between two small parking lots to the baronial entrance where bellhops and parking valets greeted the guests.

I skipped the parking lots, found a spot out front on the drive.

You can't make a fast exit with valet parking. The fine lobby has large saltillo floor tiles of the kind we imagine in Andalusian castles, and dark wood furniture from the same image of medieval Spain. As I crossed the lobby toward the stairs up to the second floor and the room number Chavalas had given me for Madrona's room, I saw the Major.

Playing the rich tourist, he lounged tall and at ease in one of the high-backed chairs where he could watch the door. When he noticed me he didn't seem surprised to see me, nodded toward the bar. I followed him through the lobby to a table in the secluded window nook. This early in the afternoon, the other two tables were empty.

"Mr. Dan Fortune, private eye. Christ, give me a break." He waved for the waitress. "Out from New York one year, lives with a tall career lady he isn't married to, is into what he shouldn't be and up to his neck in trouble he can't even imagine. You want a drink?"

"Anchor Steam."

"*Dos.*" He held up two fingers to the waitress.

In informal resort wear to blend into the rich Biltmore scene. A brass-buttoned navy blazer, tan slacks, black half-boots, open blue shirt. In good light he was a clean and boyish forty-odd to go with his six-two-or-three. Thick black hair blown dry, deep eyes that had seen sun and wind, a scar across the back of his left hand. A relaxed businessman on vacation who tipped the waitress when the beer came, raised his glass in a toast.

"To the troops, right?"

A picture of the young executive on his way up. Vice president of a medium-sized corporation. Tennis and health clubs, Europe or Asia or Latin America every year. A lot of money and benefits, but in fashionable debt from slick leveraged buyouts. The right beer and the perfect martini. A second wife. Pot in the past, some discreet cocaine, the latest VCR. His job is essentially hot air, his company is a middleman. If he is with a larger company it probably has an actual product, but that is remote, what the corporation really does is buy and sell stock, make financial deals. His work takes too much time and devotion. He prefers to play, is always looking for an angle.

"You do your homework."

The false note was the blazer buttoned even while he was sitting at the table. It didn't work. The faint bulge at his waist was all too clear to someone who expected him to have a gun. The new service Beretta was too big, or he didn't have enough experience at concealed work. Probably both. Only it wouldn't be the same Beretta.

"I told you in that warehouse, Fortune, I've got friends. A lot of friends who can get anything done and fast."

I drank the beer. "For the good of the country. You want to convince me, tell me how Madrona was a threat to the country, Major? How Paul Valenzuela is a matter of national interest? You have a name to go with the rank?"

"Hill. Major Harvey Hill, U.S. Army, retired. You don't need to know what Madrona was, or what Paul Valenzuela is, okay? It's not your business. It's not even close to being your business. I told you, walk away. We mean it."

"Somehow that goes over better in a dark warehouse. Tell me enough to convince me I should leave Paul Valenzuela to you, and I will. Convince me you had to kill Sylvestre Madrona. I'm part of the country too, right?"

"Don't be an asshole." He drained his beer, looked for the waitress. "I didn't kill any Sylvestre Madrona. I wasn't in any warehouse two nights ago. I wasn't in Santa Barbara or even in California. I can prove it. Believe me. Witnesses, photos, records, the works. You were hallucinating. You and Esther Valenzuela both. Go home, Fortune."

"And the Beretta's melted down or in the Guam Deep." I got up. "Thanks for the beer."

The Major shook his head, leaned across the lounge table. "Look, there's nothing you can do, should do, or would want to do if we could tell you what we're doing, believe me. Just a waste of your time to no good purpose. That's the truth."

I leaned on the table, bent down in his face. "I've got a client who's young and worried and even scared. She wants to know what's happened to her husband. I think she's got a right to know, or to be told why she can't know, and my time is what I'm paid for."

He looked at me the way he would look at a bug he'd like to squash. The buttoned blazer bunched even more over the gun on his belt as he hunched forward to outstare me. Then he shrugged, caught the attention of the waitress and raised one finger. I was dismissed. He was finished talking to me, had no more time to waste. But I wasn't finished with him. Maybe it was the arrogance, the elitism, the secretiveness. He and Cole were doing something I couldn't be trusted to know. Esther Valenzuela couldn't be told about her own husband. A murder had to be hidden even from the police. Or especially from the police.

"No more threats?"

"It's a free country and your time. I've tried to reason with you, Dan, not threaten you. Now you're on your own." He even smiled as I left him.

I wondered about his sudden backing off. He didn't seem like a man who would change direction without a good reason. I passed the waitress with his Anchor Steam on my way out. The waitress smiled at me. It's the missing arm, women want to mother me. Especially younger women. And poorer women. Rich women see only something incomplete, of no use to them.

On the second floor, Sylvestre Madrona's room was in front on the ocean side. It had three doors. A full suite. The businessman had been paid well. Either that or Mayan Imports ran large expense accounts. Maybe Sylvestre Madrona had been independently wealthy.

"You want?"

Chavalas had said it. She was some kind of assistant for a businessman. Small, soft-eyed, an angelic but skinny face tanned to a velvet brown under silver blonde hair pulled back in a loose bun tied at the nape of a slender neck. She wore a chic Rodeo Drive backless silver cocktail dress at eleven in the morning. Her shoulder bones were sharp as a bird's. Balanced on high silver pumps, she looked at me from a sad face that was worried, maybe even scared, but not distraught.

"My name's Dan Fortune, Miss Shay. Can I talk to you about Mr. Madrona?"

"He has die. Two days. I am sorry."

It was, despite her poor English, the right word. Whatever there had been between her and Sylvestre Madrona, it hadn't been love. Sadness but no tears.

"I know he's dead. I want to talk to you."

"To me?"

I nodded. She seemed surprised but stepped back into the living room of the sunny suite, stood in the middle of the big room still looking up at my face. It wasn't only her English that was poor, it was her whole understanding of the country she was in, its ways and customs and power structure without someone to tell her what to do.

All at once I saw an entirely different woman under the chic, expensive silver. She wasn't tanned and she wasn't blonde and she should have been ten pounds heavier. Her face was meant to be a soft full oval. Her hair under the expensive bleach was thick black, her brown velvet color was her own.

"Where are you from, Miss Shay? Mexico? Whose idea was it: the new name, the clothes, the blonde hair? Madrona's?"

"It is what Don Sylvestre want, *si.*"

"How did you meet Madrona? Where did you meet him? In Mexico?"

She blinked, unsure, and I tried it again in my broken New York–East Harlem Spanish.

"*Si*, Mexico. Both come Mexico. Don Sylvestre *mucho grande.*"

"Come? You're not from Mexico?"

"*Si*, Mexico." She gave me a big smile. "I get good job. Make dress, clean good. I learn typewrite."

She smiled and watched me, her flat brown eyes half scared and half eager. A thin, très chic silver blonde in a gaudy silver dress and silver high heels surrounded by the elegant furniture of an expensive Biltmore suite who talked of sewing in some garment sweatshop, cleaning offices, maybe even reaching the heights of a typist.

"Madrona made his money selling imported arts and crafts?"

"Much money, Don Sylvestre and Señor Ty they have."

"Importing crafts."

"*Si.* I don't know. I no go with Don Sylvestre."

"Not even here? You stayed in the hotel all the time?"

"*Si.* In hotel."

"Do you know a man named the Major? Major Hill?"

She nodded, smiled. The name meant nothing to her.

"Paul and Esther Valenzuela?"

"Valenzuela? I don' know."

"Paul and Esther," I said slowly. "You know them?"

She shook her head. "I don' know."

The sound came from behind the closed door of the suite bedroom. Metal against wood. A single sharp sound. I stepped lightly to the inner door, opened it. The back of a hotel maid's uniform hurried toward the open outside door of the bedroom.

"Hold it!"

The maid turned. She had the small stature and brown skin of most hotel maids in California, her hair hidden under a floppy dust hat. She didn't have the eyes of a hotel maid. Or the face and manner. Cool gray eyes, a high Castillian nose and an amused smile. Her slender hand was steady with a Walther PPK pointed at my chest.

"You should practice your Spanish more, Mr. Fortune. It is really quite awful."

Despite the smile, cool eyes and banter, she was tense and wound tight. Edgy, on an action high. I made no sudden moves, returned the smile, held my lone hand in front where she could see it was empty.

"Why not come in and help me out then? We both might have learned more."

Her smile widened but was somehow less amused. "Don't be too clever, Mr. Fortune. It's unprofessional."

"What profession is that? National police? Secret service? Military intelligence? Mexico, or somewhere else? I'd say somewhere else. Sylvestre Madrona was from somewhere else. Maybe the same other country down there?"

She laughed aloud. "*Don* Sylvestre? Our little *campesina*'s benefactor? That's the trouble with *gringos*, all Latin Americans look alike, sound alike. Another country, eh? But it isn't the wench who is dead, is it? The little wench seems to be doing quite well. The endurance of the *campesina*, eh? You don't have any real idea where she is from, do you? You don't have any real idea about anything at all. I think you should return to your divorces and runaways. This is all too much for you."

Another one who wanted me to go away, leave whatever it was to the professionals.

"It was an old-time French premier who said war was much too important to be left to generals. And it's a runaway I'm working on. You know where he is, maybe?"

She smiled that amused smile, shook her head in a kind of wonder. "Well, it's been real. Wait a few minutes after I'm gone. *Adios, hombre.*"

Her Spanish was a derisive imitation of my crude New York Puerto Rican Spanglish. She laughed again, closed the door.

5

You never know about people with guns. My judgment told me she wouldn't shoot in as public a place as a crowded hotel, but I had been wrong before. It all depended on who she was, what she was doing and for whom, what her level of need and desperation was. I gave her a minute, opened the door and looked both ways.

The corridor was empty.

I took the back stairway down and went out the employee's entrance and across the sloping lawn to my car on Channel Drive. The ersatz maid would turn back into herself before leaving. That was my theory. Herself or whoever and whatever she was pretending to be beside a maid. My second theory said that whatever persona she had adopted would go in and out the front door, not the employee's entrance. My third was that I would recognize her whatever her guise. I had about a fifty-fifty chance of being right on all counts.

I fished my binoculars out of the glove compartment, focused on the entrance across the lawn, had two false alarms. A sleek redhead in a tennis outfit who walked down the driveway and crossed the drive to the Coral Casino, and an imperious brunette with two Afghan hounds on a single leash who tapped her foot as she waited for the valet to bring up her white Mercedes 450SL convertible. Neither rang my bell. The third did. A brunette in a slim plum jumpsuit and high heels who walked briskly but did not call particular attention to herself as she came out, smiled at the two waiting valets. The same smile she had given me in the suite: thin, amused, confident, a shade arrogant. She walked down the driveway to an unobtrusive dark gray Acura Legend on the shore road ten cars in front of me. She didn't trust valet parking any more than I did.

I pulled out and drove past the Legend with my face turned away, slowed until I saw her behind me, then drove on ahead of her. The drive was a loop with only a few side roads and one exit where Cabrillo Boulevard came from Montecito and under the freeway at the bird refuge, headed toward the beaches, the zoo and the oceanfront hotels and motels in Santa Barbara proper. She didn't turn off anywhere behind me, signaled a left toward Santa Barbara as I reached Cabrillo. I turned ahead of her.

In high heels she wasn't going to the beach or zoo, showed no sign of having spotted me, maintained the speed limit. I watched the rearview mirror as we passed the Sheraton and the rows of East Beach motels to the stoplight at Milpas. She didn't turn into the Sheraton or any of the motels, did not signal a turn on Milpas toward the freeway entrances. I drove on to the Red Lion Inn, the newest monument to mediocrity built for mid-management business conventions and traveling salesmen. It stretched for a complete city block as an example of what a great drama critic once called not good taste or bad taste but no taste at all.

She did not turn into the Red Lion.

People strolled in the spring sun in Palm Park, bicycled on the bikeway, sat on the beach trying for an early tan or watched the boats out at sea. Ahead were Stearns Wharf with its shops and restaurants, the motels and restaurants of West Beach, the marina and breakwater, City College and the Mesa.

She signaled a turn at Santa Barbara Street behind me and was gone.

I swung hard into Anacapa Street, jarred my teeth over the railroad tracks. Made a right on Mason, a left on Santa Barbara toward where it crossed the freeway. She was three cars ahead of me in the line waiting at the light.

We all got across when the light changed, the Legend went on up Santa Barbara to Cota, hung a left and then another on Anacapa Street, turned into the new parking lot before Haley

Street. Near noon, the lot would have been full if it were farther uptown, but the lower State Street mega-mall was still being built, the lot was relatively empty, and I saw the dark gray Legend pull into a space in the second row nearer to Anacapa than State. I found a slot in the last row. When she got out of the Legend, walked toward Anacapa, I almost missed her.

She had covered the wine jumpsuit with a long gray duster, wore a hat pulled down to hide her hair and shadow her face as she hurried in the spring sun and turned right into Haley Street. In front of the Faulding Hotel three winos leered as she passed, slurred obscene remarks. This is the lower East and Westsides, on both sides of the freeway and State Street, the closest to a decayed and derelict slum and polyglot ghetto there is in Santa Barbara. It isn't East Harlem or East Los Angeles, Watts or the South Bronx, the Minnesota Strip or the Tenderloin, but it's enough, will serve.

She crossed State Street. Four ragged men sat on the sidewalk against the wall of a grocery/magazine store, backpacks and shopping carts beside them filled with all they had. They looked at nothing from dead eyes. Four who lived on the streets, in the flophouses and single-room hotels, rescue missions and Salvation Army shelters, dilapidated one-story houses and littered yards. Among the abandoned shops and old warehouses, boarded windows and empty doorways. The wandering homeless, the lost and sick, among the broken bottles, the wino bars and the crack houses.

Across Chapala she walked in her high heels over the bridge above concrete Mission Creek where no water had run this drought year. The two derelict gray bungalows set back from the street behind bare and littered yards, boards nailed across the windows and painted black, were crack houses raided by the police a year ago for the third time. I passed the bungalows. Children played behind them. The doors were open. People moved inside again.

They had tried jailing the owner, but no one could prove he knew whom he had rented to. When the judge suggested he be more careful about his tenants, the balding Latino shrugged. There was no way he was going to ask the crack dealers or needle merchants what they planned to do in the houses, tell them they couldn't rent them if they were going to sell drugs, speed, angel dust, the big C, horse.

She turned into a yard hidden by high hedges dusty and gray in the drought. Pre-teen children played on mounds of dirt from the freeway reconstruction. Their play was to smash bottles one by one methodically with a jagged piece of concrete ripped up from the old freeway. To silently pile debris and set it on fire, stand and smile as the debris burned in the sun.

She walked up onto the sagging porch of a two-story house. The door opened, she went inside.

There were two windows along the side of the battered house. She stood in the empty room, her duster and hat off, and laughed with two other people. The Major, his blazer open, the Beretta visible at his belt, and a man in a dark suit who could have been one of those who came to the Goleta warehouse the night Sylvestre Madrona died.

I knew now why the Major hadn't threatened me more in the Biltmore lobby, had backed off. He had been there working with the Latin woman, guessed what I was there for, and figured I might have a better chance to get Dolores to talk. His ally upstairs would listen, report to him, he'd never have to appear.

In the room, the woman and the Major were doing the talking. All I could hear was a drone. There are times when I wish I was high-tech—a contact microphone would have helped. The trouble is that unless you carry all that junk with you at all times you never seem to have what you need when you need it. The little gray cells are still the most important equipment an investigator, public or private, has. The most important equipment anyone has. Mine were telling me something inside the room wasn't right.

I circled the house to the rear looking for a way to slip inside without being heard. He was waiting for me. The second dark suit. What my brain had tried to tell me. They always work in pairs, the silent men in dark suits, as they had the night at the warehouse. He stepped out of the rear door, gun in hand.

"Inside."

It was a small automatic, a SIG/Sauer P230. He had the manner of a cop: unsmiling, authoritarian, impatient. People become what they do, give themselves away. But with a small foreign pistol he wasn't a policeman or FBI. Not anymore. At least, not a working policeman. My guess was CIA.

"Paul Valenzuela walk away with some national secrets, or just embarrass a government or two?"

He had the gun, size, two arms and authority. That made him superior, the boss, and in the right. He stepped down from the rear steps, grabbed my lone arm, pushed me stumbling ahead of him. Pushed, but didn't let go. Holding me in his grip made him feel even more powerful, king of it all. It was a mistake. It usually is.

The blond man who stepped out of the bushes around the rear yard wore a jaunty camel's-hair sport jacket. He moved softly behind the CIA agent whose focus was strictly on holding my arm in his viselike grip and shoving me up the back steps. The sleek newcomer raised a length of two-by-four in both hands and swung it like someone who had once played decent baseball.

The SIG/Sauer flew like a soaring bird, the agent went down on both knees, dropped forward onto his hands, managed a loud bellow. Rolled over onto his side and held his head in both hands rocking in the dirt.

"Run!" That was me.

"Back fence!" That was my rescuer.

Something ripped on my old tweed jacket where the sleeve hung free as we plunged through the overgrown and unwatered high brush at the rear of the yard. The fence behind the brush was low. He took it like a hurdler, I rolled over. The next yard was clear and clean with patio furniture behind a newly painted green-and-white house. Shouts erupted behind us.

"*Back fucking fence!*"

The front fence was white and low. I jumped this one a step behind the blond rescuer.

"Left!" The pursuers seemed to worry him as much as they did me.

"*Left! Left! Cut them off!*"

On the far side of Bath Street the blond vaulted into a low, sleek black convertible with its top down. I tumbled into the passenger bucket seat. Like a shock, I felt the engine come to life behind me with the deep power sound of a jet. In the side mirror I watched the Major and one dark suit stare after us out in the middle of the street already a block behind.

6

"Where to?" The guy grinned at me.

I breathed hard, checked my arm and clothes. The arm was fine, the tweed jacket had lost one pocket and the empty sleeve. Somehow the blond commando had come through untouched. His clothes—the camel's-hair jacket, finished off by an open-necked navy blue silk shirt and slim brown slacks—were probably a lot better quality. He continued to grin, drive, said nothing more.

"You want to tell me the story?" I said.

"Of where you want to go?"

He laughed at his own wit, seemed to drive aimlessly in the powerful car that looked like a Ferrari but wasn't red or really a Ferrari. Under the black paint and new shape was what had been a Testarossa, but so much had been changed I couldn't even begin to guess exactly what. Enough that no original Ferrari marque badges remained anywhere, replaced by a simple KS on the steering wheel hub, Koenig Specials on the floor mats, and the name Koenig on the red flat-12 engine behind us that was displayed like the jewel it was under a Plexiglas cover. I'm not a car buff, with one arm I've never been that sure behind a steering wheel, but I knew the work of Willy Koenig, the West German car tuner, and I knew the price tag. For something like this—$400,000, give or take forty or fifty thousand depending on materials.

"Of what you were doing at that house, and the shining-armor rescue. A name would be nice, too. I suppose you know mine. Everyone seems to."

He pulled over to the curb, cut the engine and offered me a cigarette. I shook my head. He lit one, blew smoke, his other hand still on the steering wheel.

"Tyrone Earl. Call me Ty, okay?"

Close, the president of Mayan Imports had as much gray as blond in his hair, had it barbered long enough to barely touch his ears and collar. The exactly right length to show both his independence and his solid financial standing. The hand on the steering wheel had blunt fingers with nails as hard as horn, was tanned the color of café au lait. On a wrist tanned as dark, he wore a $25,000 Rolex. A gold rearing horse with a wild mane and emerald eyes hung on a gold chain in the graying chest hair at his open collar.

I said, "You came about Sylvestre Madrona?"

"I came to bury Caesar, but some praise for an old friend might be in order too." He smoked, looked up and down the street. His tanned face was too strong to be really handsome. What they call craggy, with a heavy nose and brows, a wide mouth with deep creases at the corners. "Take care of Dolores, too. She'll be lost in this country without Sylvestre." He looked back at me. "Maybe find out what happened."

"How come you were at that house? You know the Major?"

"Major? What the hell's some damned Major got to do with what happened to Sylvestre?"

His eyes were blue-gray, narrowed by sun and wind even more than the Major's, set deep in the dark tanned face. A man who had lived outdoors a great deal at some time, maybe still did.

"If you don't know the Major, how did you happen to be at that house? The woman? You know her from Central America?"

He tossed the smoking cigarette into the street, looked up at the blue and sunny afternoon sky.

"Never saw her before."

"Then what were you doing around that house back there?"

"Following you."

He grinned. He was mercurial. From light to dark in split seconds, back just as fast. He expected a reaction. I didn't give it to him. Mercurial types have little patience. He lit another cigarette with a short wooden match from a small box of European matches. Mercurial in contradictions too. A $25,000 watch but no gold lighter. He waved the match out.

"I got to Dolores just after you left. She told me you'd been asking a lot of questions about Sylvestre, didn't know who the hell you were or what the hell you wanted. So I went down to the lobby to see if you were still around. From the bar I spotted you crossing the lawn. You're pretty easy to spot, right? I saw you get into your car, but you didn't leave. You sat in the car with binoculars and watched the front door. That gave me time to get my car out of the lot and take after you. A couple or three cars back, of course."

"Did you know I was following that woman?"

"Not until I saw you go running out of the parking lot. Who the hell is she? Where does she fit with Sylvestre?"

"I think she's some kind of government agent from down in Central America. National police. Maybe you can tell me where she fits with Madrona. He wasn't originally from Mexico, was he?"

"Came from Guatemala. National police? Christ, what do all you people think Sylvestre was doing?"

"What was he doing?"

"Selling masks, baskets and weaving! That's goddamn all he was doing. I thought the police here said it was a robbery."

"What do you say, Mr. Earl?"

He shook his head. "If it wasn't a robbery, I don't know what the hell to say. We're businessmen. We import handicrafts from all over Mexico and Central America. We live most of the time in Mexico, but that's all we do." He tossed the second cigarette out into the street. You could be arrested for doing that in Santa Barbara. "What do you say, Fortune? You know something I don't?"

If he believed Sylvestre Madrona's death could only be a robbery, why was he trying to find out what had happened? It was a good question, not necessarily one with all bad answers. If my partner and friend had been shot down in an apparent robbery I would want to know more. At least help catch the thieving killer or killers.

"What about his personal life?"

Tyrone Earl wasn't dumb. "You don't know anything? Or you don't want to tell me?"

"Let's say it's too early to know what I know."

"Hell, Dan, you're a private detective, right? You have to connect to Sylvestre somewhere, or why the hell would you waste your time talking to Dolores?"

A long way from dumb. I had to give him an answer that would sound honest, but not tell him anything he didn't already know if he were in Santa Barbara to continue what Madrona had been up to. If he were fishing, I didn't want to tell him anything I hadn't told the police. "A woman whose husband seems to have disappeared from our embassy in Guatemala hired me because she was being watched by a man called the Major. The Major has some connection to the State Department. State is also worried about Paul Valenzuela. Or one State Department official is. Your Madrona seems to connect to the Major too."

"Jesus," he said. "What the hell was Sylvestre into?"

"That's what I want to know. You're sure you never heard him talk about the Major? Anything suspicious?"

"Hell, no. On both." He shook his head, looked at his watch. "I'm supposed to talk to a Sergeant Chavalas at two. You want me to take you back to your car?"

"Thanks."

The low black car's turbocharged engine had the deep sound of unlimited power. Earl never shifted it out of second as we drove across town, turned south on Anacapa Street. He drove easily, gently, with a delicate touch and the sense of a man who loved automobiles and knew the wonder of the car he had.

"How fast can it go?"

"With the tall gearbox, two hundred and seventeen. I've got the small gearbox. It goes a hundred and ninety plus."

"You're conservative."

He laughed aloud. "Only two in the whole country. A Koenig Competition Cabrio. Want to try it out on a road?"

"A little too gaudy and macho for me. Where can you even get close to driving it that fast?"

"In Mexico."

"That why you live there? Fewer rules and regulations?

"Wild and woolly. Hell, I just like it down there. Life is more basic, nearer the bone, right?"

He slowed when we reach the Cota parking lot, turned in. The fake Biltmore maid's Legend was gone from the lot. Earl parked beside my Tempo. He was polite, didn't laugh. He did smile.

"I have to talk to Chavalas too," I said. "I'll meet you there. Life nearer to the bone. Is that what Madrona liked too?"

"Sylvestre grabbed at the good life, no way out of that. Anything money could buy. He liked the ladies. *Latina, gringa* or any other kind. He played the field. The hunting is good in Mexico, refugee *campesinas* to the rich *gringa* playgirls."

"Dolores Shay was one of the field?"

He thought about that. "Sylvestre had it special for Dolores. There's a wife back in his old village, but he never talked about her. Maybe Dolores tied his two worlds together. The old and the new. We never discussed that kind of thing. He went his way, I went mine. But he did talk about Dolores."

"Did he have other women up here?"

"He had some fast dinner and nightclub lays, but Dolores kept him home." He sat in the Koenig, looked out at the spring sunlight of Santa Barbara. "I'll tell you about Dolores. Maybe it'll give you some of what you want to know about Sylvestre."

7

Three years old when her grandfather is sent to a labor camp on the coast for continuing to speak of El Presidente Arbenz after he is deposed by the *generales*, Dolores Rios is the last of ten children. She is five when this grandfather is killed trying to return to the village from the camp. She cries for the man with the soft white mustache who played with her in the sun in front of the tin-roofed house while her mother worked the hand loom, her father cut wood to sell and her brothers and sisters tended their plot of corn and beans near the mountain village.

When she is six she goes with her mother and sisters to sell weaving in the market town of Chichicastenango a day away. She sees her first *norteamericanos.* They frighten her with their strange sounds, but her mother and sisters rush to join the other villagers who surround the pale aliens. Her father sells his wood and disappears into a *cantina* with the other men until the sun is behind the mountains and it is time to return to their village. He is illiterate, her father, drinks too much, boasts of all the children he has made and will make, but he is a hard worker and many village women envy her mother.

Dolores goes to the coast for her first harvest season when she is eight. Most of the village goes to pick cotton or coffee, to cut sugar cane, on the vast plantations of the *patrones* and the American companies. It is the only way they can earn the real money they must have in addition to the beans and corn to survive. But when she is ten the Indians of the Guerrilla Army of the Poor come to the district. The general who is *presidente* sends the soldiers to attack the guerrillas. It becomes too dangerous to go to the coast for work, there is no money, her father drinks himself to death.

At thirteen Dolores is married to an older village man. The new *presidente*, who sleeps with a *norteamericano* bible and a machine gun beside his bed, sends more soldiers and machines of war to destroy the guerrillas. The soldiers and war machines burn many villages and kill many villagers, the young men are taken by the army or run away so they will not have to be killed. Some go to the cities to find work where it is safer. Dolores has two children with her older husband who chops wood to sell like her father, works on the beans and corn like her absent brothers. She is fifteen when her husband is killed by a patrol of *kaibiles* who say he threatened them with his axe.

Her children die when she is sixteen. The doctor at the clinic in the market town tries to save them, but he does not have the skill or the medicines, tells her that in Guatemala, where a child dies every fifteen minutes, most women lose half their children to curable diseases brought on by malnutrition. She has been unluckier than most. Or perhaps luckier. One of thirty-two widows in her village where there are no men to marry and the soldiers do not let the families leave to earn money at the plantations on the coast, at least she is childless, can slip away one night to walk to Guatemala City. She is seventeen.

In the capital of the country there are too many people from the villages. Dolores has little money, at first she must live on the streets. Young and healthy, she soon meets a man who has a factory job and a clean shack only a little smaller than her family's house in the village, finds work at night cleaning the offices of an American company in one of the tall, shining new buildings of the city. She walks home to save the money of the bus. The man she lives with, Hector, works long hours for not much money, drinks too much and cannot marry her because he has a wife and children back in his village. But he is a quiet man even when he drinks at night while she is at work, gentler to her than most men she has known. With both of them working they can afford to buy enough food even after they send money back to their villages.

She has two more children. When the girl is born, Hector wants to name the infant Dolores after her.

"That was the name of my little girl who died," she tells Hector, "we will name her Josefina for my mother."

Hector understands. It is the custom to name the firstborn son for his father, but they had named the boy Venicio to honor Hector's brother. The son Hector has back in his village is named Hector.

Hector loves the children, stops drinking for a time and cares for them while she is at work. They make him sad, too, and when he is laid off from work, can't make enough money scavenging at the city dump, starts drinking again, she knows he will go back to his village. He cries, he does not want to go, but he has heard that life is better in the mountains now, he misses his family, she cannot feed them all on what she makes.

"You must find another man," he tells her when he leaves.

Dolores is twenty years old. She cries over Hector, then learns that two of her brothers are dead, her mother has lost their house in the village and remarried a man with ten children of his own. She knows that it is not another man she must find. She has two children, a home she cannot go back to, a job that has no future, can barely feed her children, and that she can lose any time for any reason to a thousand other illiterate women eager to take her place for less money. She will live the way she is for the rest of her life, will die at forty, and so will her children if they live past five.

A thousand miles north is a place where there is work and they pay a week's wages for an hour. Where there are real houses and running water and sewers. Where children do not die every fifteen minutes, can live even eighty years. When Dolores has saved $400 by scavenging and begging in the day, has found two women whose husbands have gone north to take the children and a man who knows how to go north, she kisses Josefina and Venicio and walks from her shack and the city. She is twenty-two.

It is a long walk. She is offered rides by men who drive trucks, rural bus drivers, rich men with cars, and even villagers with carts and burros, but it is safer to walk and she will take a ride only if she can walk no farther. Once American tourists drive her all the way to Chichicastenango where she cries because her village is only a day away. She must hide whenever she hears a motor because it could be the police or a patrol of soldiers who will arrest her and send her to a model village if they don't shoot her as a communist when they find she does not live in the district, has no papers to say why she is walking north alone. She must hide from the guerrillas, they need women to carry and cook food, they are men too.

She has walked two weeks when the *kaibile* patrol finds her. The officer is a polite young man who orders his laughing men to leave her alone.

"My apologies, *señora*, but, alas, I must take you with us. I have my orders, this district is infested with the subversive communist rabble we are hunting, you would not be safe alone to continue wherever you are going."

They take her to a village. There are many other travelers the *kaibiles* have caught on the road, the silent *campesinos* of the village, and six battered and bloody guerrillas tied at the end of the single street. The young officer points to the sullen guerrillas to show her the danger on the road in this part of the country, puts her with the other frightened travelers. It is nearly dark when he returns to them. He tells them he needs help against the subversive guerrillas and the *campesinos* he suspects of concealing the communists and their supplies.

"We must know where these animals have hidden their guns and their food, who works with them in this district. We must make them tell us. I have a plan that will get them to talk to us."

He explains that he has threatened to shoot villagers and guerrillas alike, but they don't really believe him. If they see him shoot all the travelers, they will believe he means what he says, and at least the *campesinos* will talk. He is going to take the travelers out to the edge of the village near the captured swine and have his men pretend to execute them. He wants the travelers to fall over and lie very still when his men shoot. He asks if they all understand? They nervously nod that they do.

"Good. Remember to act frightened, and lie very still. You will be doing much for your country, and afterward you can go on to wherever you are going."

The young officer smiles and calls in his patrol. There are more travelers than *kaibiles*. The *kaibiles* herd the villagers and prod the guerrillas to make them watch as the young officer steps up to put his pistol to the back of each traveler's head. When the first traveler falls he does not lie still. His feet jerk and twist. Dolores does not wait.

She is up and into the forest at the edge of the village before the *kaibiles* know what has happened. The others follow her. The villagers scatter. Only the guerrillas can do nothing. The *kaibiles* open fire, pursue, but Dolores has run as fast as she can, knows the mountain terrain well, and is not discovered hidden under a forest thorn bush in a deep *barranca* the *kaibiles* do not see in the falling dusk.

She waits in the forest all night. Hears the screams of those who do not escape, are shot on the spot. By morning the forest is silent, the soldiers are gone. She travels slowly in the forest for two more days before she returns to a road. She meets other women, and at the end of three weeks they are at the village near the border of Mexico where she is to contact the *coyote* she paid the man in Guatemala City to send her to.

She pays the *coyote*.

She wades a river.

She hides.

In Mexico everyone knows at once what she is.

"Hey, *chica*, you come live with me I send for your children in Guatemala, eh?"

"Go back to Guatemala. We got enough troubles here."

"My brother is chief of police, *chingada*. You be nice to me or I tell him and they send you back!"

Two of the other women are raped.

"Catch that fucking *chica*, asshole!"

"Fuck her, Manolo, we got two live ones, who needs that one?"

She is hungry and cold.

"You need a coat, *señora*." He is an old Mexican with a fat, smiling wife and a small hacienda. "You must eat, sleep. In the morning you can continue your journey."

The coat from the good man and his happy wife keeps her warmer, but she is always afraid.

"You have money. Give us your fucking money, little hen."

"Shit, she ain't got no money. The *coyote* or the cops took it all. Cut her fucking throat."

She hides her money well. But not well enough to fool the rural police.

"We know you have money, *chica.* You want to stay in our jail until you remember where it is, eh?"

There are no more soldiers, but there are many police and many bandits and many men on the roads from the border. When she arrives three weeks later in Mexico City all her money is gone and she is afraid of everyone who looks at her. The city is so big, there are so many people. It is raining. The puddles are yellow in the streetlights. She is afraid to speak to anyone. They will know she is from Guatemala and send her back. She is afraid to beg or ask for food. They will put her in jail. She is afraid to look for the name and address she has been given by the women whose husbands went north. People will see her look, know she is not from Mexico even though she doesn't speak, put her in jail or send her back or rob her or rape her.

But if she does not find the name from Guatemala she will soon starve or freeze in the fog and cold rain of the city. It will not matter if she is robbed or raped or sent back.

The apartment is in Azcapotzalco. The bright sun is out. Azcapotzalco had once been a town with churches and graveyards and haciendas like the towns on the coast in Guatemala, the ruins still there surrounded by the sprawl of a giant oil refinery and modern Mexico. The apartment is above a noisy *cantina,* but the woman from Guatemala can put her up until she finds a place, get her a job in the factory where the woman and her sister work. Five Guatemalans live in the three-room apartment. Dolores gets up in the dark, waits on the dim streetcorner with twenty others for the bus to the factory, does not make enough money to get her own place and still send money home for Josefina and Venicio. After a month she sees it is not that much better in Mexico. After two months she knows she must continue north.

There will be no *kaibiles,* but there will still be police and bandits and men. And *la migra.*

She must have a Mexican identity. To be caught by *la migra* and identified as Guatemalan will mean being sent all the way back. A

Mexican is arrested and driven back to Tijuana to try again a day or an hour later.

She must lose her soft accent, learn the hard sing-song speech and slang of Mexicans.

She must have money. For the false papers in Mexico and in the United States. For the next *coyote*. For food and bus fare to the new border. That far even Dolores cannot walk. For good clothes that will avert suspicion when the bus is stopped by the Mexican police or immigration. To pay back the good sisters.

Dolores has no one to borrow from, will have to work, send no money home until she has the money. It will be many months.

The sisters tell her they know a rich *don*. A *hidalgo* from home who lives in a magnificent hacienda in Cabo San Lucas where all the *norteamericanos* come to swim and lie in the sun and do nothing all day. This rich *don* often helps his countrymen to go north, comes often to Mexico City on business, has a party for his fellow Guatemalans at a big restaurant in the country outside the city. They take Dolores to the party at the restaurant that is in a great garden decorated like a fiesta, and she meets Don Sylvestre Madrona.

The sisters want Don Sylvestre to help Dolores go to the United States so she can earn money for her children at home.

Don Sylvestre wants Dolores.

This does not happen instantly. Don Sylvestre Madrona has many women at the party more stylish and sophisticated, better dressed and more dazzling than Dolores Rios. It does not begin until Don Sylvestre graciously agrees to talk to her alone in a corner of the garden. Dolores, who has worn her old Guatemalan *huipile* instead of the new Mexico City clothes the sisters have loaned her, is shy and scared and nervous and grateful that the Don will perhaps help her. They talk and Don Sylvestre promises he will help her, and she goes home with the sisters.

Next evening when Dolores returns on the long bus ride from work the flowers are waiting for her.

They are waiting the next day.

And the next.

Don Sylvestre himself appears on the fourth day. In his big white car with the driver. He takes her to a restaurant in the best part of the city. She is the only woman there dressed like a *campesina*. She is still scared and nervous, but the waiters are polite, the police respectful, important men friendly, and Dolores soon realizes that if she is with Don Sylvestre it does not matter where she works or lives or has come from.

The fifth day he arrives in a small red car that he drives himself, drives her to a country *cantina* far from the city, tells her that he will take her north to the United States personally. He wants her to come north with him. He wants her to come to his hacienda in Cabo San Lucas. He wants her. He is a lonely man who will be good to her and give her money to send to Guatemala for Josefina and Venicio. He will give her money to pay the sisters who have helped her.

Dolores goes to the hacienda in Cabo San Lucas.

"I have many *huipiles*," he tells her when they are alone in the hacienda, "you will wear a different one every day."

She wears the *huipiles* for a month.

"Now you must lose weight," Don Sylvestre says.

Dolores loses weight, becomes thin and angular.

"You will be blonde."

Dolores becomes blonde with long loose hair like a *norte-americana* cinema star.

"Now we will go north," Don Sylvestre says.

He gives her a blue American passport. Her name is Dolores Shay. She was born in Los Angeles. They drive north in his big white car with the driver. At the border Don Sylvestre shows his papers and her passport. She smiles, the guards smile and she is in the United States. They live in a fine apartment in Newport Beach, travel a great deal. Don Sylvestre takes her with him wherever he goes on his business except to Guatemala as if he is afraid that if she sees her children she will want them. She does want them, but the money she sends is enough to pay her brother and his wife in Quetzaltenango to have Josefina and Venicio in the family, and Don Sylvestre is good to her.

Dolores does not know what made Don Sylvestre choose her, or why he brought her north and made her a thin blonde with cinema-star hair and silver and gold clothes. She does not think about it. She does not think about where he is when he is not with her. She knows he has other women, older women, but when he goes out to parties he takes her. He does not like her to leave the apartment when he is not with her, does not want her to find work or learn English or learn how to read. But he gives her much money to send to Josefina and Venicio, she learns some English by watching the television in the apartment all day, learns to read a little by watching a program on Channel 34 where they speak Spanish, and Don Sylvestre is good to her.

When he is shot to death in Santa Barbara while they are on the business trip, she is frightened. She is alone in the hotel room, the police come and ask many questions she cannot answer. But they are polite, do not ask to see her papers, let her stay in the room. Alone in the empty hotel suite, Dolores is sad. She turns on the television, practices speaking English with the faces on the screen, thinks that perhaps now she can get a job, even bring Josefina and Venicio to the United States. Or make enough money to go home and buy some land and build a little house for the three of them. Her dark eyes under the blonde hair stare at the bright faces on the television. She is twenty-five.

8

Sergeant Chavalas said, "What the hell are we getting around here, a banana republic war?"

I had told him about the "maid" in Sylvestre Madrona's suite at the Biltmore, about her meeting with the Major and the men in the dark suits, about Earl's rescue of me. He looked at my tweed jacket without a sleeve or pocket, then at Tyrone Earl.

"You don't believe it was robbery-murder? Decided to snoop on your own?"

"It's all I have to believe, Sergeant, but when Fortune came around questioning Dolores it sure as hell looked like he didn't believe it. I wanted to find out what he maybe knew and I didn't."

"Did you?"

Earl smiled at me. "I know some of what he thinks, I'm damn sure not all. I just don't have any notion of how Sylvestre fits with any of it."

"A businessman," Chavalas said. "Nothing else."

"Not that I ever saw or heard, and we're a small company."

"How small?"

"Me, Sylvestre, agents in all the Latin countries who spot the handicrafts and close the deals with the villagers. Some warehouse men, a receptionist, an accountant and a lawyer on retainer in L.A., another receptionist, accountant, lawyer and warehouse guys in Mexico City."

"So you're saying, really, a two-man business."

"That's about it, Sergeant."

"No smuggling, no *coyotes*, no politics, no drugs."

"Christ, no."

I said, "You're that sure about Madrona, Mr. Earl?"

"Ty." His blue-gray eyes seemed to turn inward under the heavy brows, he leaned forward in his chair in the afternoon office. "You tell me what says, even whispers Sylvestre was doing any of those things."

Chavalas said, "Where we found him was no place a tourist should be late at night, and nowhere a robber would be at any time."

"Hell, Sylvestre could be crazy as a loon, and who says a thief—"

"He wasn't killed there anyway," Chavalas said. He watched Earl like a hawk. The importer only sat back in his chair.

"Where was he killed? How do you know?"

"Dan?"

Chavalas was as aware as I that Earl was trying to pump us while we questioned him. The sergeant would give him enough to make him think he was winning the game, maybe relax and get careless and tell us more than we told him. Maneuvering for the advantage. The twentieth-century game in work, leisure, war and love. I told Earl how I'd found Sylvestre Madrona that night in the warehouse.

"You know why he was there? You know anything about that warehouse?"

"We don't have a warehouse in Santa Barbara." He said it, but he wasn't thinking about it. A fact he could deal with while he thought about what he couldn't deal with. "This Major shot him? Why?"

"I don't know what the Major did. I heard shots, saw the Major standing over Madrona when I went in."

Earl turned on Chavalas. "What does this Major say?"

"We're looking for him to talk to him."

"But Dan saw him in that house—" Earl stopped.

I nodded. "Yeah, he won't be there when the police get there. They've only got my description of what he looks like, no idea where he's living in town."

For the time being I would keep my knowledge of the Major's name to myself. You take what advantage you can get today.

Chavalas said, "That brings us full circle—why would the Major, or anyone besides a mugger, want to shoot Mr. Madrona?"

"And I still don't have one damn idea in hell why."

I said, "Biltmore suites, big Cadillacs, sports cars, houses in Mexico City and Cabo San Lucas, grand parties, forged American passports, all the women he wanted."

Earl laughed again. Big, loud, exuberant, uninhibited laughter. "You've been listening to our Dolores too much. Sure, Sylvestre was a high roller, but he was a fraud too. In the first place the hacienda in Cabo and the big mansion in Mexico City weren't his, they belong to the company. We all use them. The cars are leased to the company, so is the apartment in L.A. Mine too, for that matter. He didn't even have a place of his own in Mexico City. I do because my wife lives there."

"The Koenig too?" I asked.

"Sure. Name of the game, right?" Grinned. "The IRS might be after Sylvestre, but not the INS."

"A forged American passport?"

"Hell, forged papers are a cottage industry in Mexico. In L.A. too these days. A passport is top dollar, but that only means a nice *mordida* in Mexico, and Sylvestre liked to impress the women. In Mexico it doesn't take billions or even millions to be a high roller."

"Much money," I said. "Ms. Shay's exact words were, Don Sylvestre and Señor Ty have much money."

Earl looked down at the floor of Chavalas's office, suddenly serious. The mercurial shift again, the dark side of him. "To a *campesina* like Dolores, much money is goddamn little, believe me. Sylvestre probably spent more on a dinner party than she ever saw in a year." He shook his head, his craggy face somewhere between sad and angry. Then looked up at us and smiled. "Mayan Imports does just fine. Buy cheap from the villagers down there, sell high up here. Pay the agents on commission off the purchase price, keep the overhead down, end up with one damn nice profit margin. It's a sweet business." His face shifted once more, almost dark. "Money was no problem for Sylvestre."

"Or you?" Chavalas said.

"Or me."

I said, "What was his problem?"

"He was a human being like the rest of us." Then he gave that big, loud laugh. "He didn't have any problems, Dan. Not the kind you get killed for. Unless maybe by some irate husband. He liked the ladies, liked making money, liked living well, but that's it. A businessman, legitimate and hardworking."

"What about his personal life?" Chavalas asked. "The irate husband. Did he have a lot of Miss Shays? A wife, maybe?"

"I told Dan all about that, Sergeant."

"Tell me."

He told Chavalas what he had told me in the car about Madrona's personal life, the story of Dolores Rios-Shay.

Earl stood. "I better get back to the Biltmore before Dolores wonders if I'm dead too. If you need me, I'm staying at San Ysidro Ranch."

"What can you do for Dolores Rios?" I asked.

"Take her back down to L.A., straighten her out with INS and find her a decent job. Back to what she was before Sylvestre made her over. Don't think she ever really liked it."

"Why'd she let him do it?" Chavalas wondered.

Earl looked at him, the serious face again. "She didn't really have any choice, did she? Not if she was going to stay alive, send money to her kids."

He nodded to both of us, walked out of the office. Tyrone Earl was a charmer, looked and acted more like an aging tennis player than a businessman, smooth yet down-to-earth. He'd been pumping us and giving very little. Not that he'd gotten much either. He had a way of backing off and sliding away just when he might be in danger of being pinned down, but before he got any real information. I had the odd feeling he didn't really want, or maybe need, anything from the police or me. He was here for another reason.

"He's not telling us something," Chavalas said.

"Protecting Madrona or himself?"

"One, both or maybe even someone else." Chavalas looked out his window at the beautiful lavender blooms of the jacaranda. "This Major and a foreign agent sound like politics."

"Or smuggling. Guns, ammunition, something like that. They

are importers, have warehouses and probably trucks. Even jets nowadays, get the merchandise up here faster."

Chavalas still studied his tree. "You're sure about the agent?"

"Educated guess, that's all. You learn anything new since this morning?"

Chavalas looked down at an open file folder on his desk. "We got your Major's name from the State Department. Major Harvey Hill, U. S. Army, retired. A military intelligence and counterinsurgency specialist. Worked with the State Department and CIA on detached duty from nineteen eighty-four through nineteen eighty-eight, details still top secret."

"He worked with the CIA? That could really be who the two dark suits are. On duty or maybe on their own."

"I thought about that too," Chavalas said. "State referred me to the Pentagon for the record of his military career. Usual stuff—led a platoon in Vietnam, assigned to special forces. One tour in Germany and another in Panama, then sent to foreign posts until he went on detached duty. Retired in 'eighty-eight, works now for a civilian company, World Military Incorporated. They supply the services with reports on foreign military units, tables of organization, new equipment, training methods and chain of command."

"You check on the company?"

"Works out of D.C. It's small, headed up by a retired air force general, the whole staff are ex-officers."

"How big a staff?"

"Ten, twelve."

"Shit," I said. "That means library work, a boondoggle. They get published reports, compile them, put them in a jazzy plastic cover and deliver them. Add a touch of spice with a few phone calls to personal contacts."

"Doesn't sound like what the Major's doing around here."

"No, and it doesn't sound like it rates a government car. Who'd you talk to at State?"

"Your deputy assistant secretary, Mr. Max Cole. Washington confirmed he was out on the Coast. Down in L.A., they said, and declined to tell me what his business was. Cole declined to tell me anything at all. When I asked about Major Hill being in Santa Barbara, he said he knew nothing about the Major since he left the service, gave me the number of World Military in Washington. They told me Major Hill was on an assignment in Mexico, had been for a week, would I like his number? I would, and I called. A man answered, said he was Major Hill, had never been in Santa Barbara, had been in Mexico all week, had fifty witnesses to prove it if I didn't believe him. Just for fun I asked some questions about his record I'd gotten from Max Cole and the Pentagon. He answered them all."

"Surprise," I said. "No voice check, of course."

"This is Santa Barbara, not the FBI. Maybe someday, but even then we'd have to be ready with a comparison. Right now all I've got is your story about someone you say is Major Hill."

"Which one is the real Major Hill, and how do I prove it, right?"

"How do you, Dan?"

"I don't. Maybe the Major Hill up here is a fake. I don't think so, but I can't prove it without checking him out. We know Max Cole is real. The guys in suits look and act like CIA. So if my Major Hill is a phony, then Cole and the others are in on the fake." I looked out the window at the lavender blooms on Chavalas's favorite jacaranda. "Maybe I'm lying about the warehouse. Or at least mistaken."

With no other witness to the warehouse shooting, even if my Major were the real one, it would be my word against fifty unimpeachable witnesses in Mexico, a whole company of ex-heroes in Washington, and the State Department.

"Are you, Dan?"

"Which?"

Chavalas considered his favorite jacaranda once more.

"Mistaken."

Chavalas is a decent man. Not many cops love the beauty of trees and flowers the way he does. But he meant either one. No cop can rule out anyone lying in a murder case. If he does, he's not doing his job.

"No. The man who calls himself the Major was the one in the warehouse standing with the gun over Madrona's body."

"Not a stray fingernail in that warehouse, Dan. No blood, no bullet holes, not a sign of breaking in. Not even bullet chips out of the concrete pillars. That's a hell of a coverup."

"That's a hell of a lot of clout and manpower."

"The warehouse belongs to a solid local businessman with no connection to Mayan Imports or Latin America. He's lived here most of his life, is a hundred percent legitimate. The Omaha trucking company's had it leased for ten years, does no business in Latin America, never heard of Sylvestre Madrona, Tyrone Earl or Major Harvey Hill, has no connection to the State Department."

A hell of a coverup, or I was a liar, crazy or both.

"The gun?"

"No trace. Cartridge cases are standard army issue for the new Beretta."

"What did Deputy Assistant Secretary Cole say about Paul Valenzuela?"

"On a trip. State Department business."

"A straight-out lie. Keep it simple."

"You don't know that, Dan."

I didn't, not for sure.

9

Esther Valenzuela wasn't at her parents' house. The Major was.

He sat in a big flowered armchair, with Mr. and Mrs. Conrad side by side on the matching couch, Deputy Assistant Secretary Max Cole across the room in a brocade chair beside a mahogany end table. The Conrads stared at my tweed jacket with its torn-off sleeve and missing pocket. No one else did.

Any questions I had about the men in the dark suits being CIA disappeared the instant I saw who stood behind the Major in the living room. Walter Enz, a CIA man I'd bumped heads with on a case a year ago.

"Still shaping the universe in our image, Walt?"

The man who'd captured me at the empty house on the lower Westside stood near the marble mantelpiece, a bandage barely concealing a livid bruise on his head.

"The same stupid shitass, Fortune?" Enz said.

The Major looked from me to the small man stiff as a ramrod behind him. "How do you know Fortune, Enz?"

"He stuck his nose in where it didn't belong once before," Walt Enz said. His manner hadn't improved, but his wardrobe had. A well-tailored blue suit and the self-satisfied expression to go with it.

"The Major your new keeper, Walt?" I said. "What happened to our pal McIver?"

"He got old and slow and soft. He got a desk, I got his job. I ain't old or slow or soft. It's a new ball game."

"Looks a lot like the same old Gestapo game to me."

I talked to Walt—the macho banter he understood and expected—but I watched Esther Valenzuela's parents. George Conrad was a solid, compact man in suit, shirt and tie even at home on a warm afternoon. His wife was thin, wore a flowered dress and low heels. She had a sensitive face like her daughter's, with short, matronly gray hair. They sat bolt upright and faced Max Cole and the Major like kids in awe of the teacher. I guessed that Cole had pulled rank on them, given them a story about top government business that couldn't be revealed, we're sure you understand, but we need your cooperation.

"Don't be a bigger asshole than you got to be, Fortune," Walter Enz said.

"All right, Enz." The Major turned his attention to me. "We waited here for you, Dan, as we've explained to Mr. and Mrs. Conrad, because Esther wanted us to be sure you understood the whole situation before you walked away. She feels she owes you that much."

I looked out the archway into the entrance hall for any sign of Esther Valenzuela. An open door to the left showed an empty dining room. I listened for sounds that would reveal another person in the big house. I saw and heard nothing.

Max Cole shifted restlessly in the brocade chair. "I say it's none of his damned business. The less anyone knows the better."

"Dan knows how to keep his mouth shut," the Major said.

I smiled. "How about Esther explaining it to me?"

"Esther talks to no one from now on," Max Cole snapped.

The Major leaned forward. "Dan, I want your promise that what I tell you goes no farther than this room. I have Mr. and Mrs. Conrad's word. Okay?"

I said nothing, did nothing. I was going to get the story he wanted to tell me no matter what I said or did. His eyes hardened a hair, I wasn't playing the game right. But he had his story.

"You think you saw me shoot Sylvestre Madrona. You didn't." He leaned back in the armchair, frowned over how to explain a serious and difficult problem. "We don't know who shot him. That's one of the things we're trying to find out. The people we suspect are skittish as virgins with a squad of Marines, we're afraid you could have scared them into lying low already."

"Speaking of Marines, it's a coincidence the murder weapon was a service Beretta M9, the same as you carry?"

"A lot of people carry our nine-millimeter Berettas, from guerrillas to bank robbers."

"You still have yours?"

He reached under the navy blazer, pulled out the big service pistol. "Want to give it to police ballistics?"

"Would it do me any good?"

"Since I didn't shoot Madrona, no."

"You weren't even in Santa Barbara," I said. "In fact I guess you're not here now, right? Still down in Mexico."

Walt Enz swore. "Shit, Major, you're wasting your time on a goddamn hardhead like Fortune."

The Major ignored the CIA man. "I flew up this morning, Dan. You want the number of the flight?"

"I'll pass." Whatever they were doing was arranged, organized and covered. He wasn't worried about his gun, the flight would check out. "Which was Madrona? Guerrilla or bank robber?"

"He was a fucking poison peddler, that's what he was," Walt Enz said. "A heavyweight dope shipper and seller out to suck our kids dry and toss them in the garbage."

The Major turned. "Mr. Cole and I can handle Fortune, Enz. Maybe you and Moretti should take a swing outside, make sure he came alone and no one tailed him."

The silent man, Moretti, moved toward the archway out of the living room. He would be the number-two CIA man. Walter Enz hesitated, aware he was being gotten rid of, and yet aware that it was a good idea to be sure I'd come alone. The problem was that someone else had told him to do something, and he didn't accept that. After all the years leaning on walls and waiting as the number-two man, he gave the orders now.

"I'll take care of any tails, you and Cole make damn sure you don't give Fortune too fucking much. Understand?"

It was pretty lame, but it served his purpose, at least to him. After the two CIA men had gone, the Major seemed to think about some insoluble problem, such as co-workers with more dedication than understanding, more belief than brains, before he returned his attention to me.

"Madrona was a major drug lord, Dan. Tied into the Medellin cartel on the highest level and using his position with Mayan Imports as the perfect cover. What he was doing up here, who he was meeting in that warehouse, we don't know but we will."

"Are others at Mayan Import involved? Tyrone Earl?"

"That's something else we're investigating. So far Earl looks clean, doesn't seem to have a clue to why Madrona was killed."

"He was exactly what Madrona needed," Max Cole said. "A legitimate businessman as the perfect cover for his illegitimate business."

The Major scowled. "It's not a business, it's a war. An open war on the integrity and future of this country. A dirty and ruthless war. A war we have to win, Dan, and we need all the cooperation we can get. Right now that includes you."

"Does it include Paul Valenzuela?"

"Especially."

"How?"

Cole said, "That's precisely what we don't want you going around asking or even talking about. This is no business for amateurs, Fortune. Let those who know what they're doing do it."

They both sat there in the sedate, dignified, conservative old living room of the Conrads, watched my face with the fierce intensity of Joan of Arc listening to her voices. Mr. and Mrs. Conrad watched all of us, their eyes bright with admiration, the thrill of secondhand excitement. We were better than a movie on the VCR. The safety of the nation was at stake. We were all warriors for the national security against the forces of evil.

"Let Big Brother's troops save us?"

"You wouldn't let a layman treat your cancer, would you, Fortune?" the Major said.

I said, "Don't throw national security at us every time a government official wants to do what he isn't sure he has the right to do. Tell us what you're doing and why."

Max Cole got up abruptly as if barely able to control his anger. "The CIA is right, Major. We're wasting our time."

He made me think of the former official of ex-Panamanian strongman General Noriega who, having trouble with members of his now-opposition party, complained that in the old days he would simply have purged them. All governments in all places at all times would like to simply purge. The only difference is that for some governments it's a first choice and for others a last resort. No established power goes out easily.

The Major nodded to the Conrads. "I'm sorry, but I think we'll have to ask you to let us talk to Fortune alone."

Have you ever noticed when officials and civilians occupy the same space or time it is the civilian who is asked to move? Even in a democracy where the official is the elected servant of the civilian. It says something about all governments, and about most civilians. The Conrads jumped up as if shot.

"Of course," George Conrad said. "Come, Ethel. We'll be in the kitchen if you need us, Major."

"I'll make coffee," Ethel Conrad said.

"It's very kind of you," the Major said, glanced toward where Max Cole stood at the mantelpiece, all five-foot-seven of him still angry. "Cole?"

"Very kind," Cole said, tried to smile but didn't quite make it. He was more than angry. He was worried, maybe scared.

While we waited for Mr. and Mrs. Conrad to exit their own living room, I thought about the Major's tone with Cole. No matter who had the title, the Major was in charge. The nominal civilian not the official. And when the three of us were alone, it was the Major who fixed his serious eyes on me.

"All right, Dan, we're going to tell you the whole story, okay?" He paused to give me a chance to enthuse, but went on smoothly when I didn't. "It all started down in Mexico about two weeks ago. We got a tip that a big shipment was coming into L.A. through Mexico along the Trampoline route. Our canary used a name no one knew: Madrona. We didn't have a clue who or what Madrona was, it looked like a new team in the league right in the middle of the crackdown. We alerted all the troops from Medellin to La-La land and waited."

"Who's we?"

"DEA, State, Mexican police, INS, the Pentagon, the CIA, some FBI up here. The whole—"

"Which one is World Military Incorporated a cover for? Military intelligence?"

"World Military is a civilian research company that works with the Pentagon and not a damn thing else. I still work on my own for State when they call on me for intelligence or counterinsurgency problems in Latin America where I've got the contacts and know the scorecard. Okay?"

"What have intelligence and counterinsurgency got to do with the drug war?"

Max Cole said, "Major, I told you—"

"We're using everything we can against drugs, Dan."

I said. "When do we get around to Paul Valenzuela?"

The Major stood up to pace. "Paul Valenzuela stumbled over some dangerous information, gunmen came after him, he ran off and hid before he could give us the information."

"How do you know that?"

"Valenzuela called Cole in Washington."

"Before or after he ran?"

"After."

"But didn't tell Cole where he was?"

"He was scared." The Major continued to pace for a moment in silence, then stopped and looked at me. Verbal punctuation, we all do it. "What he'd run across was a hot lead inside the embassy to a Guatemalan drug king named Madrona. That's what he told Cole on the telephone."

"And why you flew out here?"

He nodded, sat down again. "We wanted to talk to him and protect him. He'd panicked when he ran and hid. He was in more danger out there alone than he would have been if he'd come to us. It seemed logical he would contact Esther, so I came out. But that was only part of it."

"What was the other part?"

"Our original pigeon in Mexico picked up some additional information—the unknown Mr. Madrona was going to meet another man involved in the deal in Santa Barbara. We traced the meeting to that warehouse, but someone else got to Madrona before we did. The rest you know."

He shrugged and sat back. I looked toward Max Cole. He was leaning on the mantelpiece lighting a cigarette. It was the first time I'd seen him smoke.

"That's it?"

"That's all we can tell you."

"What was the lead Paul Valenzuela stumbled over? Did he think it meant someone at the embassy was mixed up in drugs? Who are the thugs he ran away from? Why is he hiding from you?"

"Those are all nothing you need to know."

"The Latina snooping around Dolores Shay. What is she? Who's she working for? Besides you."

Cole said, "You're being told to stop asking questions for your own and your country's good, Fortune. Why not just do it?"

As if to emphasize the deputy assistant secretary's message, the Major's advice and concern for my welfare, Walter Enz and the second CIA man came back into the room. They took their silent posts around the elegantly papered walls. The four fixed me with their solemn eyes like the silent weight of a team of basilisks.

The Major said, "Claudia Nervo is with Guatemalan security. They're fighting the drug dealers as hard as we are. The drug kings create havoc in those small countries with their money and private armies. We're all together in this. Okay?" He smiled man to man. "Come on, Dan, let go of it. This is our job, we know what we're doing. Go home, do what you do best, don't worry about Madrona. Your client is safe, your job is over."

They all stood and smiled at me in the big, sunny living room with its small-figured wallpaper. A comfortable room in a rich city under a fine spring sun. Reassuring smiles, solid and substantial. Confident.

I said, "I don't worry a lot, Major, but I really begin to worry when people tell me I have to be ignorant for my own good. It's too dangerous for me to know what's going on, let them save me from some great evil I can't even know about. I worry when I can't help a woman find her husband, or know what he's involved in, because I might harm the public interest."

"You can stop worrying about Paul Valenzuela," the Major said. "We've found him, he's safe with us, and Mrs. Valenzuela is with him. That's why she wanted us to explain what we could to you, and why she sent money to pay your bill in full. Enz?"

Walter Enz walked to me, held out an envelope with the cash sticking out of it as if they'd been counting it. It looked like a nice bundle, more than what I had done for Esther Valenzuela was worth. I looked at the Major in his flowered chair.

"Who's the guy in the limo? The one with you at the warehouse where you never were."

At the mantelpiece, Cole exploded, "For God's sake, can't you hear? This is serious government business! Paul Valenzuela is safe. Esther wants you off the case. Now take your money and—"

"He's only an undercover FBI man, Dan," the Major said. "You're starting to get paranoid, see shadows."

I watched them all. "I'd like to talk to Esther herself, have her tell me, before I quit."

"All right," the Major nodded, stood up. "I'll tell her as soon as we leave here, have her call you at your office."

"That's fine."

The Major nodded. "Enz?"

Walt Enz handed me the envelope of cash.

10

They all came out separately.

Walt Enz and Moretti drove down the driveway in what looked to be the same black car that had driven up to the warehouse the night Sylvestre Madrona was shot. They'd parked it behind the Conrad house. Cole was next. A deputy assistant secretary of state rated an official car. Not a big car, but a free car with a driver. It hadn't been there when I arrived, the driver off for coffee or maybe a fast line of big C.

The Major came last, paused in the doorway at the top of the brick steps to thank Mr. and Mrs. Conrad for their hospitality. He walked around the corner to his black Buick that belonged to the government just as Cole's car did, but the Major's car didn't announce the fact or have a driver. They had been expecting me to come calling, were waiting to tell me their story.

The Buick turned on Anacapa Street, headed downtown toward the ocean. He showed no more sign of being aware of a tail than he had that first night. Traffic was heavy in the late afternoon, the lawyers, bankers, real estate salesmen, shoppers and tourists heading for the freeway and home or some motel. The black Buick drove easily, unhurried, moved with the thick flow of cars without pushing or weaving or running any yellows. Twice red lights stopped me, but I picked him up again at the next light. An advantage of staggered traffic lights.

The cars bunched up more as we neared the freeway lights that are the last bastions remaining between Los Angeles and San Francisco. Monuments to the power that was, and maybe still is, Santa Barbara, they are to be removed after a long fight between the state and the city. For forty years the state was adamant on putting the freeway up on steel legs that would cut the town off from its beachfront, harbor, wharf and marina. For the same stubborn forty years the city refused to have anything but an entirely sunken freeway invisible to citizens who strolled oceanward. For forty years travelers north and south cursed their way through Santa Barbara every holiday weekend and every rush hour. Now it was almost over. The outcome? A street-level freeway with three underpasses at a hundred times' greater cost than either original idea.

I braced to force my way through the lights if they went red after the Major and before me. But the Buick turned right on Haley. Across State and Chapala on the same route the Guatemalan security woman, Claudia Nervo, had walked earlier. Turned among the lower Westside streets and stopped in front of the same two-story house. Hidden up the next block, I watched the Major get out and stride into the house, out of place down here in his blue blazer, tan slacks, expensive shirt, half boots.

No one else appeared.

After ten minutes I moved through and across the barren yards of the worn and paint-peeling cottages along the concrete banks of Mission Creek. No one stopped me or spoke to me. If they watched me I didn't see them. Any stranger who hurried through the yards was either a cop, a crook on the run, an unknown junkie or a dope dealer, and the people down here wanted no trouble with any of them.

Across the silent yard I saw no movement inside the gray house. The shadowed sunlight of the late afternoon had begun to cool toward the evening chill of Santa Barbara. Traffic noise was heavy from the nearby freeway as the frustrated rush-hour drivers burst loose after the long delay at the stoplights, covered any sound that might have come from the gray house.

If I was right, and the Major was so anxious to get rid of me he would go straight to Esther Valenzuela and have her call me, he should be in there now dialing my number, listening for me to answer before handing her the phone with an unspoken warning to tell me only what he had instructed her to say. When there was no answer, he would hang up and wait for maybe ten minutes before dialing again. He would wait in the house with Esther until I answered. I would wait for dark.

I was wrong on both counts.

Just after five, the sun low behind the bluff of the Mesa close above the house and the freeway, the Major came out the front door and down the steps. He was alone, walked out to the street. Beyond the hedge the door of the Buick opened, slammed. The engine started, the car pulled away and faded into the steady roar of the freeway.

Somehow you can sense an empty house. Maybe it comes from those ancient days of prehistory when another human meant a hope of safety in the night of a thousand other beasts stronger than we were. The early seconds of the brief moment we have been on this tiny planet around a second-class star. I sensed, in the old gray house, no human aura. No light, no movement, no life. I've been wrong before. Those old senses are muted now that we have nothing to fear but ourselves.

I waited a half an hour, then went in, briefly checking with my lone hand for the old cannon in the remaining pocket of my torn tweed jacket. There was no light, the front door was unlocked. Inside, low-angled sunlight came in through the dusty, uncurtained windows that faced the south and the sea. Dusty old furniture that had been cheap when it was new. Dusty floors, an empty kitchen with an empty refrigerator that wasn't working. Dusty dining room too small for more than six people at the table if it had had a table. A house built in that era of the thirties and forties when the poor were rising into the middle class and had to have, even in miniature, all they saw in the Hollywood movies where the rich lived in elegant mansions with a room for every purpose.

Carpetless stairs up to a dustier second floor. A narrow hall to a small front window that faced west and the now-orange glow behind the dark Mesa. There were four doors off the hall. I listened. Only the steady sound of the stream of motors on the freeway, the soft creak of boards beneath my feet, the faint rasp of my own breathing.

The first two bedrooms were empty. The third door was a half bathroom with a dirt-caked toilet bowl and spiders in the corners. The final door had been the master bedroom. Larger than the others with two windows that faced the Mesa and the light of the setting sun and its own small bathroom. As empty as all the other rooms in the dusty house.

No one was a prisoner in this house, nor had been recently.

From the window at the end of the upstairs hall I looked down at the street in front. Four skinny black men drank beer on the sagging porch of a cottage across the street. Two small girls played with makeup and long dresses. An older Latino with a long white mustache and a sombrero walked quietly. No sign of the Buick or the black car of the two CIA men. No limousine waited along the shabby block.

Downstairs, the only telephone was in the empty kitchen on the sink drainboard. It was pushbutton, had no dust on it and was operational. I listened to the dial tone over the heavy drone of the freeway, dialed my office and used the remote to see if Esther had left a message. There was nothing.

In the dusty and empty kitchen I thought about why the Major would come to an empty house to make his telephone calls. Calls he didn't want Deputy Assistant Secretary Max Cole, or even the CIA and FBI, to hear? Reports to someone else?

No one bothered me on the return trip through the bare yards above the dry and littered concrete channel of Mission Creek. No black Buick or limousine was parked on this block. I pulled away from the curb, watched my rearview mirror.

Far back the black Buick appeared from nowhere.

On Bath Street I speeded up. Passed the first corner and turned sharply right at the second, pulled into a long driveway beside a house turned into a pet clinic. Hidden, I stood at the corner of the pet clinic house from where I could see the corner of Bath and the cross street. The black Buick went on up Bath Street without turning east.

He knew now that I hadn't believed his story of Paul and Esther Valenzuela and the death of Sylvestre Madrona. He knew I would not drop the case. If I had believed him, I'd have gone home to wait for Esther Valenzuela's phone call, not tailed him and searched the abandoned house. Not tried to trick him and been tricked instead. Outfoxed and outmaneuvered.

Kay would be back tonight from Los Angeles. I drove home to Summerland. The evening sea wind wasn't the only chill in the Santa Barbara air.

We eat dinner, Kay and I, in the dining room of the Spanish hacienda we rent in Summerland, the raffish beach enclave of Montecito. With the silverware she had picked up over the years, the crystal stemware and bone china and flowers. But not one of us at each end of the long table. Near enough to touch. Tonight even closer, and with candles because she had just returned after four days. Because the Major knew I was still working for Esther Valenzuela.

"What can he do, Dan?"

She is a tall woman. In heels taller than I am and a lot slimmer. Her angular face under the dark auburn cascade of hair has wide-set eyes that watched me steadily in the soft light of the candles. She likes candlelight. I don't. But we like each other so I have to work on that.

"I don't know," I said, dipped an artichoke leaf in the margarine that tasted almost like butter. "But there's a hell of a lot of power behind him. He can prove he was in Mexico when he was here. He can lose a service pistol where no one will ever find it. He can whistle and a more-or-less high State Department official appears."

"Perhaps you should leave the case to him."

Since I came to live with her in California she has been calmer about what I do, but not that calm. She knew what I had to do, would do. She didn't like it any more than I like candles, but she had to work on it too.

"I can't believe their story, there's too much they won't tell. There has to be someone higher up. Someone with a reason to worry about Paul Valenzuela. I want to find Paul Valenzuela, get his side of it."

"You don't believe they really found him? Have him hidden safe somewhere?

"I believe they have Esther Valenzuela safe somewhere. Safe for them."

She twirled some spaghetti on her fork. "Was this Madrona what they say?"

She is a wonderful cook who has little time for cooking. Her modeling and acting agency keeps her busy between Santa Barbara and L.A. I have no trouble with that, I don't wash the car or mow the lawn, and I don't support her any more than she supports me. We eat out a lot, just as I did in New York. When we do eat in it is always something special. Tonight it was her spaghetti. She makes the sauce when she has time, freezes it for coming-home dinners. I like it with artichokes.

"Probably," I said, "but there has to be more. If Madrona was at that warehouse for a meet, and the Major and the man in the limo surprised it, what happened to the other man or men? I heard the shots from outside, no one came out except the man who whistled up the limo and driver, and no one was in the warehouse except the Major."

"No one you saw, Dan."

"If anyone else got out some way I didn't see, why didn't the Major go after them? If someone was still inside the warehouse, why wasn't the Major hunting for him or them instead of standing over the body? If the Major or the man in the limo had shot Madrona, and someone else was still there, why didn't that person try to use my help, say something from hiding? The Major didn't act as if there was any danger in that warehouse except me, and he thought I could have been with Madrona." I nodded over a forkful of spaghetti. "It's more like the Major and the man in the limo had been meeting, and Madrona was the intruder."

I saw that night in the warehouse again. The Major stood over the body of Sylvestre Madrona. The dead man's blood was still spreading, shot only moments before. The Major had heard me and turned, firing. As if a sudden sound at that moment could only be an enemy. But not an enemy he already knew was there. *If you came with Madrona you're already up to your ass in shit. Don't make the same stupid mistake, end up the same way.* Something close to that. As if Madrona had surprised the Major in the warehouse, had made the mistake of—what? Drawing a gun? Refusing to cooperate?

"The coverup was so fast and complete. Why cover up the shooting of a drug dealer?"

"To hide it from other drug dealers he worked with?"

"They didn't hide it from other drug dealers. They didn't cover that Madrona had been shot, only *who* had done the shooting, where and when. Why do government agents want to hide that they shot a drug dealer? The only reason I can come up with is that if they admitted the killing they'd have to explain why they did it, and that's what they don't want to do. Why?"

Kay had no answer. Neither did I. We didn't get any farther over the ice cream and tea.

"I don't believe a Guatemalan security agent would come up here after a simple drug dealer, no matter how big. Down there, drug dealers are more likely to be protected than chased. In too many cases the generals and politicians *are* the drug dealers, or at least on their payroll." I drank my tea. "National security, maybe, but how and where does Paul Valenzuela fit?"

The dishes are mine. With an automatic dishwasher even a one-armed man can handle them. The kitchen was quiet, the single light muted, the routine task soothing. Traffic relatively light on the freeway on a weekday evening. The spring night wind moved the trees outside, the soft pound of the surf across the freeway and the railroad tracks hovered like the purring of some giant animal. Dishwashing is a time to think.

Someone didn't want the murder of a drug dealer known, and wanted Paul Valenzuela. Someone with power. I thought about power. About people who make power, position, fame, greed so all-important. More than a woman, a home, pleasure. More than work, than life itself. Power here and now. Today. As if it could last. Nothing could last, not even the universe. From the big bang that started what we call the universe, to—what? The big shrink back to a hot ball of matter? Where did the matter come from? What is nothing? What is the universe in? What is unending? Our minds can't really think about any of that. So maybe they're right, the people who want to win, be big, be rich, be powerful here and now.

If I believed that I'd shoot myself. What matters is what you can taste, smell, see, feel. Other people. As long as we last. I started the dishwasher, went to my office to write up what I'd done on the Valenzuela case today before I looked for Kay again and the possibilities for the evening.

The message light of the answering machine on my office line was blinking. It had not been blinking when I came home. I keep the office ring too low to hear from the dining room.

"This is Esther Valenzuela. They told me they'd found Paul, he was with them. They made me go with them. I don't know where I am. Help me. I—"

A scared voice. Cut off by a hand clamped down on the receiver cradle.

Kay's voice was behind me. "They kidnapped her?"

"They wouldn't call it that."

She wore her soft white robe open over a pale green nightgown I hadn't seen before.

"You did some shopping in L.A."

"It'll keep."

"I'm not sure I will."

She smiled. "What can you do to help her?"

"Try to find her. Maybe her parents know more. Maybe they left some clue at her house."

"Then find her."

11

There was light only in the living room of the big house on the upper Eastside. The Conrads waited alone and nervous for their daughter to return. Ethel Conrad answered the doorbell at once.

Her eyes were bright when she saw me. "Have you heard from Esther?"

"I'm sorry, Mrs. Conrad."

Her face and shoulders sagged. She turned away, walked ahead through the entry hall into the big, comfortable living room. A warm room, well used and enjoyed by good people who had done everything right and done it well. They did not understand what the Major and Cole were doing, but they could not question it. They could only sit and wait. George Conrad in his high leather armchair in front of the flickering TV in the soft light of the single table lamp. He didn't look at my jacket this time, notice I'd replaced the old tweed with an older orange-brown corduroy.

Ethel Conrad sat on the other side of the lamp table, forgot to ask me to sit down. The show on the television was a bright and frantic comedy of many bouncy young people. Neither of the Conrads laughed.

"What did Esther say to you when she left?"

George Conrad glanced at his wife. "Sit down, Mr. Fortune, please." His solid face under the fringe of neat gray hair and behind the rimless glasses was apologetic. His wife had failed to ask a guest to sit.

"I'm so sorry, Mr. Fortune, forgive me." She didn't care about a lapse in propriety. Her mind was on her daughter. "She left without saying anything."

George said, "We didn't actually see her go, Mr. Fortune."

"They went into George's study to talk, and we didn't see her again before she left," Ethel Conrad said.

"Who's they?"

"She and the Major," George said. "Secretary Cole stayed in here with us, told us about Paul having some information against those drug criminals so they had to protect him and Esther. We understood that, of course, but it is worrisome."

"Whose idea was it to talk in the study?"

They looked at each other in the muted light of the room. The colors of the television flickered. Ethel finally said, "I believe the Major's. Yes, I'm sure he wanted to speak to Esther alone and I suggested George's study."

"Where were those CIA men?"

"Mr. Enz and Mr. Moretti came in about half an hour later," Ethel said.

George Conrad said, "Secretary Cole talked to us for some time in here while the Major was with Esther in the study, told us about some drug kingpin named Madrona. Enz and Moretti came in later when the Major returned to wait for you."

"I believe they were in the study," Ethel Conrad said. "Or up in her bedroom."

The Major had wanted Esther Valenzuela alone in the study. I guessed that the two CIA men had been searching the study and Esther's bedroom. All three had probably taken Esther somewhere and returned to wait for me.

"Was there anyone with Cole and the Major besides the two CIA men?"

"No," George said.

"Can I look at the study?"

"Of course," Ethel said. "It's the last door on the right as you go along the hall. Across from the small sitting room."

Away from the street at the back of the house, the study was larger than the small sitting room from where I'd watched Esther

Valenzuela and Max Cole the first night. Everything proper and in its place: dark wood-paneled walls, soft light, mahogany desk and tables, maroon leather couch and armchair, books shelved from floor to ceiling around high windows that overlooked the garden.

I saw the side door.

Outside a brick path curved through the garden toward the street. It had to be how Esther Valenzuela left the house without the Conrads seeing her. Left or was taken. The CIA men, Max Cole's driver or the limousine man could have come and gone unseen with Esther. There was no sign of a struggle in the perfect order of the study, but how much fight would she have given the Major and his allies? How much could she have given?

In the immaculate study all surfaces were clean and bare. The answering machine had no messages. There were no scribbled notes, nothing unexpected in the desk drawers.

In the living room, the Conrads still stared at the television without really seeing the action. There was an aura of paralysis about them. They were worried about their daughter and son-in-law, but knew they had no reason, or even right, to worry. It was a matter of the national interest, and Esther was safe under official care. They should not be worried. But they were.

"Can I look in her bedroom, Mrs. Conrad?"

She got up. "I'll show you."

George Conrad seemed almost envious as she led me out to the hallway again. She had something to do.

"It's at the far end of the hall. Over George's study. It looks out on the garden and the big pepper tree. She was always a quiet girl, liked to sit and watch the garden, the birds. Daydream, I suppose." She smiled. It was a wan smile, sad and even nostalgic, as if she knew that whether her daughter were safe or not, came home again or not, after the events of the last few days she would not be the same.

"I won't take long," I said.

She left reluctantly. She had nowhere else she wanted to be, and watching me was better than bad television.

"I'll make some coffee."

The room was that of a child occupied by a returned grownup, a child who had gone away and whose mother had kept it as it had been. The child had come back for a visit and lived in it but was not of it. As if the room itself were under glass and the returned child, older, lived on top of the glass. The possessions and furnishings of grammar school and high school neat and in place. The books and air tickets and traveling makeup kit and jewelry and perfume and clothes of the returned married woman spread over them without really touching them.

Two dresser drawers were open, half empty and a mess. In the closet hangers dangled empty, the remaining clothes scattered and on the floor. There were two suitcases of what I guessed was an expensive matched set trimmed in leather. A present of doting parents to a traveling daughter. The midsized one was gone. All the signs of hasty grabbing and packing by ham-handed males who couldn't have cared less what the clothes would look like later. Esther Valenzuela had taken clothes with her, but not all her clothes. She expected to be gone a few days, but she expected to return. From wherever she was. There were no clues to where or why. I had not really expected there would be. Not in the study, and not here. The Conrads had said the two CIA men had probably been in both rooms after Esther had gone.

Downstairs the show was another comedy of grotesque faces in overacted closeup. George Conrad watched it all with rigidly open eyes. His wife had given up, sat with a magazine.

"If she does call, or come home, let me know right away."

Santa Barbara is a small city where few people or cars move on the side streets at night. When I want to think I take the back ways. Freeways are not for thinking, or for watching the night. The lush streets of the Eastside, shadowed by the big old Victorian and Mediterranean and Monterey-style houses, were dark and silent and empty in the cold spring wind. Sycamore Canyon Road curved pale along its dry creek, the scars of the great fire still black on the eucalyptus and last few abandoned ruins.

It looked like Esther Valenzuela had gone with the Major more or less voluntarily, but not exactly gone on her own. They wanted to keep her away from me, but that wasn't the only reason. They were sure that sooner or later Paul would come to her or contact her. If he could. It was still Paul Valenzuela they were after, not drug lords. Not directly or immediately.

East Valley Road twisted through old Spanishtown over Cold Spring Creek that had once been the only constantly running creek in Montecito. The road straightened through the dark Montecito Village to the turn down San Ysidro Road toward the freeway and the sea. Somehow I sensed it had always been Paul Valenzuela the Major and Max Cole wanted, not drug lords or Sylvestre Madrona. Not directly.

North Jameson Lane paralleled the freeway, the blue roofs and lights of the Miramar Hotel on the other side. Ortega Hill Road, dark and rural except for the night hum of the freeway, spiraled up and over its steep hill and down into Summerland.

The only lights in our rented hacienda were over the front door and up in the bedroom.

The shadow moved behind our house.

I parked on the next block.

In my work it's always wise to know your own neighborhood. A narrow driveway ran from the cross street to a pair of illegal rentals our neighbor had built behind his house back in the raffish days of the beach community when no one gave a damn. It took me unseen behind the cover of thick hedges and a high fence to where the fence ended at our yard. I had my cannon in my lone hand. The shadow was at the outside entrance to my office.

Bent and busy over the lock. I hoped whoever it was knew the work well enough not to alert Kay and bring her downstairs, make me move in before I wanted to. We had no alarm system, I won't live behind self-imposed bars in a prison of privilege or fear. But we had good locks, I'm not a fool, and I maneuvered closer, slow and silent and covered by the intruder's concentration on the work of picking a tough lock. When the door finally popped open and the shape slipped inside, I sprinted the last few yards and went in close behind, my pistol touching.

"Keep walking in."

I closed the door, flipped the light switch with my elbow. She walked away from my gun without turning around, sat down and faced me, smiled that amused smile. The fake maid from Madrona's suite at the Biltmore. According to the Major, a Guatemalan agent. Claudia Nervo.

"Have a seat," I said.

She laughed. "You're quite good. Intelligent and light on your feet. I'm impressed."

"So am I. You pick a mean lock. I didn't know Guatemalans

trained their secret police so well. But I guess all of you down there are trained by the CIA, right, Miss Nervo?"

She wore the same plum jumpsuit she had when she left the Biltmore. A good dark color for night work, utilitarian with pockets and enough looseness to cover a gun the size of a PPK, and not something that would turn heads on the street the way all black could. Slimmer than she had seemed in the maid's uniform, and smaller, what looked like long and thick dark brown hair swept up and held by a purple turban. But the gray eyes were suddenly not so cool, and the high Castillian nose was pinched and angry in her arrogant brown face.

"How do you know my name? No one except—"

"The Major happened to mention it when he was telling me how you were all battling the drug war together."

She held her hand up, pantomimed smoking, indicated her pocket. I nodded. She drew a cigarette from her jumpsuit. Her eyes were hot and her voice ice. "The trouble with Americans is they think everyone in the world must be an American patriot. The United States is the whole world, the universe, so everyone should be eager to serve it. Everyone would have to be, right? That other people might have different ways and interests and goals never occurs to you. We're all tools to be used for the glory of America."

"Not all Americans."

"All Americans I've had to work with." Her eyes flashed in the light of the office, anger replaced the ice in her voice. "You remember your Senator McCarthy and the Soviet agent Gubichev?"

"Joe or Gene?"

Her gray eyes inward on her furious memory, she heard only then not now. "One of your ridiculous public spy trials. A woman named Coplon, something like that. She worked in some Pentagon office, passed secrets to her Russian lover, Gubichev. Valentin Gubichev, that was his name. They were both caught, went on trial. They were both convicted, as far as I remember. I think Gubichev was eventually exchanged for some American spy caught over there. It doesn't matter."

She smoked in the silent office. Distant music played upstairs in the bedroom where Kay waited for me. I pictured her up there naked in the bed, her thick auburn hair spread out on the pillow. Down here Claudia Nervo smoked, talked, had no sexual aura for me at all. She was my work. Sometimes I wonder which is the more powerful: sex, work, curiosity, or fear. It seems to depend on the particular moment, the intensity of the instant.

"What matters," Claudia Nervo said, "is your Senator Joseph McCarthy. While the Coplon-Gubichev mess was going on, this eminent high government official of this so-big, powerful nation of yours was making a speech to denounce the sinister laxness of the administration in power, in which he was correct, but that's something else." She waved the burning cigarette, her anger became scorn. "During this stupid speech he continually referred to Mr. Gubichev and Ms. Coplon as traitors. Over and over he ranted against the traitor Valentin Gubichev. It never occurred to your honorable Senator that far from being a traitor, Mr. Gubichev was a fine, loyal, brave and successful patriot. By the senator's own standards, Gubichev was a hero. But a Russian hero, and that was a concept Mr. McCarthy and most Americans seem to have great difficulty grasping. Gubichev the Russian had acted against America, therefore he had to be a traitor. The United States is the universe."

"Not Guatemala?"

She looked around for an ashtray, I produced one from my desk drawer. She stubbed out the butt. "The Mexicans have a proverb, Mr. Fortune: *Poor Mexico, so far from God, so close to the United States.* It applies in Guatemala also. We are too small and unimportant to imagine we are the world." She smiled, looked straight at me. "But we don't imagine the United States is the world either, and I don't work for the Major. I am not up here to help the Major no matter what he thinks. I am here for my own country. Perhaps you and I can deal."

"Deal for what?"

"Information. That is why I was at the Biltmore, why I came to search your office, right? I want to know what you may have learned about the life and death of Sylvestre Madrona, and the whereabouts of Paul Valenzuela."

"His *life* as well as his death?"

"His friends, family, associates. Inside Guatemala and here in the United States."

"The Guatemalan secret service is enlisted in the great U.S. drug war the way the Major says?"

"We are enlisted against what might harm Guatemala."

"Guatemala or the generals?"

She took out another cigarette. "We have a civilian government now."

"In Guatemala the only civilians are the poor."

"Ah." She blew a stream of smoke. "You must have heard the so very sad and so largely imaginary story of our 'Don' Sylvestre Madrona's so-very tragic little *campesina.* Or another heartrending story very like it, eh?"

"What makes you think Dolores Rios's story is imaginary?"

She shrugged. An eloquent Latin shrug with arms and head and hands to enhance the shoulders. "The famous magical realism. Rumor, imagination, dreams are as real as reality. A rumor of atrocities runs through the villages like diarrhea. I have heard so many such fantasies."

"The biggest single cause of death in Guatemala, diarrhea," I said. "Even more than gunshot wounds the last I heard. At least among children."

"Believe as you wish. Fortunately, *we* rule in Guatemala."

"Who is we, Ms. Nervo?"

"Those who can rule. Not the Dolores Rioses."

"Not the drug kings like Sylvestre Madrona?"

"Madrona did not sell drugs in Guatemala."

"What did he do?"

She smoked. "He was suspected of supplying the subversive militants with guns, aiding the communists who want to destroy our country."

"That gave you a good reason to 'talk' to him, didn't it? Maybe out in that warehouse. Maybe he wouldn't talk. You're not in Guatemala here, right? You couldn't just take him somewhere and make him talk."

"Talk to, yes, but not shoot. He was no use to me dead, and I did not find him until he was dead in the local morgue. I don't know when or how or in what condition you found him, do I?"

"You're still up here."

"There are others, associates. Any information you have found on who he worked with would be valuable to me."

"Was Paul Valenzuela someone he worked with?"

"I ask you the questions. I have the money."

"Or did Valenzuela know someone Madrona worked with in Guatemala? Someone who doesn't want to be known to U.S. officials and Valenzuela could spill the beans?"

She crushed the second cigarette in the ashtray, stood up. "If you have any information, I'm at the Santa Barbara Inn."

"I have the gun, Ms. Nervo."

She looked at the old pistol in my hand. "You won't shoot me, Fortune. Not here in your house, not anywhere."

She walked past me and out the side door.

The fusillade of gunfire exploded in the night.

12

Claudia Nervo vanished.

I lay face-down.

Half inside the door, half outside on the steps.

The noise of many weapons firing at once makes you want to cover your ears to escape. Bury your head. Curl up behind some safe wall and wait for it to end. Stop hammering, hammering.

On an old bucket I sailed in long years ago in a faraway war we offloaded a cargo one night in a North African port. A hundred tiny red points of flame spat at us from the dark. We clawed for cover, the gun crews opened up, the skipper screamed frantic orders. Only after a full volley from the deck's 50- and 57-mms, all of us down flat behind the gunwales, did we hear the captain screaming at us to stop. "Cease fucking fire! Stop! It's the unloading crew! Stop!"

Fifty men smoking at night across flat land looks like an army firing at you. Many guns firing through the dark look like many men smoking cigarettes.

Except for the noise.

The hammering that suddenly stops.

Silence.

I raised my head, fired at the shadows that moved across the night in the next yard.

"Ah, Jesus Christ!"

Shadows down the next driveway to the street.

Across the dark yard I hoped I remembered a clear path to the street as I ran.

One of them limped.

Four men or maybe six men. Two cars.

I fired again.

The limper screamed and went down.

They dragged him into a car. One faced me and the front yard. I went down. The pistol shots whined overhead.

When I raised my head the cars were gone. The stench of gunfire and burned rubber in the cold night.

Lights were on all along the street. Faces wary at windows. A few braver people inched out into their front yards.

"Dan!"

Kay at our front door, two steps out and searching the night.

"Dan!"

Claudia Nervo lay on the ground near the open side door, her head and back half-propped against the house. Blood spattered the house, glistened on the ground around her in the weak light of the single window and open door. Twisted and awkward against the house, she stared ahead in the dark night. Her gray eyes shined flat and empty. I bent to straighten her, make her more comfortable.

"No." Her voice was a hoarse whisper as flat and empty as her eyes. "Don't."

"Dan! Where are you?"

"Side door! My office!"

Claudia Nervo breathed carefully. The pain like ridges on her face but no sound on her lips. She heard Kay come to stand in the open side doorway, turned her head slowly. It seemed to focus her for a moment. She stared up at Kay in her nightgown and white robe in the night. Liquid bubbled inside her chest.

"Did you . . . kill any of them?"

"I hit one. They took him away."

"Did you . . . see . . . ?"

"Four men, maybe six. Two cars. That's all. It was too dark, too fast."

"The Major." Hate bubbled with the liquid in her throat. "The *cochino* Major. Swine."

Kay squeezed my hand. "For you then, Dan. They were after you."

I said, "We don't know that. It could have been anyone. Madrona's friends. Drug dealers. Her enemies. I don't know what she was really doing, Kay. She—"

Claudia Nervo said. "You can never trust them. *Yanquis. Animales.* Protect Madrona, all of them. They want help, kiss the devil. Then, *pffftt, finito.*" The fury in her eyes flashed. She tried to rise, cried out in pain and fell back. "You cannot trust them, *mi generale.* Today they hug you, tomorrow they stab you. Tell them nothing. The fucking *yanquis.* Peasants. Mongrels. They have no breeding, no bloodlines, no culture!"

I said, "The Major protected Madrona?"

Claudia Nervo breathed hard, sucked at air, closed her eyes.

"I'm calling nine-one-one." Kay went inside.

I had been listening for the sound of sirens. Someone among the startled houses along the quiet block must have called the police. But there was no sound in the distance, only the hum of voices on the dark street and the heavy rasp of Claudia Nervo's labored breaths, her whisper.

"My hair. I want my hair . . . down."

I loosened and removed the purple turban. The dark hair spread over her neck and shoulders. She reached up to smooth it, shape it, but she was too weak. She could only touch the hair with her fingertips, stroke it like a lover's hair.

"I better call the police," I said. "The paramedics will be here soon."

She tried to shake her head, but it was pressed against the wall of the house and she couldn't move it. Instead, she moved one hand from her hair to touch me. "Don't leave."

Her other hand continued to caress her hair. "They come into your country, the *yanquis.* They buy and make you wealthy. They help you control the peons and the Indian scum, but always they must tell you what you have to do. They do not care about you, only about themselves. They make you fat and lazy and suck you dry."

"How did the Major protect Madrona? Why?"

The first siren began to echo across the night from the direction of the freeway through Montecito. It could be the sheriff or the paramedics. Claudia Nervo didn't hear the sirens any more than she had heard me. Liquid bubbled into the hoarse whisper of her throat. The fear in her eyes was like a pit to infinity that slowly turned into a depth of anger even deeper. A despair and rage that filled the liquid whisper. "It is all ours! All mine. They take it away. Fucking peasants, stupid Indians. Animals without understanding. Pigs, idiots. They have to be destroyed, eliminated. It is ours, all progress is ours, everything . . . ours! All gone. *Jesu Christo*, all lost . . . lost . . . *Maria madre de Dios* . . ."

The sheriff's cars and the paramedics arrived at the same time. The deputies spread along the block to hold the curious away. Claudia Nervo hadn't waited for them. She was gone from behind the dead eyes that held no more light. I went out to the street.

"Back at the side door," I told the patrol sergeant. "A woman. She's dead."

The pair of paramedics pushed past us, trotted with their bags to where Claudia Nervo still lay propped against the side of the house. A patrol deputy pointed to blood on the street where they had dragged the man I'd wounded into the car. I told them about Esther Valenzuela hiring me to help find her husband, the death of Sylvestre Madrona and the attack, but not about the warehouse or Claudia Nervo's guess about who had attacked.

"You never got a look at them?"

"Four men, maybe six, that's all I could see. Just shadows in the dark with guns."

"You don't know who they could have been? No idea why they shot the woman?"

"No," I said. "I think she was some kind of Latin American agent, maybe she had enemies who followed her up here. Sergeant Gus Chavalas over at SBPD might know more."

I was known to the police in the area. I knew the two deputies by sight, but my story had an unsatisfactory ring. They held me for the Major Crime and Crime Scene Investigation detectives to show. Kay watched me, took her cue, said nothing about who it could have been. When the Major Crime detectives did arrive with the coroner's detail they listened again to my story, didn't like it any better, took me in. I told Kay to call Sergeant Chavalas in case the sheriff's people forgot while they talked to me for a day or so.

The county jail is out in Goleta off Calle Real close to the dump. They held me in booking detention until they booked me, then put me into one of the single holding cells. I wondered if that was because they wanted me safe or wanted me to be alone. Probably both. It's a relatively new jail, and not too bad, but there is no such thing as a good jail. Not for a free man. (I know there are those who somehow can only live inside the joint, whether from fear of the outside or need of the inside for the danger and violence itself, but they are not really free men. If any of us are.)

The detectives let me stew an hour or so, came to question me in relays. I told them everything without naming names or giving any of my guesses. It wasn't hard, there was so little to tell beyond guesses and theories and the stories of other people that might or might not be true. They didn't like what I told them, or believe it, but except for the attack it wasn't their case and they didn't know enough to prove anything against me.

It was after ten P.M. when Sergeant Chavalas sat down in the cell and a corrections officer locked the door behind him. The officer didn't look pleased. "I only got your lady's message an hour ago. The county boys out here handed me the red tape for another hour. They're not happy with you going around them to me, they don't buy your story, they don't want to let you go even on my say-so until the sheriff okays it and he can't be reached until morning."

"What did they tell you?"

"They got five calls about a gang war in Summerland. They found you and a dead woman and blood in the street. You'd fired your pistol. You told them you were working for a woman whose husband in the State Department was missing. You hadn't found him, didn't know who shot the dead woman or why except maybe she was a Latin American agent. They identified the victim as a Guatemalan businesswoman, Claudia Nervo, haven't reached the Guatemalan officials yet, haven't been able to locate the Esther Valenzuela you say is your client. Where is Mrs. Valenzuela?"

I told him where I thought Esther Valenzuela was and what Claudia Nervo had said about the Major protecting Sylvestre Madrona.

"Who the hell is this goddamn Major Hill?"

"I've got a hunch it's not who he is, but what he does and for whom."

"The guy in the limo?"

"Maybe."

"So what is it? Drugs? Guns? Both? Something else?"

"It sure isn't an importer of Central American peasant knick-knacks," I said. "But we've got something to look for now. At least you have."

"The wounded man?"

"I think I hit him bad enough to need immediate treatment and fast. He wasn't walking."

Chavalas stood. "I'll find him if he's in the county. Sit tight, I'll get you out by morning."

The sheriff's detectives came back. I told them the same as I had before, added maybe they should cooperate with Chavalas and the SBPD. They didn't take to my suggestion. They came back in shifts until midnight. Then they got tired and went home. I'd keep until morning.

I dozed to the endless hum of jail noises through the small hours of the morning. The shuffling feet and protesting voices of the newly arrested. The constant drone of the arresting deputies and corrections officers. The footsteps and the door closings and rasping of wheeled carts of the corrections officers and orderlies. The whining and cursing and singing and groaning of the prisoners in the eight holding cells. Even the sound of the spring night wind somewhere far away.

I thought about Claudia Nervo. Her rage at losing all she had by dying. She had everything, and now it would be gone. The peasants and communists had taken it away from her by forcing her to risk her life to fight them. She had said Guatemala wasn't the world to her, as the United States was to men like the Major. Not Guatemala, only her class. The rulers. The landowners and the generals. It was their country and their world and their universe. A disease of our species, and one that could, probably would, be fatal to us all someday.

Somewhere around two or three I fell asleep. To dream of the shifting faces and floating bodies of Kay and Claudia Nervo. Blood and nakedness, the half-awake voices and cries and groans of the jail. When I woke up, Chavalas was looking down at me.

"You get out in an hour."

His dark Greek face that passed so easily for Latino was almost pale with fatigue. Fatigue and something more. He sat down on the bunk and looked away out the barred cell door. His hands were clenched so tight the knuckles were as pale as his face. He was in a rage.

I sat up. "You didn't find him?"

"I found him. And I lost him. I found him, and I couldn't touch him."

13

Gus Chavalas does not like the Madrona case from the beginning. From the moment the body is discovered by the two early-morning lovers, he knows there is a coverup. It is no robbery, it did not happen at the bird refuge. When Dan Fortune comes with questions, he finds out who is behind the coverup but not why. Mr. Tyrone Earl says Madrona was in Santa Barbara to sell handicrafts, hasn't a clue to why he was shot, but Madrona's "assistant," Ms. Dolores Shay, who barely speaks English, is a very strange assistant for a simple businessman.

When he goes to the warehouse in Goleta it has no trace of a shooting or forced entry. Whoever has cleaned up the blood and covered any bullet holes is an expert. A team of experts to do it in two days. When he puts the lab on it they come up with chips and traces, but what does that prove? Madrona had a common blood type, people are always being injured, floors and pillars damaged in warehouses. The ownership of the warehouse seems to connect to no one involved with Madrona. The man, Major Harvey Hill, U.S. Army, Ret., whom Fortune thinks shot Madrona is in Mexico, or someone who says he is Major Hill is in Mexico, and the State Department guy Dan says came to pressure his client denies ever being in Santa Barbara. Someone is lying or there are a lot of mistaken identities. Chavalas trusts Fortune, so unless Dan has made the mistakes, it is a hell of a coverup.

He checks on hotels, motels, bed and breakfasts. He turns up no Major Harvey Hill, no sign of a man in a limousine Fortune has said is lurking around. If they are in Santa Barbara they are hidden in a private house and keeping low. The CIA denies knowledge of anything and everything. He has no grounds to call in the FBI. The State Department insists that Deputy Assistant Secretary Mr. Maxwell Cole is in Los Angeles not Santa Barbara. Dolores Shay can tell him nothing, and Tyrone Earl is nosing around asking questions but not giving out any useful answers. There are no leads in the bird refuge where the body was found. Chavalas gets nowhere. He has other cases. The Lieutenant is impatient.

"What have you got to back up this Fortune's story? It's a two-bit mugging, for Christ's sake, Chavalas. Work on it, okay, but you've got bigger cases. What's happening with—" and the Lieutenant lists the other four cases Chavalas has on his docket.

It is like trying to hold the morning fog, pin down a snake. Chavalas knows it is a coverup, and he doesn't like coverups. He doesn't like pressure to get off a case from the Lieutenant. He likes the truth and the law. They are important to him, have been ever since he was a boy.

Augustus Caesar Chavalas grows up in Santa Barbara, the son of a Greek fisherman who owns his own trawler and makes a good living. The elder Chavalas never becomes rich, but is able to buy a nice, solid little house on South Jameson Lane in one of the less wealthy enclaves of affluent Montecito. He lives comfortably, gives his children the normal childhood of a clean, almost ideal small American city.

Young Gus and his siblings go, of course, to public school. On South Jameson Lane this means Montecito Union where his classmates are almost all from well-to-do middle-class business and professional families. This makes no difference to Gus or the other kids and families except for the usual small minority of snobs. The snobs are the only noticeable minority at Montecito Union in these years, young Gus enjoys school.

South Jameson Lane also means Santa Barbara Junior High. The school is located in the heart of the small but definite hispanic *barrio* of Santa Barbara. It is also the nearest junior high for the elegant upper Eastside and for Montecito. This creates a dynamic, even bizarre, mix to the student body and the parents associations which will probably be beneficial in the long run and the future. It is not beneficial when Gus arrives at the school.

At the time, there is a deep split, even antagonism, between the well-off anglos and the poor hispanics and few blacks of the *barrio*. It is a time of divisiveness through the nation, and the children reflect this as they usually do. A mutual divisiveness. In small and large. The Montecitan anglos flock to the theater groups that put on plays and musicals, the singing ensembles, the science fairs, the band. The hispanics and blacks take little part in school activities. The upper Eastside and Montecito parents join all the PTA groups, they are the boosters and class aides. Hispanic and black parents rarely come to the school even when summoned. Some anglo parents complain about the expenditures on special courses in Spanish. The hispanic students switch to Spanish the instant they are out the school doors. The Eastside and Montecito kids come and go in car pools. The hispanics walk.

The anglos are in the majority, the hispanics move in tight groups. There are confrontations. Even a few mini-riots. They are easily handled, it is a small *barrio*. The hispanic students, male and female, dress much older, macho and sexy, which annoys the anglo parents. The anglo students run the school, ignore the interests of the hispanics and blacks, which angers the hispanic community. Rebellious Montecito kids flaunt associations with hispanics of the opposite sex, which angers both communities, but worries the Montecitans and Eastsiders more. Rebellious *barrio* kids tend to drop out of school which worries their parents and the police.

For young Gus Chavalas it becomes a special problem. His name, stocky build and dark complexion that meant nothing in Montecito where there were no *barrio* hispanics, now mean a great deal. To the anglos who don't know him he is hispanic. To the kids from the *barrio* he is hispanic too, until they find he speaks no Spanish, lives in Montecito. There are verbal incidents and physical confrontations. Snide remarks and whisperings and challenges and dangerous misunderstandings. In the corridors when he walks alone the militant anglos see a hispanic without his gang group. When he is with his Montecito Union classmates the hispanics see a traitor. In the heat of mass confrontations and mini-riots the school officials and the police herd him with the hispanics away from the anglos.

He learns in those three years a lot about injustice and how the law can ignore it. He learns about the need for law, and the importance of order, of being sure what you think is true and being careful how you act on what you think. He learns order is not justice, but it is the beginning of justice. That justice is more than the law, but that without law there is rarely justice. He learns Spanish in defiance of the arrogant anglo majority, and refuses to join any hispanic groupings to stand up to the narrow *barrio* minority.

In high school, where there are more poor anglos and everyone is older and concerned with their individual futures, it all changes, but he has already been set on a path. Gus Chavalas has learned the horror of injustice and of not knowing what is really true. He has come to believe very much in the need for justice, and truth and law. He becomes a policeman. He likes his work, and he doesn't like the Madrona murder at all. It doesn't seem to have much truth in it and less law.

He is working late when the report of the Summerland shootup comes in. Kay Michaels calls. Chavalas guesses at once that the Guatemalan businesswoman who has been killed is the same woman Fortune told him was working with the Major, the agent of some Latin American country. Kay Michaels says the dying woman had accused the Major and CIA of the shooting, that Dan isn't sure, it could have been anyone, and is being held by the sheriff's department. Chavalas tells the Lieutenant he is going out to the county jail to talk to Fortune, get him out.

"Sounds like a county case to me," the Lieutenant says.

"It has to tie into the Madrona murder."

"Is that what Fortune says?"

"It's Fortune's house they shot up. He thinks they could have been after him, not the woman they killed."

"Fortune thinks a lot of things," the Lieutenant says.

"It's a residential neighborhood. Family houses. Ordinary citizens. You want to just forget it, Lieutenant?"

"The county'll handle it. You have enough work."

"Fortune didn't make it up. The woman's dead. The people are out on the street."

The Lieutenant says nothing. Chavalas leaves, drives out to the county jail. The Lieutenant's opposition is vague, hard to get hold of, but Chavalas is uneasy. He feels the coverup under it all, the elusive snake, the fog. The deputies oppose him, but this is easy to grasp—he is the city and Fortune has gone around them to him to put pressure on them. They are annoyed, hold him up an hour, refuse to release Fortune without orders from the sheriff himself who is out of town at least until morning.

Fortune gives him the wounded man.

If the wounds were bad enough, they could not have gotten the man out of the county so fast. It is his first possible break. The hospitals quickly turn up blank. He gets everyone in the office to call doctors, puts out the word to all his contacts throughout the city and Goleta. They wake many of the doctors up, most are annoyed, none admits to treating a gunshot wound. The Lieutenant watches from his office.

Chavalas expands the calls to Ventura, Oxnard, Solvang, Santa Ynez, Buellton, even Lompoc. It is a long, slow process. No doctor who did treat a gunshot wound and failed to report it is going to admit it now. The night drags on.

As the lists run out, people go home. The Lieutenant goes home. Chavalas thinks of Vandenberg Air Force Base. His contact there knows nothing. Point Mugu and Port Hueneme wash out. It looks like an even slower door-to-door sweep by a team tomorrow, which will probably be too late even if the Lieutenant lets him have the personnel.

The call comes at 3:30 A.M.

"Sarge?"

He recognizes the voice as an orderly at a private drug rehab clinic out beyond Goleta who keeps an eye on the junkies sent there. For a price.

"Hear you lookin' fo' a gunshot hidin' out?"

"You got one?"

"Same nut?"

"Tomorrow."

"Room six. No paper. Like, that there room it's empty, check? They watchin' the do'."

"Who?"

"Two dudes in suits. Diff'nt times."

A wounded man with no record of admission in a room listed as empty with two other men guarding the door in shifts. Chavalas drives the late-night freeway north past the last Goleta exit. When he arrives, the clinic is locked tight. There are a few scattered lights through the building on its parklike grounds, his stoolie orderly is nowhere in sight. Chavalas did not expect him to be, it is not part of the price.

The lobby inside the glass doors is dark and deserted. He has no warrant, has no way of knowing for certain the man in room six is the right man, how much his stoolie has embroidered and imagined. If it is the attacker Fortune shot, the two guards will be armed, and Chavalas cannot be sure, after the wild and random shooting out in Summerland, that they won't shoot even a policeman.

He needs a reasonable certainty it is the right man. Enough for a warrant, or at least to convince the Lieutenant there is cause to suspect a crime and go in without one. Chavalas circles the dark building slowly to find a way inside, looks through the windows into the rooms. Most of them have nightlights, the dark is terror for junkies. He finds what he thinks is room six, and there is a man in it lying silent in the bed, another man seated facing the door. The man on watch wears a dark suit, is reading, there is a small automatic on the table beside his chair. In the parking lot Chavalas sees a limousine with a dozing driver.

The Lieutenant does not appreciate being awakened, tells Chavalas to come to his house. When he arrives, the Lieutenant is not alone.

"Madrona?" the Captain says.

Chavalas tells them what his pigeon has told him and what he has found at the clinic. "I think it's enough for a warrant."

"An unidentified limo, and a guy in bed with another guy in his room reading? A guy you think has a gun?" the Lieutenant says.

"I saw the gun, Lieutenant."

"Did you see the wound?" the Captain says. "Did you talk to either man? You don't know it's even a gunshot. You don't know anything. They could be Federal agents doing their job, couldn't they, Gus? Cops from anywhere."

"It all fits what Fortune told me. Fortune's never steered me wrong. It's worth taking a look at."

"Tell county, it's their territory, damn it," the Lieutenant says. "Maybe it's drug dealers, maybe it's a gang war."

The Captain says, "Have you ever seen this Major you keep talking about?"

"No, but Fortune has."

The Lieutenant says, "Maybe we should bring in Fortune. Talk to him."

"Gus," the Captain leans forward where he sits on the Lieutenant's living room couch. "You have a shred of evidence Madrona was anything except a businessman got mugged?"

"Fortune—"

"Fuck Fortune!" The Lieutenant is redfaced. "He better watch his goddamn step around me."

"Cool it down, Orel," the Captain says.

Chavalas looks at them in the small room dim inside the night windows and realizes they are angry, yes, but they are also embarrassed. They are under pressure, they don't like it, but they believe it is legitimate pressure from higher authority and they have a duty to do what they have been asked to do.

"What about the woman in Summerland, Captain?"

"County says the State Department and the Guatemalan embassy have taken over. It's their problem, Gus," the Lieutenant says. "Looks like they've got rebels down there, the fight came up here. They want to keep it under wraps."

"Fortune thinks the shooting could have been aimed at him. If it was, they could try again. Don't we protect our people?"

"Fortune could be up to his gonads in his own shit," the Lieutenant says. "I never knew a private who wasn't."

"Fortune doesn't even know who the shooters were," the Captain says. "Anyway, it's county. Fortune's theirs."

"Madrona's ours."

The Captain says, "You got nothing to go on. It's a dead end. I think we should close it out."

The Lieutenant says. "It's a federal case, okay?"

"Our local problems aren't all there is, Gus," the Captain says. "Sometimes you have to bend for the bigger good, the more important problem. For the good of everyone."

"Not everyone," Gus says. "Just special someones."

The Captain says, "The right someones, Gus."

"Trust us, for Christ's sake," the Lieutenant says. "You're not the only one who knows something, Chavalas."

"Go home, Gus," the Captain says.

14

Chavalas sat on my bunk. He looked tired as he listened to the morning noises of the county jail.

"I've got a murder I can't chase. I don't like that. I've got a dead woman and people being shot at on a public street because they're somehow connected to that murder and it's not my problem. I don't like that."

I listened to the morning noises too. From the hacking and spitting and coughing that went on and on, to someone singing and the screech of the inevitable wheeled carts, the rattle of mops and buckets.

"They believe what they're doing."

He looked down at the floor as if studying his shoes or the jail floor itself. "Nothing that's wrong in principle is right in practice. You can't break your own law for the good of the country. That country isn't worth saving."

Up all night, he wasn't a man ready to go to bed. He walked to the cell door and looked at the wall across the corridor the way an admiral stands on his bridge and stares out to sea as he plans his battle.

"There was a limousine at that clinic. The driver waiting in it. The Major's Buick wasn't there, but the wounded guy and the two guards sound like your CIA men. I think it was you they were after, Dan."

"If it was the Major," I agreed. "They figured they had to stop me after I tried to tail the Major to Esther Valenzuela. I might as well have hung out a sign saying I didn't believe their whole yarn."

"Say it is the Major and his people, then they must be holding the Valenzuela woman somewhere in town or close to it."

I nodded. "They expect her husband to come looking for her, or to call her. They've probably got the phone in her parents' house tapped and monitored, will tell him to come and talk. That means they have to keep her close. Make it as easy as possible for Paul Valenzuela to come to them."

Chavalas continued to examine the far side of the corridor through the bars. "No one's looking for the man in the limo."

"You have an idea in mind?"

"It's a small town in a lot of ways." He turned, gave me a thin smile with not much humor in it. "It's hard to hide a limo. I'm on my own time now. I'll get back to you when I've got something. They release you in an hour. I talked to the sheriff."

It was an hour and forty minutes. The sheriff said nothing to me except to stay in town in case they found who shot up my house. I assumed someone had leaned on him too, and he was in no mood to be pleasant or to tell me anything. I only asked to use the phone. I called Kay to say I was out and okay. I told her about Chavalas, said I'd be home later.

"How much later, Dan?"

"Don't plan breakfast, lunch or probably dinner."

Morning fog had rolled in over Montecito, hung as far inland as the edge of the mountains and San Ysidro Ranch itself.

When people accustomed to staying at the San Ysidro Ranch arrive without reservations, find it unexpectedly full, they reluctantly go to the Biltmore. The San Ysidro is one of those special hotels, its prices prove it. As with most of us, it has had its ups and downs over the years, but overall it has maintained a quiet elegance and class since the last century. The kind of hotel where presidents and kings went in the days when there were kings, when presidents traveled more privately and not like emperors. The only place I know where *both* Winston Churchills signed a guest book in one of its cottages.

These cottages are the key. They are large, exclusive, rustic, but with everything anyone could want for comfort from entry halls, sittings rooms, fireplaces, kitchens, private decks with Jacuzzis, fine furniture, the works. Service. Privacy and service. The cottages are hidden among thick native trees and shrubs along secluded paths. There are trails for walking among the mountains, riding trails, tennis courts, but no golf course although that can be arranged. A four-star restaurant and a quiet lounge for tête-à-têtes.

After the kings had stopped coming, if not entirely the presidents, it was a haven of the stars for licit and illicit liaisons in those golden Hollywood times of high public illusion and rigid studio control. Now the clientele is anyone who can appreciate its low-tech elegance and afford it, even businessmen. As I walked along the path under the trees and fog I saw that Tyrone Earl had one of the larger cottages. The mask and basket import business was booming.

"How do you like your eggs?"

He walked away through the entry hall and living room into the kitchen. A short, dark, muscular man without age stood at the stove. Tyrone Earl sat at a small table draped in a blue and white tablecloth from Guatemala, set for two with real silver and bone china. He pointed to the second chair, waved to the man at the stove.

"Another coffee, Mito."

The thousand-dollar camel's-hair sport jacket and sleek slacks were gone. He lounged on a basket chair in worn Levi 501s, dark cowboy boots and a battered flight jacket from the Vietnam War era against the morning fog and chill. Only the medallion of the rearing horse still hung in the open collar of a blue work shirt. The silent cook brought my coffee. He wore the same Levis, a heavy handwoven blue shirt, and up close his Indian face showed even less what age he was. The coffee smelled strong and earthy.

"Nicaraguan," Earl grinned. "The best there is. Name your style of eggs, Mito cooks like a dream. I never travel anywhere without him."

A private cook, his at-home clothes, his own tablecloth, china, and silver. Mr. Tyrone Earl traveled even better than Sylvestre Madrona. All that was missing in the cottage was the silver blonde.

"Over easy." The aroma of the coffee made me realize I was hungry after a night in jail.

Earl gave my order in a language that wasn't Spanish. The fog rested white on the empty deck outside, and over a sloping lawn that reached to a dense stand of trees with tops lost in the drifting white. In the gray morning light his skin seemed less tanned, the veins and wrinkles clearer. He looked tired too, the long blond hair grayer and ragged, his craggy face heavier and more lined.

"So? You didn't come for breakfast, Dan." His open smile was as easy as before, the gray-blue eyes tired but relaxed.

I waited while the dark man, Mito, put down a plate of three eggs over easy, a basket of hot corn tortillas wrapped in a cloth that matched the tablecloth.

"They say that Madrona was a drug king. Someone else says he was supplying guerrillas with weapons, ammunition."

"Not a Soviet agent? An international nuclear terrorist? The secret leader of China?" He drank his coffee, ate some egg. "Who are *they*?"

The eggs were as good as Earl had said, the *tortillas* homemade. "The Major, State, the CIA, Claudia Nervo."

Behind me, Mito had stopped cooking, seemed to be watching and listening to us. He leaned on the counter, his back to it, his arms folded like Walt the CIA man. He was more than a cook, but if he had a weapon I couldn't see where. Maybe he didn't need a weapon.

"What the hell's a Claudia Nervo?"

"My guess is Guatemalan secret police."

He laughed. "Christ. The real heavy artillery. They sure must think Sylvestre was up to something big."

"He was killed for a reason, the murder covered up for a reason. Claudia Nervo came up here after him for a reason."

"You want me to tell you Sylvestre ran drugs. Maybe I run the stuff too, right?"

"Do you?"

He stood and walked to the windows that overlooked the lawn, the slope, and the trees half lost in the fog. "You ever live in South America, Dan? Central America? Even Mexico? I live in Mexico, go around the villages buying in Guatemala, Honduras, El Salvador, even Nicaragua." His back in the jaunty flight jacket sagged as he stared out at the fog drifting across the lawn and around the trees. "You get a different angle when you're down there. They've chewed coca leaf and peyote, smoked marijuana, for a thousand years. The *campesinos* can't live on what the rich let them grow, so they grow coca leaf and marijuana to kill the pain of hunger, and sometimes to sell to live. If we'd help the real people down there instead of living off them, we wouldn't need any drug war."

A faint gold had begun to tinge the fog. The tops of the trees at the edge of the lawn were almost visible. Mito hadn't moved a muscle at the counter, leaned as quiet and motionless as a jungle cat, or the Indian who hunted the jungle cat. Earl turned and sat again across from me at the table. He had picked up the coffee carafe on the way, poured cups for both of us.

"People've always used drugs, Dan. It goes back to before the pyramids. Most of the time it's the rich, the outlaws, the dreamers and the artists. That's how it was here twenty, thirty years ago: the rich and artsy did coke, the crooks did heroin, the kids did grass, everyone else did booze. Once in a while the poor start doing the hard stuff, and it gets to be an epidemic. It was that way in China a hundred years ago, it got that way here in the nineteen eighties. The reason's always the same." He drank the rich coffee, held the hot cup in both hands to warm them. "The poor get poorer. They get left out. Low pay and a dead end, or no pay and no hope at all. In this country today you have a big underclass with no way out, and it's growing. Three thousand bucks a week pushing dope looks a hell of a lot better than minimum wage or two-bit welfare, and the poor are going to try to feel good the best way they can on what you pay them. Right now, that's a five-buck crystal of crack. You want to stop drugs? Stop poverty."

"The drug war's the wrong way to handle the problem?"

He was silent for a time as the sun thinned the fog beyond the windows of the cottage. "It's a phony drug war. The government doesn't give a damn about the poor using all the drugs in the world." The hot cup close to his face, he breathed the steam and aroma. "The government didn't give a damn in China or the U.S. until the stoned poor got to be a problem for the solid citizens. It's only when crime starts to scare the good people, when sickness cuts into work time, that government moves in. The government drains the swamps, Dan, only when the mosquitoes come out and bother the rich."

I drank, looked out to where the fog was lifting rapidly, looked at Mito still half asleep against the counter. "You learned all that on buying trips in Central America, Mexico."

He put the cup down. "Like I said, living down there gives you a different look at everything, especially the U.S. You know, you can still get real service in the hotels down there, lots of help all over. Ten little brown people to move your chair, hold up your skirt when you pee." He studied me, mockery in his cool gray-blue eyes. "A couple of years ago I took a train up here. Through the Rockies, beautiful run. There was this old couple in the dining car moaning low. The rose in the vase on the table used to be real, now it was plastic. The plates, cups, knives were plastic. There was no service. I explained to them that the U.S. had gotten wages up so high no one could afford to pay people to serve the middle class anymore, only the real rich. The service they wanted, the old middle-class life, depended on a lot of poor people who got paid so low they had to do anything to stay alive. In the U.S. that was gone. Of course, they could still go to El Salvador or Honduras to get their service."

He smiled in the sunlight breaking through the fog. "You have a lot of poor people here, sure, but you pay them welfare to keep them out of your world and that lost you your servants. You can't win 'em all, right? But take heart, Dan. The way it's going, U.S. business moving its manufacturing to Asia and Africa and anywhere that has nice cheap labor, you're getting a two-level country again with only skilled or service jobs. With all the refugees from the little wars all over the world, a fine big underclass of poor with no skills is building again. Service could get a lot better up here and damn soon. Once you get all those poor folks off crack, of course."

At the counter, the dark and silent Mito almost smiled.

"And Madrona was just a businessman," I said. "No drugs, no guns, no guerrillas, no politics."

He laughed. "Pretty damn soon you'll have me and Sylvestre hiding Che Guevera who really isn't dead, raising an army to free all Latin America from the landowners and the U.S."

"Are you? That would explain Claudia Nervo."

Earl shook his head. "You know, I think it's time for me and Mito to get out of this crazy country and back down to Mexico where people are real." He looked at his watch, stood up. "I have to get going, Dan."

I stood. "Madrona was still shot for a reason."

"In Guatemala you can get shot for giving a stranger a drink of water. Maybe that's what Sylvestre did."

Kay wasn't home when I got to our hacienda in Summerland. Jail isn't the best place to sleep. I lay down on the couch in my office and thought about Tyrone Earl and the great American drug war. *The government drains the swamps only when the mosquitoes come out and bother the rich.*

15

The pound of the surf far off where I swam in blackness. The ringing in my ears as I went under. It took four more rings to remember and grope for the telephone I'd put on the floor beside the couch.

Sergeant Chavalas's voice. "Hope Ranch, a big house up on a hill over by the ocean." He gave me an address on Via Roblada. "Park up the road, walk in. We'll spot you."

"We?"

"I picked up some volunteers."

The bedroom was dark, silent and still. The clock read 8:10 P.M. The only sound was the distant surf and the closer drone of traffic on the freeway. Kay wasn't home yet. It was one of those times when my hand still automatically reached for a cigarette. Smoke, pull myself out of the weight of sleep, get myself together and ready to act. I got up and had a Sierra Nevada ale in the kitchen instead.

More structured than Montecito, with an entry arch over the main road in, the Hope Ranch enclave's range of socioeconomic status is narrower than Montecito's—from very well-off to the mid-range of pretty damn rich.

They came out of the night and bushes along the road that curved uphill toward the lights of a large house at the crest. Two sheriff's deputies in uniform. Hope Ranch is in the county.

"Dan Fortune."

"Up this way."

Chavalas stood in the shadows of a grove of old native oaks at the edge of the wide lawn of a big fake French farmhouse. It was at the upper end of the Hope Ranch economic scale, had size, lawn, seclusion and view. Both mountains and ocean. Two million cash at least. Chavalas wasn't thinking about how much the house had cost or was worth.

"Diego spotted the limo in Hope Ranch, tailed it here. I staked out the clinic. I figured whoever they were they'd move the wounded guy as soon as they could. They did. They used the limo, brought him right to this house. There's a woman alone in a back bedroom in there, the wounded guy in another room, and two like your CIA guys."

"Not the Major? The man in the limousine?"

"We haven't spotted anyone else. The limo left right after they moved the wounded guy in, all we saw was the driver."

"Who's we?"

"My partner over there. Sol and Diego from the county."

"Sheriff's deputies are your volunteers?"

"It's the county out at the clinic and here. They got the same orders we did, they're as pissed as I am."

I looked at the big, lighted house that shouted money into the Hope Ranch night. "You're taking a big risk. Captains and sheriffs don't like to be crossed. You have a warrant?"

"Compelling evidence that a crime's been committed."

"What evidence?"

"Your testimony, the limo, the wounded guy, what we saw through the windows." He looked again toward the house that loomed massive against the night sky. "We figure to make waves too big for anyone to sweep under the rug no matter who asks. If we prove these people are endangering civilians, committing some serious damn crimes like kidnapping for whatever reason, our bosses have to back us."

"You hope."

"They're good cops. They'll move when they know these guys

are out of line. Besides, they'll have to cover their own asses once we blow the lid off."

In countries with a strong and accepted rule of law, the glaring light of public knowledge can be a powerful weapon. If the public media is honest and tells it. If anyone cares. If the other side leaves anything for the light to reveal. They know the power of public knowledge too.

"How do we blow the lid off?"

"We walk up to the front door," Chavalas said. "We're the cops, right? With a little back door cover just in case."

The *we* going to the front door turned out to be me, Chavalas and one deputy. His partner would cover the back door. The second deputy would take the attached garage and its connecting door into the big house. Chavalas gave the backup time to get into position, then marched up the driveway and long brick walk to the front door.

I had my hand on my cannon in the pocket of the orange-brown corduroy jacket I had to wear until I got a new tweed.

No shots. No challenge.

Chavalas rang the bell. Rang again. Again.

"Police! Open or we come in."

The Major had changed back into his uncomfortable suit and tie, saw me when he opened the door. "Is this one of Fortune's games, officer?"

"Sergeant Chavalas." He showed his wallet with the shield. The deputy was in uniform, his badge was obvious.

The Major didn't bother to look at either badge. "What do you want, Sergeant?"

"To talk to Esther and Paul Valenzuela."

"Why?"

"We've had a complaint they're being held against their will, have reason to think they're in this house. You the owner of this house, sir?"

"No."

"Can we speak with the owner?"

"They're not here."

"Who are they? You know their names?"

"They're friends who believe in America and those who serve it, Sergeant."

"America," Chavalas said, "is somewhere you don't kidnap citizens no matter what patriotic reason you think you have."

The Major looked at me and shook his head. "I'm getting tired of Fortune's fantasies, Sergeant. Mrs. Valenzuela is under my protection of her own free will. Now if you'll—"

"We'd like to talk to her."

"She is not in this house. Her whereabouts are none of your business. If she were here you couldn't talk to her. Unless, of course, you have a warrant. So now, again, if you'll—"

Walter Enz the CIA man appeared in the doorway behind him. His suit coat was open, his right hand somewhere around his belt inside the coat. The deputy moved away from us to the left, his hand rested on his pistol in its holster. Chavalas looked at Walt, then back at the Major.

"You're Major Hill, right? Major Harvey Hill, U.S. Army, retired."

"I wouldn't believe everything Fortune tells you, Sergeant. Especially what someone told him."

"Can I see some identification?"

"I don't think so. You have no warrant I've seen, you're trespassing on private property, you're—"

The loud crash of something metallic, and the single shot from inside the mammoth house sounded like a nuclear bomb in the quiet Hope Ranch night.

"*Help!*"

Chavalas and the deputy both had their guns out. "I guess we're going in."

Walt Enz and the Major ran ahead of us into a living room the size of a basketball court. It had a cathedral ceiling that looked like a rustic barn, and a second-floor indoor gallery of dark, roughhewn beams all around. Chavalas's partner was already in the room from the back door, gun out. He pointed to our left. "That way!"

They were inside the oversized garage. Four cars were parked inside including the black Buick, and the garage doors were still closed. The deputy and Esther Valenzuela crouched behind the nearest car, a silver Rolls Royce. One of the big old ones. The deputy had his gun out. Down behind a heavy workbench next to the open door from the house into the garage, the number-two

CIA agent, Moretti, watched the two behind the Rolls Royce. He held his Sig/Sauer. An overturned garbage can and cover lay in the no man's land between the bench and the Rolls.

Walt Enz barged into the garage. "Moretti?"

"He was waiting in the garage, Walt, suckered me with the can and grabbed the woman."

Chavalas called, "Who shot, Sol?"

"Him," the deputy behind the Rolls said.

Moretti said, "He wasn't going to take her out of here until I had orders."

The deputy, Sol, said, "He come out o' the house door with her when you guys rang the bell. He was headin' for one of the cars, I guess. I knocked him over with the can, grabbed Mrs. Valenzuela. He took a shot at me to cut me off from the outside door."

Behind the Rolls, Esther Valenzuela stood pale and drawn, but her dark blue eyes had a new anger in them. Angry eyes that watched only the Major and Walt Enz as they hurried to Moretti. Chavalas and his partner, the second deputy and I, stood out in the garage between them and the Rolls. We had Esther Valenzuela, but they had us held inside the garage. The firepower was close enough to equal if we tried to break out on our own. All the makings of a Mexican standoff. I looked toward Esther.

"Is Paul in the house?"

"No." Her voice shook, but I heard the anger in it too.

Chavalas said, "Are you here of your own free will, Mrs. Valenzuela?"

"No."

"Do you want to leave here?"

"Yes."

Chavalas faced the Major who stood behind the workbench with the two CIA men. "Looks like we'll be leaving, Major. Unless you want to face an obstructing police officers charge if the kidnapping doesn't stick."

"We need her here, Sergeant. You don't understand. We—"

"Try us," Chavalas said. "Tell us what the hell you're doing, maybe we'll understand. Maybe even help."

Walt Enz said, "It's too fucking important for local cops."

"He's right," the Major said. "A federal investigation, an international matter, as I told your captain."

I said, "You know, Major, another thing I worry about is an investigation that has to be hidden from the local police, that has to operate outside the rules."

Walt Enz said, "You never know who's on the take, who's mixed up with the dealers and sellers."

"The local authorities will be fully informed when the time comes," the Major said.

If you take a good look at history, you'll find it's the people in power who want to break the rules in the name of order and safety and national interest.

"What we're doing is for the protection of the country, Sergeant. Your protection," the Major insisted. "You can't do what we can do, don't you understand? There's a national danger out there."

He reminded me of another State Department man who got into a fight with an old reporter I knew in New York. Bill Worthy was in China for the *Baltimore Afro-American* back in 1957 when John Foster Dulles was telling everyone the Communist government was crumbling in the face of an angry populace. Thousands of Chinese peasants were starving, their bodies were being picked up in government trucks every night. The countryside was in turmoil. Worthy looked around, saw no dead bodies and no trucks coming at night, no turmoil, Mao in firm control. He reported what he saw, and Dulles picked up his passport, ordered him out of China. The truth didn't match what Dulles wanted Americans to believe. The Major wouldn't care about truth, only about what he considered best for the country.

"What country, Major?" I said. "Yours or mine?"

Chavalas said, "You're sure it's the country you're out to protect, not yourselves?"

"Shit," Walt swore. "What the hell kind of cop are you? What kind of goddamn American? We're the U.S. government, for Christ's sake. You're as bad as fucking Fortune."

The Major said, "It's not your job to question the government, Sergeant."

I said, "Loyalty is our honor?"

"You're damn fucking right it is," Walt exploded. "You got the loyalty of a wet turd!"

Chavalas said, "Why not work with the police, Major? Why not trust us? We know the area better than you do."

"What we're doing has nothing to do with this area or your local problems, Sergeant. You have to work by civilian rules."

"Murder and kidnapping in my town have something to do with the area," Chavalas said. "We're taking Mrs. Valenzuela with us. If you don't like that, you can try to stop us. Sol, Diego, take her out of here."

The Major said, "We'll be talking to your captain and the sheriff."

"You do that," Chavalas said. "Maybe that way we'll get the whole thing straightened out."

I didn't think they'd try to stop us now, but you couldn't be sure with superpatriots or secret police. It would depend on how important to their mission they considered this to be, how much they thought they could get away with. I knew now that they were probably working for the government, yes, but for their part of the government on some project of their own. A project they considered far more important than anybody's constitutional rights.

The deputies escorted Esther Valenzuela out of the garage. Chavalas, his partner and I waited until they had reached our cars, then left, too. It was a long walk across the night lawn.

16

"They said I had to go with them. For Paul. Paul was in danger and I was too. They had to reach Paul before the others did, the same ones who killed that Madrona. It was vital, and I could help them by being with them. I told them I wanted to wait here in the house for Paul where he knew I'd be. I didn't want to leave my parents alone. But the Major took my arm and almost dragged me out the door with those two CIA men behind us. They walked me out through the garden to a car. At that house they kept on talking to me about Paul until they thought I'd fallen asleep and that was when I called you." She shook her head as if wondering how she could have let them take her to the Hope Ranch house. "I didn't want to go with them, but I did. I let them take me to that car, so I don't know if you can call it kidnapping."

Chavalas and the deputies took the remote tap off the house phone, told Esther to call them if anything more happened, and went home to wait for calls from the captain and the sheriff. I didn't think those calls would come. Now the Major would have to tell a lot more than I thought he wanted to, explain too much to the captain. He would be more likely to try to grab Esther again.

"They just kept asking me to tell them everything I knew about what Paul was doing, who his friends were, who he knew down there in Guatemala. I had to go over that phone call again and again and again until I couldn't think."

"They still don't know where Paul is?"

"I don't think so." She rubbed her eyes where she sat in the leather armchair of her father's office, looked at the tall grandfather's clock.

"What did they want to know about Sylvestre Madrona?"

I sat in the other leather armchair, the empty chair behind the desk between us like a missing interrogator.

"Had Paul and I known him. Had we ever met him, perhaps down in Guatemala. With some other men called the Mexican, the Irishman, or Don Pablo. I told them I'd never heard of Madrona or any of those names, and I was sure Paul hadn't either. They seemed quite sure Paul had heard of them, went on asking me to try to remember if he'd mentioned any of the names."

"You don't?"

"No, none of them. Do you?"

"The Mexican was Gonzalo Rodriguez Gacha, one of the leaders of the Medellin drug cartel. He was killed recently in Colombia. Don Pablo's probably Pablo Escobar, another Medellin kingpin."

A few days ago she would have been horrified, even scared, at the thought her husband could know men like that. She was still outraged, but now she didn't seem scared, could think about it. "I'm sure Paul doesn't know any of those men, but I have a strong feeling the Major does."

"And the CIA," I said.

She shuddered, looked at the clock again. "I'm sorry, Mr. Fortune, but I really am exhausted. I'm afraid I have to go to bed, early as it is. I guess I'm not that strong, this has all taken a great deal out of me."

"We'll talk more tomorrow."

The light in Esther Valenzuela's upstairs bedroom went out half an hour later. I settled in the front seat of the Tempo, listened to some music.

The Sixth is my favorite Mahler. The Tragic. Solti and the Chicago. A portable compact disc player that works off batteries was Kay's Christmas present to me last year. With the headphones it's silent as a tomb.

Half an hour later Esther Valenzuela's green Subaru backed erratically out of the Conrads' driveway. Her foot on the gas pedal and brake was nervous, eager or both.

People who have never had any reason to hide, have never hunted their fellow humans, don't even think about someone who might be following them. That's one reason CIAs and KGBs handle civilians so easily. But the Subaru paused in the middle of the dark and quiet Eastside street as she looked both ways, looked again, before driving past where I was hidden. People who have never hunted or been hunted don't know what to look for.

At Mission and State she pulled into the Arco station. From the time it took her, I estimated she pumped about five gallons into her ten-gallon tank. She was going far enough to be worried that half a tank wouldn't get her there and back. It meant the freeway. I drove ahead of her. She was a basically cautious, conservative person, would signal in time for me to choose the north or south entrance. We went north. On the freeway I led her for a mile, then let her pass. She didn't look at me, soon pulled off on the San Marcos Pass, Highway 154 exit.

I drove on. The car that had come on the freeway behind me at the Mission Street entrance, and now sat two cars back, was a black Buick. The next exit was El Sueño Road. I took it, hit my brake at the stop sign, then went through without stopping and speeded up along Calle Real. The Buick had to sail through the stop and speed up also or lose me. It was a chance he'd had to take, and he'd lost. The chance I had to take was that Esther Valenzuela was going over San Marcos Pass into the Santa Ynez Valley. If she wasn't, I'd lose too.

On Turnpike Road I made a right, led him deep into the back streets. I lost him in the maze of small streets and dead ends, slipped along Yaple Avenue, out to Cathedral Oaks Road and up Old San Marcos Pass Road. The Major himself, or one of the others, he didn't know the town as I did, would have no idea how to pick up me or Esther Valenzuela again tonight. I hoped I did.

I'd lost some time, took the old road as fast as I could to where it joined Highway 154, the new San Marcos Pass Road. This was where the last big fire had burned through to go deep into the city itself, the charred brush and stumps and ruins like a war zone in the night on both sides. Long after rush hour on a weekday night, there was little traffic climbing up the dark curves of 154 toward the top of the pass. It is a two-lane highway going up with the mountains close above the winding road on the right, sheer drops and the sweeping view of the lights of the coastal plain to the left. I didn't pick up the green Subaru until almost at the top, settled in one car behind her.

As we crested the pass she ignored both East and West Camino Cielo, and old Stagecoach Road where it led down to Cold Springs Tavern. We went on over the Cold Spring arch bridge that had shortened the old curving route down the pass. It looked like she was headed into the Santa Ynez Valley toward Solvang or Santa Ynez or Los Olivos. I relaxed, missed her turnoff into Paradise Road. Too close to make the turn after her, I drove on without slowing until I reached where the old Stagecoach Road comes back in at the bottom of the pass.

The old road intersects Paradise Road about a mile back. I turned into the pitch-black backcountry and hit the gas as hard as I dared on the road narrow in the beams of my headlights. She could have suckered me, returned to the highway as soon as I was out of sight. To do that she'd have to have spotted me, or be a lot more experienced in the shadow world than I had reason to think she was, and I wouldn't find her anyway. My judgment told me she was somewhere ahead on the dark road into the canyons of the Santa Ynez River. Experience and judgment sometimes count for more than power and muscle. Sometimes.

I caught up to the taillights between Fremont and Paradise campgrounds. Drove close enough to see it was a green Subaru, dropped back to occasional-glimpse range past Los Prietos campground and the ranger station, closed up again as we neared the point where the remote road forked. The headlights of occasional vans or jeeps entered the road, most coming toward us on their way out of the backcountry.

Twice other vehicles pulled between us, but soon went off into side roads or campgrounds. One took the left fork into Oso Canyon. She took the right fork toward Gibraltar Reservoir. I cut my headlights, followed her twin red points in the darkness. They turned off into a dirt road not long after the fork. She had driven the whole time at a steady, medium-fast pace with no signs of being aware of anyone behind her even when the road had been empty of all but the two of us, my lights visible if distant. All her attention was on where she was going.

It was a cabin alone in the deep night shadows of a grove of native evergreen oaks. A quarter mile in from the paved road where I saw the long beams of her headlights and twin red points of the taillights suddenly go out. I parked, sat in the night waiting for my eyes to adjust before I got out and walked ahead along the faint silver of the dirt road. There was no moon, only the glow of the cosmic night sky far from any city or town. There is still an atavistic sense of awe, delight, beauty, alone under the vast dark sky of the universe. And a sense of total solitude, even fear, with the sweeping menace of the night everywhere.

The Subaru seemed to jump out of the night and smash into my knee and chest. I held to it to keep from falling, listened. There was no sound, not even a wind. The car had been nosed into the trees half off the road in front of the almost-invisible shape of the cabin. I circled the cabin, slow and cautious among the trees and through the thick brush. Shadows moved inside across the small light that came through cracks around the shuttered windows of the unpainted cabin. There were voices. The spaces between shutters wasn't enough to see more than the vague shadows. The voices only a wordless drone.

There was only one door to the cabin. It had no commercial lock, only a latch that lifted from both sides. The bar had not been lowered inside, the latch lifted easily to my touch. Esther Valenzuela sat at a wooden table, a mug of hot coffee in front of her. The rest of the one-room cabin had a bunk bed against one wall, a worn-out brown corduroy couch, two wooden chairs, a sink with a pump, a gas stove that used bottled gas, and a portable cooler on the floor. The light was two kerosene lanterns and a battery-operated camp lantern.

"Mr. Fortune!"

I said. "How long have you known?

Paul Valenzuela said, "This is the detective?"

"Since just before they came to the house and took me with them," Esther said. "He'd been calling, not leaving his name."

She was learning, getting tougher, holding back. Her husband stared at her.

"He followed you?"

"I never saw him, Paul!"

I said, "You weren't supposed to." I turned to Paul Valenzuela. "She's new to all this. I'm not. No one else followed her or me."

"You're sure, Mr. Fortune?"

"I'm sure."

He stood uncertain in the small cabin. I didn't want to alarm him by telling him that someone had tried to follow me from Esther's parents' house. A slender young man in a Los Angeles Dodgers' windbreaker, chino trousers, high-top basketball shoes. Tall for a Latino. In his late twenties and getting older fast from the dark shadows around his nervous eyes, the deep lines at the corners of his mouth. Black-haired with Indian eyes, he wasn't that dark and his lean nose, long face and thin build showed the caucasian mixed with the Indian. The legacy of Tenochtitlan and Maya, Aragon and Castile. The uneasy mix that is the modern Latin American *mestizo, ladino.* For him triply complicated by the culture clash of the *chicano,* the Latino born and raised north of the border in an Anglo-Saxon culture.

"How did you know?" Esther said.

"It's my job." I watched Paul Valenzuela. "You want to tell me the rest of the story of that phone call in Guatemala?"

17

In the message room of the Guatemalan embassy, Paul listens to the loud, arrogant American voice on the ambassador's private line. He is nervous, this is not the kind of call that usually comes in on the ambassador's personal line. Those private business and social calls the ambassador has taped because he likes a record of everything, a habit he got into at his company back in Minnesota.

"I have no idea what you're talking about, Mr. O'Neill, and I don't have time—"

Paul is frozen. He can't move to leave the message room or touch the switch that will silence the machine. It is the voice. So bold and blunt, so American, so angry with the ambassador on a call that is not from Washington, not on the top secret or even the official line that the CIA monitors, but local from here in Guatemala on the personal line.

"I'm talking about past, present and future, Mr. America. Chapter and verse. The whole enchilada. Who we helped, who we supplied, who used our pipelines, facilities and routes. Who paid us and who we paid. When and who Washington is playing goosie with next. I'll blow the whistle on what's really been going on and is going on down here yesterday, today and tomorrow unless D.C. calls off the dogs and their local trained fleas."

"If this is business, Mr. O'Neill, you should call on the official line and go through the proper—"

The ambassador's voice is shaking, and not with anger of his own. The ambassador's voice is protesting, apologizing to the insulting voice. To Mr. O'Neill, a name Paul has never heard at the embassy or anywhere else in the State Department.

"I don't want the official line for the official goddamn runaround. Why the hell do you think I'm calling on your private line? I want you to talk personally to Washington. You, no one else. My boss is dead and I'm tired. Tell Washington to find another grandstand play or they'll be hearing a chorus and verse nobody wants on the air. This is one sucker Washington and the Company don't kiss and cuddle and toss over when it fucking well suits them."

There is a long pause. In the message room Paul looks around nervously. The tape machine hums as it turns. He stares at it like a mouse mesmerized by a snake. There is something about the brash, irreverent American voice that sends a chill up his spine. This O'Neill is not supposed to be calling the embassy. He is not a normal caller. Something is wrong about this man, and the ambassador is scared. It is there in the voice of the ambassador when it comes next.

"You better talk to Carl Foster. Let me put you on hold, I'll see if he's in the embassy. I don't think he is. I believe he is out on some field work, but I'll—"

"Don't put me on hold, Mr. Official America, you're not selling hardware now. And no Carl Fosters. I've talked to Carl Foster. Old Carl doesn't want to talk to me. Carl doesn't have the time of day for Jack O'Neill anymore. Carl and I go back to when he was still wetting his pants in the trade, but that was yesterday and Carl has his orders. Forget Carl, Mr. Ambassador. You're the boss, you talk to Washington and you do it right now. You tell them the Irishman wants a top summit meeting with the people who can say yes and make it stick. An airtight deal or the music's going to hit the air. And, Mr. Ambassador? You tell them the Irishman has it all in black and white and color. I do mean everything."

The silence in the code room is almost as loud as it must be in the ambassador's office when the phone goes dead. Paul stares at the tape that stopped automatically when the caller hung up. Who is O'Neill? What is his relation to Carl Foster? He clearly doesn't know the ambassador, but does the ambassador know him? His name, at least. Paul takes the tape from the machine, slips it into his pocket, inserts a fresh tape. He resets the machine, turns the audible monitoring switch off, hears the door open behind him and someone stop just inside the door.

"Valenzuela?"

The ambassador is in the room, pale and staring at Paul.

"I was checking the machine, sir. The audio was open—"

The ambassador blinked. "You heard?"

Paul nods. The ambassador hesitates, wipes his face with one hand, holds out the other hand.

"All right, it can't be helped. Just don't talk about it. I'll take the tape."

Paul removes the false tape from the machine and hands it to the red-faced diplomat. Should he tell the ambassador? Give him the real tape? He takes a deep breath, takes a chance.

"Sir? Who is he? I mean, Mr. O'Neill, sir. What was he talking about? What grandstand play? What did he do for us? I mean, he's an American, he says he's known Mr. Foster a long time, but he talks about Washington as if it's the enemy."

Paul expects the ambassador to be angry, to ignore his improper questions. Instead, the ambassador sits down and wipes his face again. "How do I know what he was talking about? What do I know about anything in this crazy country? Except that this kind of shit I don't need." A small man in a blue tropical suit, the ambassador looks up at Paul. "What in God's name could I know, Valenzuela? I'm a goddamn hardware manufacturer from St. Paul who raised a bundle of cash for the party, put the screws on in the right places to get our man elected. Now I'm up to my ass in generals, guerrillas, death squads, Amnesty International, the Mayor of Berkeley, and characters like this O'Neill." The pale and angry businessman turned diplomat stands up. "This I turn over to our good CIA station chief's capable hands as soon as he gets back from wherever the hell he went today, and you and I will conveniently forget everything we heard, you understand? I mean, we're civilians, right? What do we know?"

Paul watches the ambassador leave clutching the tape. He sits down at the tape machine, but continues to stare at the closed door where the ambassador has vanished. He watches the door as if both expecting someone else to come in and trying to make up his mind about a course of action. No one comes in, and he glances up at the clock on the wall of the message room.

He stands, walks out of the room, locks the door behind him. He hurries along the corridors to his own office, picks up the telephone receiver, dials a long series of numbers. He tells the smooth and neutral female voice that he wants to speak to Deputy Assistant Secretary of State for Latin America Max Cole. The female takes his name, location, and the general nature of his business—which he states as a possible problem in Guatemala.

"Valenzuela?" The voice of the deputy assistant secretary is surprised. "Paul? What is it? Are you all right? What's wrong down there? Did the ambassador tell you to use the emergency code for—"

"No, sir. I . . . there was a phone call here, sir. A local call to the ambassador. An American named O'Neill."

"O'Neill?"

"Jack O'Neill. He talked about some Irishman who wanted a meeting with someone in Washington. The ambassador told me to forget what I heard, said we should both forget what we heard and let Carl Foster handle—"

"The Irishman? A meeting?"

"He seemed to be saying he had information the ambassador wouldn't want made public. Is that a specific person, sir? The Irishman?"

"You heard this call?"

"We tape all incoming calls on the ambassador's personal line, the audio happened to be open—"

"The ambassador tapes his private calls?"

"He likes a record, sir. Not the official or top secret line, of course. Mr. Foster monitors those lines. That seems to be why this O'Neill called on the ambassador's personal line, he didn't want—"

"All right, Paul, never mind all that. The tape of this call is still in the machine? Give it to Carl Foster, and—"

"The ambassador came to get the tape as soon as the call was over, sir. He seemed nervous, upset. He said he would give the tape to Mr. Foster—"

"Fine." Cole sounds relieved. "Then there's no problem. I'm sure Foster will get to the bottom of whatever the problem is. Now—"

"I didn't give the tape to the ambassador, sir."

Silence. "What do you mean you didn't—"

"I gave him a different tape." Paul swallows in the small space of his office. "Sir, I think you should hear the tape. Maybe the chief should too. There's something very wrong about this O'Neill, sir. He sounds dangerous, and the ambassador is afraid of him. He . . . O'Neill sounds like he's had some kind of dealings with Carl Foster. I . . ." Paul hears himself as he trails off. Why doesn't he trust the ambassador? Or even Carl Foster? Why doesn't he want to give the tape to the CIA chief? Why is he so sure that this is something he should show only to Max Cole, perhaps the Assistant Secretary himself? "It was his voice, sir. So angry at Washington. The way he talked about Carl Foster, as if he knew him so well. The way he talked to the ambassador. So . . . so disrespectful . . ."

He trails off again. He holds the receiver and waits for Deputy Assistant Secretary Cole to say something. Max Cole was his mentor back in Washington when Cole was only a department head, has always been a friend.

"All right, Paul," Max Cole says finally, his voice quiet. "Why don't you take the first plane out tomorrow in the morning. I'll tell the ambassador I wanted to talk to you. You can be here by tomorrow afternoon, can't you?"

"I think so, sir."

"Do that then. I'll listen to your tape, and we'll talk."

"Sir? Who is this O'Neill? Is he the Irishman he talked about?"

"We'll talk tomorrow."

Paul's hand shakes when he hangs up. But he is sure the strange call is something they should know about in Washington. It could be days before the ambassador or Carl Foster got around to reporting it. If they ever did. Paul doesn't like the CIA man, and the ambassador is a figurehead political appointee who knows less about the country than Paul does. Whatever this O'Neill—the Irishman, if they are the same man—has been doing, it is clear it is something O'Neill is sure the ambassador and Carl Foster and even people in Washington would not want made public. That alone is something Paul is certain his superiors in the State Department should know.

He leaves the embassy, aware that Carl Foster could return at any time. The ambassador could give the tape to the CIA man,

Foster could play it, and both would realize at once what had happened and who had the real tape. He decides he won't wait until morning, drives home to pack a bag and try to get on the next flight out to anywhere in the States from where he can get a connection to Washington.

At the nice suburban house he and Esther have in a good residential neighborhood he sees the man walking around the house. The second man is looking into the garage. He recognizes them as two of Carl Foster's CIA agents, drives on past without stopping. In the rearview mirror he sees them walk out of sight around the house, leave their gray car parked at the curb. He drives straight on to the airport. Carl Foster somehow must know about the tape already, it may even be too late for the airport.

Soon after he leaves his own neighborhood, he thinks a large white car might be following him. He watches it behind him all the way to the airport, but the two men who get out are Latino strangers and show no interest in him. He is cautious and alert in the terminal, sees no one he knows, especially not Carl Foster, and no one approaches him. His diplomat's passport gets him a seat on the next plane out. He notices that the two men he thinks were in the car that could have been following him are on the jet too, but they do nothing, sleep most of the flight. By morning he is at Dulles International in Washington.

He doesn't see the Major at first. Or he doesn't know he has seen the Major.

It is only when he is in the telephone booth to call Esther in Santa Barbara and tell her where he is and what has happened that he realizes the man he becomes aware of watching him from across the terminal is the special liaison officer he met a few times at State Department functions and knows only as the Major. In the next instant he also realizes that he saw the man, the Major, the moment he came through the arrival gates. Saw him again when he stopped to buy a cup of coffee and a doughnut before coming to the phone booth. Now the Major stands across the terminal, but makes no attempt to approach.

Slowly, as he starts to tell Esther about the strange telephone call, Paul sees the others.

Two who lean casually against an empty ticket counter.

Another who buys coffee at the same booth Paul did.

The two dark Latino men who had been in the white car in Guatemala City and on the plane with him, and who now seem to watch both him and the Major.

"I'll call you later," he says into the receiver to Esther distant in California.

He leaves the booth.

All five men start toward him through the crowds in the terminal.

Paul Valenzuela runs.

18

Esther Valenzuela poured mugs of coffee from a chipped white enamel pot on the gas stove. Paul sat in a crude wooden chair, his hands clasped on the table. I was on the corduroy couch.

"I knew something was wrong, Mr. Fortune. The Major and those other three were there for me. And not to welcome me. It had to be the tape of that phone call. I know CIA men by now when I see them. I didn't know how they knew I was on that flight, or was even coming to Washington, but it had to mean that they wanted to stop me from getting to Secretary Cole with the tape of the phone call from this Irishman. Something was going on I knew nothing about. So I ran."

The coffee was thick, black as tar and even stronger than it looked. Coffee made by a man who didn't cook for himself. None of us objected to the vicious brew, listened to him talk in the cabin with the heavy night of the backcountry outside.

"Dulles was crowded with the morning flights, I got away from all of them. I didn't know who those other two were who'd come from Guatemala City on the same flight. They weren't with the Major, but they were sure after me too. I was scared and I had to think. I couldn't go to Esther at her parents' house, I knew they'd be there. I don't know anyone or anywhere around Washington, and I wanted to try to reach Esther, so I flew out here. I called a guy I know who has this cabin, took a flight out of Richmond, connected into Santa Maria. I didn't want to leave a trail, so I had my friend pick me up and drive me down. He gave me a change of clothes so I wouldn't stick out in my suit back here. I've been trying to think ever since."

"What have you come up with?"

He didn't answer at once. A thoughtful young man who considered what he was going to say. "How did they know I was coming? The Major and the CIA? Deputy Cole could have told them. But he didn't know I was going to take the earlier flight. Anyway, he was my friend. I thought he was."

Esther said, "He hasn't been acting like a friend, Paul."

"But he didn't know I was going to take the night flight."

"Someone called the embassy," Esther realized, "told them you were flying to Washington! That's why the CIA were waiting at the house. Those two men from Guatemala City must have heard it too. There has to be a leak in the embassy, Paul!"

I said, "There're always leaks in embassies, and only one person who could have told them you were going to Washington."

"Secretary Cole," Paul said. "He called the ambassador after we hung up. The ambassador told Carl Foster."

"You'd already left the embassy," I said, "so Foster sent men to your house. They missed you at the house, later learned you'd taken the earlier flight. Someone else heard you had the tape and had left the embassy, sent those two men. They didn't miss you, tailed you all the way to Washington where you slipped them all."

"But who, Mr. Fortune? That Jack O'Neill who made the call?"

"That would be my bet. The Irishman, if that's O'Neill himself. You have any idea who he is? What this is all about?"

"I do now. Or at least some of it." He got up, went to the sink with its pump to empty and wash the coffee pot. To have something to do. "I should have guessed from all he said to the ambassador about facilities and payoffs, from his reference to his boss being killed. But I didn't, or maybe I didn't want to."

"A drug cartel man," I said. "The boss he talked about was Rodriguez Gacha."

He walked around drying the coffee pot. "I had nothing to do here but think and try to contact Esther without alerting her parents or anyone else, so I got a ride into Solvang and looked in the newspapers and magazines of the last couple of years for anyone named the Irishman." He put the dried coffee pot on the stove, looked at each of us. We shook our heads. He opened a wall cupboard, put the pot inside with small stacks of plates and mugs and other pots. An orderly young man, and it was a borrowed cabin.

"There wasn't much, he keeps a pretty low profile. Or he did." He sat again, folded his arms across his chest this time. "His real name's Hugh John O'Neill, and he is an American. He comes from a successful middle-class Irish family in Council Bluffs, Iowa. That's from an interview *Time* did for a big roundup article on the Medellin and Cali cartels. His father, Hugh Sr., is a manufacturer, doesn't believe a word of the stories about his son.

"Jack graduated from the University of Iowa, was ROTC, went into the service and did three years in Vietnam. After that the mentions get pretty vague. No mention of when he got out of the service, what he did, marriages, anything, until he shows up as a pilot working for small airlines in Latin America that were later found to be part of the emerging drug cartels." Paul shrugged. "He must have worked his way up fast, because soon after he's listed as a suspected lieutenant in Gacha's cartel in Medellin, someone who works behind the scenes on an international level, especially with Americans."

I thought about the position of an American high up in the drug cartels now that the U.S. was pushing a massive campaign against the drug trade. Or at least that part of it run by the independent cartels and their multibillionaire bosses. Would they trust him now? Worse, was his usefulness to them over? Or was he even more useful?

"There was one other odd story." Paul spoke slowly as if trying to understand. "I remember reading reports from Colombia about the private armies of the drug kings leading raids on the leftist guerrillas and their supporters, of their paramilitary commandos attacking union workers and left-wing politicians. Reports of the assassinations of leftist leaders and officials, of coordinated operations of the army and the drug paramilitaries on guerrilla strongholds and villages suspected of sympathizing with the guerrillas."

His thin young face that was the legacy of two worlds had a kind of wonder as he heard his own voice that came from still a third world. "But there was this one report from a Colombian colonel. A strong force of his elite troops under his personal command were on a sweep to give a warning to the villages in an area suspected of being a guerrilla stronghold and came under heavy fire from all the villages. The villagers had never been armed before, now had automatic rifles and grenades. They even seemed to have some experienced leaders, beat the soldiers off, and the colonel had to retreat from the area. He interrogated some captured villagers, learned the arms and paramilitaries had been given to them by a drug king they called El Irlandés, "the Irishman." The colonel identified El Irlandés as relatively unknown in Colombia, but reputed to be Rodriguez Gacha's chief international aide."

He looked first at Esther, then at me. Serious. Expectant. Waiting for us to tell him what we thought.

Esther said, "You think he wasn't known well because he's been doing his criminal actions in Guatemala? That's why he knows the ambassador and Mr. Foster."

"Maybe he has been in Guatemala. Probably buying opium poppies, making heroin up in the mountains. There's more of it being grown all the time. But what makes me wonder is him helping insurgents in Colombia. Maybe he's something else. You can never be sure of anyone down there. There was this time I was biking up in the northeastern part of the country when an army patrol stopped me."

On his motorcycle, Paul is taken to a large finca *where the major in charge of the area has his command post. The major is busy, Paul must wait. His passport is taken in to the major, his motorcycle is placed in a fenced compound with the vehicles of the patrol and a beautiful white Mercedes Paul guesses belongs to the owner of the plantation. A tall, distinguished man in his fifties, with silver gray hair and impeccable in a white tropical suit and finely woven panama hat, waits with Paul, makes polite conversation.*

—You are American?

—At the embassy, Paul acknowledges.

—Ah? But you wish to see the country where you have been sent for yourself, eh? Most admirable. If all our diplomats would do that, eh?

The man has an accent Paul can't quite place, not any Latin language. He thinks it is German, but the special German accent of a man not from Germany. He guesses Swiss, and the man soon confirms this.

—Perhaps it is easier for those of us from countries with no position to

maintain, eh? I am Swiss myself, from Zurich, on a little motor trip to see also for myself. From Costa Rica, where I have business, to your country, where I too have business. A whim, eh? What better way to see some of this world of ours I do not know except from books.

A sergeant takes Paul in to the major, who apologizes for the delay, hands him back his passport. The major suggests that it would be a good idea to clear his travels with the local authorities, Guatemala City does not always know conditions in remote areas and the roads can be dangerous with bandits and guerrillas. The major smiles a lot, tells him how grateful all Guatemala is for the help of the great United States of America.

As Paul waits for a soldier to get his motorcycle from the fenced compound, he sees that the white Mercedes is gone. The major has forgotten to give Paul back his keys, Paul returns to get them. The Swiss gentleman is with the major. The sergeant goes in to get the keys, Paul hears the older man's polite voice.

—I demand the return of my car, Major. I have no idea what lie you plan to tell me or your superiors, but I will not accept another car for any reason. Is that quite clear?

Paul hears the major swear, shout to the sergeant to get back in there and close the fucking door. The sergeant hands him his keys, hurries back inside the major's office. As Paul again goes out to his motorcycle, three more soldiers run into the house. He hears angry voices and the unmistakable sounds of a beating. He hesitates on his motorcycle. The soldiers around the finca *look at him. He rides away.*

In Guatemala City he reports to the ambassador who informs the Swiss officials. Eventually the Swiss receive a letter from the Minister of Justice that says there is no record of any Swiss tourist in a Mercedes ever entering Guatemala.

Paul's voice has become hypnotic in the silent cabin with only trees and the night outside. "There was another time when we had a group of visiting journalists. They came down after a British magazine reported American officers in the field with the Guatemalan troops against the guerrillas. They were sniffing for dirt, I had to take them north, put them up in a rural hotel."

The journalists meet soldiers, villagers, and the American advisers, who all deny that Americans ever go into the field. The visitors see no actual Americans in combat, end their trip. The commander, a very young colonel, gives a farewell party. All the local dignitaries attend, a brigadier general is sent from Guatemala City to represent the Defense Minister.

There is a great deal of strong drink, especially the colonel's favorite rum, the rare Ron Anejo Botran Solera 1893, which he insists the reporters join him in drinking. When two of them decline, the young colonel flies into a rage. He insists the journalists have insulted his country. They have insulted him. They have insulted his brave men. They are cowardly pigs who come to his country to accuse him of not leading his own men in battle, to sneak around like dogs sniffing for lies.

The colonel slaps one journalist in the face repeatedly, beats a second, chases both through the hotel where they hide in the room of a third reporter. The colonel breaks down the door, pistol-whips all three, and chases them around the hotel and grounds for three hours. His soldiers keep any help away. The chief of police, called by the hotel owner, refuses to send any men. The brigadier general from the Defense Ministry apologizes to the beaten newsmen when the colonel passes out, but until then he has been nowhere in sight.

When the police finally do arrive they refuse to file any charges or even take down an official report. The incident never happened. The Americans were all drunk. The brigadier continues to apologize profusely, conveys the deep personal regrets of the Defense Minister and of the civilian presidente, *but it is clear that no one is going to do anything to the young colonel, who, sobering up over a massive breakfast with his favorite Ron Anejo, asks loudly what the journalists are still doing in his hotel.*

In the capital the journalists complain vociferously, take the next flight out to report the outrage to their editors. Paul goes with the ambassador and Carl Foster to see them off, on the way back finds out what has really been going on.

—That colonel is the kid brother of a top general who's maybe the next president. How do you think he got to be a colonel so young?

—Family is the magic word. The general and the kid colonel are the biggest landowning family up in that area. The Defense Minister is married to a cousin. The civilian president went to school with the general.

Paul broke the trance, turned to look at us. "That's how they act down there, the military and the landowners we support. Maybe this Irishman isn't what everyone wants us to think he is. They all know his name, and they're sure worried about what I heard. Enough to want the tape a lot."

"It looks like the Irishman wants it a lot too," I said. "Do you have the tape?"

He nodded.

I stood up. "Then let's talk to Gus Chavalas."

19

Paul Valenzuela rode with me. We would go directly to the police station, not take a chance on the Major and Max Cole watching the Conrad house.

Esther led us along the dark rural road out of the back canyons and up to Highway 154. There was little traffic in the pass this late on a weekday night, and not a lot on Foothill, and we took the back way to police headquarters. Mission Canyon Road had more as we drove past the Mission and turned downtown through the quiet upper Eastside.

All the way down Olive Street there were enough other cars out to slow us and put two cars between my Tempo and Esther's Subaru. The light caught me at Anapamu. Esther made it through and went on ahead to Figueroa. She turned when she saw us coming up behind her.

A limousine blocked her, the black Buick pulled out from the curb behind her.

"Down!"

Paul Valenzuela slid out of sight. I gunned on down Olive with tires squealing, had a glimpse of the Buick going after the green Subaru that was trying to drive around the limousine on the sidewalk.

Paul Valenzuela opened the door to jump out of the Tempo.

"No!" I braked hard, grabbed him with my lone hand. "It's you they want. They think you're with her. They won't hurt her. Stay down."

Chance. Paul was with me not Esther. She had made a traffic light, I had been stopped. Call it luck.

We slewed away down Olive before they could see their error. In the rearview mirror low headlights turned out of Figueroa on the opposite side of Olive, came after us. Wide headlights, a low silhouette. Some kind of sportscar.

I turned on Cota between a honking pickup from the west and a white-faced old man behind the wheel of a Cadillac from the east. Turned again into Salsipuedes, went across Haley and under the freeway. Corkscrewed through the back commercial streets, came out on Milpas, headed for the sea and the beach. I bounced across the railroad tracks and parked on the shadowed street between the softball field and the Red Lion Inn.

"Keep down."

The Major and the man in the limo knew by now that Paul was with me. The car from the opposite block of Figueroa could have been watching the Major or following me or both. Or I could be wrong. Right or wrong I couldn't take Paul home to Summerland. Someone would be there. Sooner or later.

"How could they know we were going to the police? How do they know I'm in Santa Barbara?"

I had to tell him about the car that had tried to tail me away from the Conrad house when I had followed Esther. "They're as good at this game as I am, Paul. They knew if Esther was going out so soon after we got her away from them she had a reason and it was almost certain to be you. I lost whoever it was, but they knew we'd bring you back to Santa Barbara sooner or later. So they covered the Conrad house, my house, the police station, who knows where else. Simple logic—where would we go, what would we do—and cover all bases they could."

"Have we lost them?"

"I hope so." I started up. "We'll go to a motel I know down here behind Cabrillo Boulevard, call Sergeant Chavalas."

We both watched four more cars pass. None of them were limos, black Buicks or sportscars. We drove to the small, almost invisible little motel behind Cabrillo between Milpas and the zoo. Kay and I had stayed in it while we were looking for a house to rent. The owner, Ted, is a friend, there's always an extra room. We took it.

Chavalas wasn't in his office. The way it was with his captain I wanted him to be there when I brought Paul Valenzuela in the first time. At his home number his wife said he was out on a late-developing case, had no idea when he'd be back.

"I'm going to Esther," Paul said.

"They want you, not her. And there's more than one *they*. They've used her all along to get to you. Don't make it easy."

"I've got to know she's all right."

"You stay locked in here, I'll make sure."

"An hour," Paul said. "No more."

"Don't answer the phone or the door, keep the door locked. Don't use the phone. When I come back I'll knock a code: three, one, three, two."

Two blocks from police headquarters I parked on Figueroa and walked. The limousine waited in the shadow of a tree between me and the police. One shadowy head at the wheel, another in back. On the far side of the station someone leaned against a building wall. There was no sign of Esther Valenzuela's green Subaru or the Major's Buick.

At the Conrads' big house on the upper Eastside there was no Buick, but the green Subaru was in the driveway. I drove on past and parked at the corner of the next block where I could watch the street in front of the house. Sat until I spotted the single watcher under a tree across the street. He would be the only one I would spot. They didn't have unlimited manpower. At least not on short notice. I drove back to the front steps, went up the walk bold and open. It wasn't me they were interested in. Not until I came out. And if they knew I was inside it would help keep them from the motel and Paul.

"Mr. Fortune. Come in."

Esther Valenzuela glanced across the night street to where the watcher was a vague shape under the trees. She had learned a lot about the world she lived in over the last week.

"Is he all right?"

Concerned, even anxious, but her movements were steady and

firm as she walked ahead of me into the quiet living room. The uncertain young woman of the first days faded farther and farther behind in some innocent world where she could no longer live. She gestured me toward an armchair. I shook my head.

"He's in a motel where I know the owner. He wanted to be sure they hadn't hurt you before we did anything more."

"They were so sure Paul would be with me they assumed he was hiding in the back of the Subaru." She smiled a faint amusement. "I pretended he was, shouted at the back seat, told him to run. By the time they realized no one else was in the car you were out of sight."

"The Major and who else?"

"Those two CIA men."

"Max Cole?"

"I didn't see him."

"What about the limousine?"

"Only the driver got out."

"Was there any other car? A low sportscar?"

"Just the two. When the Major saw Paul wasn't in the car he was very angry, but he didn't do anything. I drove home, they didn't stop me."

"He doesn't need you anymore. Paul won't be decoyed now. They'll just watch you. Did you talk to the police?"

"No." The innocent world of the young wife who had hired me was almost lost. "I'm not sure we can trust them. I don't know whose side they're on with Paul, what they've been told, who they'd believe."

"We can trust Gus Chavalas."

"I don't know that, Dan."

"Then you'll have to trust me, my word." I walked to the door. "If the man out there follows me, go to Sergeant Chavalas down at police headquarters. Tell him what's happened, tell him I'll contact him sometime tonight. If the guy doesn't move, stay in the house and wait."

They would tail me. The only question was how they'd do it. My guess was the guy under the tree across the street had already called for backup on a walkie-talkie. He'd stay where he was to keep the house covered, the roving backup would zero in on me from somewhere out of sight. As I walked down the walk to my

Tempo at the curb, I looked for the spot where they could pick me up whichever way I drove.

The Conrad house was in the middle of the dark block. Both corners or almost any driveway would do. The best was the hidden driveway I'd used the first night to follow the Major. As I drove past I looked that way. The black car was there facing out. They gave me all the way to the corner before they fell in behind, ran dark until I turned on Mission toward the freeway. Not the Buick, the CIA car that had come for Sylvestre Madrona's body at the warehouse.

It's not hard to lose a tail on a freeway once you know it's there. Especially at night. Speed up until they have to hit seventy, drop in front of a semi and slide off at the first exit. If they don't sail on past trying to find you somewhere ahead they're masters, but even if they spot you the semi blocks them and you pull right back on while they dive off at the next exit to backtrack and pick you up.

The black car sailed on past.

I pulled back on the opposite way, headed through the lights for the Milpas exit.

Paul Valenzuela opened the motel room door before the last knock of my code had stopped echoing.

"She's at home." I told him what she'd told me. "Fooled the shit out of the Major to give us some time. She'll do fine. Anything happen here?"

He shook his head. "They're watching the house?"

"They're watching everywhere they can think of and have the men for."

I dialed police headquarters again. Chavalas hadn't returned. They wanted to know my name, if they could help me. I hung up.

Paul paced the small room. "Can we trust the police?"

"Chavalas, yes."

"But not the others?" He sat down, held his face in both hands, tired out.

"The police are like most of us, Paul, only more so. They know what they grew up with. They salute the uniform, the office, the flag, no matter who is in it or who waves it."

His face was behind his weary hands. "They'll believe the Major, Mr. Cole, the CIA. Not me."

"Until they have big reasons not to."

He looked up at me. "Then what can we do?"

"We can get to Chavalas."

"When?"

"As soon as I can contact him. Meanwhile, I want to know everything we're dealing with."

"You mean that other car? The one that could have chased us after the ambush? You don't think it was the Major's gang?"

"I don't know for sure what it was."

"But you're going to find out."

"I'm going to find out."

"Then I'm going with you."

"They don't have you, and don't know where you are. We need to hold that advantage, you understand? You stay here, stay out of sight, stay locked up, answer no phone calls, get some sleep."

"What will you do?"

"Look for an Irishman."

Close against the dark mountains, San Ysidro Ranch at night is a rich glow of discreet lights scattered among the trees and bushes and hidden walks. Lights in distant cottage windows and low along the walks. A warm clustered glow from the restaurant and downstairs lounge above the narrow, unobtrusive parking lot. For a five-star hotel the office has all the glitter and glamor of a minor motel in some nameless town off a remote interstate.

The single clerk greeted me politely, but didn't ask if I wanted a room. "Can I help you, sir?"

"If you can connect me to Mr. Tyrone Earl's cottage."

"I'm sorry, sir. Mr. Earl checked out."

"When? He was here this morning. What's your checkout time?"

"Mr. Earl checked out this evening."

"This evening?"

He nodded. "About an hour ago."

"You let people check out so late?"

He looked at my empty sleeve and old corduroy jacket and

grinned. He served the rich and the beautiful, but he was a kid who shared a studio apartment downtown or a shabby cottage on the Westside. We were equals. "He got charged for the whole night, believe me. People come here don't worry about money."

"Rich people always worry about money," I said. "You have his home address?"

"I'm sorry. We can't give that out."

It had been worth a free try, but it wasn't worth any money. If Mr. Tyrone Earl was who I thought he was, the address would be the Sherman Oaks office on his card, or a nonexistent number on some Mexico City *avenida* he'd never been near. I walked back to my car, listened to the night.

The last few low voices in the restaurant and lounge, a faraway cry that could have been passion in a cottage or sudden death in the brush. The rich did always worry about money. New money worried less than old money, but neither threw cash away unless there was a reason even more important than money at the moment. Like grabbing a man who had the tape of a telephone conversation you didn't want him to have, didn't want him to give to anyone else.

The shortest way back to the freeway was down San Ysidro Road. At that late hour the only traffic on the freeway was a couple of big double bottoms making time and a few partygoers on their way home from L.A. The Cabrillo Boulevard exit under the railroad tracks is the faster way to the beachfront motels. On the oceanfront curves the traffic was heavier past the beach with its ghostly volleyball posts and couples still lying in the sand. Traffic and strollers in the clear night where the lights of the oil rigs stood out on the sea like a fleet of aircraft carriers sailing to attack the world.

In the back streets behind Cabrillo, even the motel office was closed. Cars lined the night street in the silence broken only by the sound of the surf on East Beach, the passage of the late-night cruisers all along Cabrillo Boulevard, trucks on the freeway. None of the parked cars on the street or in front of the motel office was a black Buick, a limousine, or a rebuilt Ferarri. The walks among the units were deserted.

The door to the motel room stood open.

A black rectangle as deep and bottomless as any black hole in the vast universe. It seemed to pull me toward it, suck me in. A black hole with blacker movement exploding out of it.

I ran.

They slammed across the open court after me.

I ran toward Cabrillo Boulevard.

Into a shadow that flowed up and out of a parked car as I passed, flashed in the night. Slammed into the shadow. My old cannon into bone. Flash and pain. Cold pain. Wet. Blood.

It was a knife. In my shoulder. Burned. Throbbed. They had Paul Valenzuela and no one could know. Hide where they would never find me. Hope they would never find me. Bleed where they would never find me.

Dark streets. Empty streets.

In the jungles of Santa Barbara the beasts sleep, predators crash through the night. Prey and predator. The wounded in a sea of helplessness. Pain and fear and the indifferent universe.

Bright street. Wide street. Street that moves. Flash, flash, flash.

If you have ever been hunted, you will never hunt again. If you have been shot, you will never want to shoot. Anachronism. Throwback. Warrior without need. Killer without cause.

Among the wide lights. Faces. Screams. Thunder of pain.

In England long ago when you were hanged there was no scaffold and you strangled slowly. Swung in the wind. Curled into a ball. Unborn. The black Ferarri drove squealing out of the trunk of the exploding limousine as the Irishman sang in the red and green trees and the Major laughed, laughed . . .

THE IRISHMAN

Give an Irishman a horse and he'll vote Tory.

—NINETEENTH CENTURY BRITISH POLITICAL MAXIM

20

They told me how lucky I was.

The knife wound in my shoulder had put me into shock, but had hit no major blood vessels. A relatively mild concussion when my head hit Cabrillo Boulevard, but no fracture. A cracked rib and a lot of bruises all over my left side where the car hit me when I ran out into the traffic. A heavily bandaged shoulder, sore ribs, aches and pains and a hell of a headache. Four or five days in hospital. It could have been worse.

I knew how much luckier than that I was, how much worse it could have been. It could have been my right shoulder. My lone arm. A one-armed man knows more than most how small and helpless a wounded man can be alone. Any man alone.

They found no trace of who attacked me. Sergeant Chavalas said, "Near as we can reconstruct it from the scene and what you remember, they got Valenzuela out of that room, left people to cover the rear. Two chased you when you showed, one was waiting up the block, knifed you. You must have hit him pretty hard too, we found a lot of blood on the sidewalk and not all yours."

My eyes were closed behind the headache. "I remember I hit something with my shoulder and my old gun."

"You made it to Cabrillo, ran out into the boulevard. There was enough traffic and people out walking to keep the attackers off, and not so much that the car that hit you didn't have time to brake. You were damn lucky."

Kay held my hand where she sat beside the bed. I squeezed her hand, muttered silent thanks again to the cosmos that it had been my left shoulder. But it wasn't the cosmos this time, and not luck that had sent me out into Cabrillo Boulevard. My only chance had been people and traffic.

"It was all I could think of to save myself. People and traffic. Witnesses, maybe even help."

"You never got a look at them?"

"No." It was like pushing an enormous weight to even talk. "Paul Valenzuela?"

"Not a peep. Nothing in that motel room to give us a lead. Your pal the owner didn't hear a sound. Not even when they went after you."

"Esther?"

Kay said, "She's pretty distraught, Dan, but she's hanging in. I've been going over there to do some support talk, help her wait."

Chavalas said, "The Major's vanished, and the CIA. But deputy assistant big boss Cole is still in town. Officially, this time. State Department business. How about that? Only he's been seen a couple or ten times at the Conrads' house."

I fought the headache, the throb in my shoulder, in the dark behind my eyes. "Esther Valenzuela? Your night raid to break her away from them?"

"You know, no one ever did call to complain about that. Not to the captain or the sheriff. I never mentioned it, the captain doesn't even know. I'm starting to wonder if maybe the Major's problem isn't all that official."

"Moonlighting?"

"It happens, but this feels sort of different. When I call Washington they don't know anything, but they cover. Everyone is somewhere else. No one's even been in Santa Barbara. Whatever, they've backed way off now. It looks like the war's moved away."

"Tyrone Earl?"

"Checked out of town. We called his office in L.A. No answer. You know anything about that, Dan?"

I told him Paul Valenzuela's story, all about the telephone call to the ambassador, the Irishman, the chase of Paul. Esther hadn't told him any of it. She had learned too much too fast. You have to know who you *can* trust and trust them or you'll trust no one and that is only another way to be alone. When I finished I felt like I'd climbed a mountain. "My guess is Tyrone Earl is Jack O'Neill. The Irishman. He's up here after Paul Valenzuela too. It's all that makes sense. He likes to play games. Hugh O'Neill was the Earl of Tyrone in Elizabethan Ireland."

"He's a funny man. What else is he, Dan? Don't tell me a guy who sells masks and hammocks."

"Probably drugs. Producing, manufacturing and shipping. Maybe guns and politics. They tend to go together these days."

"The Major was telling it straight all along?"

"I think Madrona and Earl are up to their ears in drugs. I don't know how straight the Major is telling it."

I lay in my own dark and thought about the Major and his phony story of Paul Valenzuela. If one elaborate story was phony, maybe everything was.

Chavalas said, "Earl and Madrona were after Paul Valenzuela too? Wanted that tape?"

"That's my other guess."

"Why? If you're right, it's a tape of O'Neill's own phone call."

"A negotiation call. In Paul Valenzuela's hands it's a loose cannon. It gets out maybe there's nothing to negotiate."

"If Earl and Madrona want to negotiate, why kill Madrona?"

"Maybe the Major doesn't want to negotiate. Eliminate them all. Madrona, the tape, the Irishman."

I waited in my self-imposed darkness with wound and headache. When he spoke again I knew he had stood up. His voice above and closer.

"Or maybe your Irishman wants Valenzuela and the tape for a kind of hostage. Insurance policy."

He was a smart cop. The tape wasn't much use to Earl, or O'Neill, or whatever his real name was, but if the Major and the CIA and State got it, a threat was removed. A threat that might hold up the negotiations, but also made eliminating the Irishman less important as an option. It had all the sound of a delicate balance. Call it power politics. And Sylvestre Madrona had made a wrong move.

"Anything you know you're not telling me, Dan?"

"No."

He heard the unsaid in my weary voice.

"But?"

I opened my eyes. "I think there's something we both don't know. Any of them could have Valenzuela and the tape."

"Or none of them." He walked to the door. "Call me when you're ready. I'll keep looking for Valenzuela. For all of them. My own time."

A man with two perfectly good legs does not need a wheelchair to go along a wide hall, ride down in an elevator and get into a car at the sidewalk. Everything is a matter of liability and insurance. Someone would sue for a stubbed toe. I often think there's little hope for our future on this planet, sometimes I'm not sure that isn't a good thing.

Kay drove. "You should go straight home and rest."

"Five days in the hospital wear a man out."

"Don't be a smart ass."

"Don't hand out rules you'd never play yourself."

"Shock and concussion are nothing to play with, Dan."

I kissed her lightly. "Drive me to Esther Valenzuela."

Mrs. Conrad answered the door. She looked ten years older than she had a week and a half ago. The real world had gotten to her. Or maybe the change in her daughter. Esther Valenzuela sat in her father's office going over a pile of letters.

"Paul's letters from Guatemala when he was first there." She didn't get up. "I'm looking for anything he might have done or seen that could connect him to this Irishman, any hint of trouble with Carl Foster or the ambassador."

"Have you heard from him, Esther?"

She looked at me. "What makes you think I could have heard from him? If I had, I'd have told you and the police."

"You didn't tell them anything about his story of the tape."

Her steady eyes didn't change. "You have to be careful who you tell anything."

"Does that include me?"

"Not yet." Now she stood up. "Nothing has happened, and there's nothing I've heard I haven't told you, Mr. Fortune, and thanks for sending Kay." She smiled at Kay. "It would have been a lot harder without her. I don't know what—" She went to the windows that overlooked the garden. "I sit here in the house and wait. For a call, a letter. For the police to tell me he's dead. For the Major to come and say it was all a mistake, Paul is fine, we'll soon be back in Guatemala City as if nothing had ever happened." She watched some bird out in the garden. "But that isn't going to happen, is it? Far more likely the police will tell me Paul is dead."

"I don't think he's dead," I said.

She watched the bird. "Why not?"

From its hop, a flash of orange red, I guessed the bird was a robin. A large western robin. "Because I think I know who has him, and I don't think they have any reason to want him dead."

She turned at the window. "It's not the Major, is it? Not State or even the CIA."

"What makes you think it isn't one of them?'

"Because Max Cole has been visiting me two or three times a day. He never asks about Paul directly, acts as if he's here to give me help, moral support. At first I thought it was because he wanted me to think they didn't kidnap Paul. But then I saw how alert he became every time anyone came to the door or the telephone rang. How he asked small, innocent questions about you, what you'd learned. About what Paul told us in the cabin. Anywhere Paul could have gone to hide again."

"As if he thinks Paul might have simply run off?"

Her whole face darkened in anger. "He acts as if he is thinking only of me. Of Paul. Our good friend. He acts as if he knows nothing about what has happened to Paul. He—"

The ring of the doorbell out in the hallway made her listen. She listened with every cell of her body. Tense as a new mother who thinks she hears the baby cry. We all listened to the sound of the door opening. Under the tension and tightness, agonized hope in Esther Valenzuela's face. The hope you don't want to admit you have even to yourself. Especially to yourself.

As the silence at the front door lengthened, her hope faded. A glance of sympathy from Kay. If it were Paul, there would have been more than silence. More than the low, soft drone of voices that came after the silence. Her mother's voice and a male voice.

Footsteps that walked past the living room toward the door of the office.

"Esther?" Mrs. Conrad opened the door and came in. "I told him you were busy with Mr. Fortune, dear, but he says he wants to speak to Mr. Fortune too."

Deputy Assistant Secretary Max Cole came into the office behind her.

21

"I was sorry to hear of your injuries, Mr. Fortune. You have recovered, I hope?"

The big voice of the State Department man still surprised as it came from the diminutive body and pink mouth under the high forehead and thin gray hair. He tried what was intended to be a sympathetic smile, but the permanent frown furrow between his eyes spoiled it. His blue chalk-stripe suit was better suited to the cool of a Santa Barbara spring day.

"I hope so too," I said, "Deputy Assistant Secretary of State Max Cole, Kay Michaels."

"Miss Michaels." Cole inclined his balding head to Kay who smiled and nodded.

Cole looked toward Mrs. Conrad. It was a dismissal. The older woman dutifully left the office, closed the door behind her. Government business.

"Where's your buddy the Major and his CIA troops?"

The frown furrow between his eyes deepened. "Major Hill had other business to attend to." They can't handle irreverence, the government people. But he had a mission, tried to overlook my tone. "Can you tell me what really happened the other night, Mr. Fortune? How you happened to be with Paul Valenzuela? Where you found him? Who attacked you?"

"I don't know who attacked me. You're sure it wasn't the Major's people?"

"I'm quite sure." His confident voice was smooth as cream. His eyes had no expression at all. "Paul Valenzuela?"

"Paul called Esther, we went out to a cabin in the Paradise area and found him there. He'd been in Santa Barbara ever since he ran in Washington. But you know that much, right? The Major tailed him out here. That's why he was watching Esther. You just didn't know where he was in Santa Barbara."

"I don't know anything about—"

"Stop it, for Christ's sake, Cole. He'd called you about the tape, gone to Washington to meet with you." I told him the whole story of the telephone call, the tape, him and the Major as Paul had told it to us. His eyes hardened into the kind of certainty he understood. He had been prepared for Paul's story.

"I have no idea why Paul is lying, Mr. Fortune, but very little of that happened." He sat down in a leather armchair and crossed his legs neatly in the chalk-stripe trousers, brushed a trace of lint from the knee. "The true story is that the CIA station chief in Guatemala City intercepted a telephone call to Paul from a known leader in the Rodriguez Gacha drug cartel who has been expanding the ring's operations into Guatemala. Foster immediately taped the call, Paul somehow found out and stole the tape. He then escaped from Guatemala using his State Department status, evaded all our attempts to talk to him. We have no idea what connection Paul has to the Irishman, what he or the Irishman are doing, or when Paul first came to know him, but we have to find out. A great deal is at stake."

Esther Valenzuela's face was white. "That's all another lie, Mr. Cole! You know it is! How many lying stories are you going to tell? The Irishman called the ambassador and threatened to expose some kind of past deal with someone. He knows Carl Foster well. You know that too!"

Max Cole shook his head sadly. "I'm sorry, Esther, but Paul is involved with the drug cartel. Perhaps he's been fooled. Or perhaps he couldn't help himself. Perhaps it is something from his past in the *barrio* of Los Angeles. We all know that Los Angeles is the main drug port of entry at this time. Or perhaps Paul is only a dupe. But we must know the truth."

She stood there in the office and faced him. It wasn't what she would have done a week ago. "You have the truth. Paul told it. I don't think we've had any truth from you, Mr. Cole."

"Why would I lie, Esther?" His voice was soft and soothing. "Especially about Paul. I think I've been a good friend."

I said, "I can think of fifty reasons for you to lie, Cole. From protecting your own interests, to protecting clandestine and maybe illegal actions, to protecting your pals' political asses."

Cole reddened. "Really? You have strange views of your own leaders, Mr. Fortune."

"People who support corrupt generals and death squads aren't my leaders, Cole."

"May I suggest you have no idea what you're talking about?"

"You can suggest all you want," I said. "What you can't do is get any of the information you want from us. You don't have Paul Valenzuela, you don't know where he is, and you won't find out from me."

His anger finally broke through the smooth surface. "I think you know exactly where Paul is, you hear? I think—"

The side door out into the garden opened, two men stepped into the office. One was the driver of the limousine. The other was the man I had seen run from the warehouse that first night to be picked up and driven away in the limousine. He came in at a quick, brisk walk, nodded to Max Cole.

"That's fine, Cole, but I think I'll talk to these people myself."

The chauffeur held the door. Max Cole went out without a word. The chauffeur closed the door. His face impassive, his hands empty, but if there were any kind of threat the chauffeur would be ready to handle it one way or another. The second man nodded to us.

"Mrs. Valenzuela, Miss Michaels, Fortune. Why don't we all sit down?"

Slim, compact, neither tall nor short, he sat behind George Conrad's desk without asking. Esther and Kay sat on the leather couch. I didn't sit.

"You have a name yourself?"

He waved an abrupt hand. I annoyed him. "Sit down, Mr. Fortune. I prefer not to have to look up at someone when I talk to him."

"I don't much care what you prefer."

He sighed. "Does that make you feel better? More powerful? Independent? Your own man?"

"Something like that."

"Good. Then can we get on with it?"

I could have asked him what "it" was, but I would find out soon enough. He wouldn't be a man who wasted time.

"When I have a name."

He shrugged. "Dobson. Martin Dobson."

I sat in one of the leather armchairs.

"Thank you, I appreciate it," he said, with more than a touch of sarcasm. He didn't think a whole lot of me. Probably not a whole lot of most people.

In a dark brown suit I recognized as featherweight cashmere, he leaned back. Trim and solid in his mid-forties. A man who worked out, jogged, played racquetball at the health club. He had not felt intimidated or out of place or nervous since he was in his teens. The suit was rumpled, but had cost five times Max Cole's suit. A white shirt, dark red-and-blue-striped Guards tie, cordovan oxfords, brown socks, and no vest. I had a hunch if it got cold he'd put a mismatched sweater on under the suit. Cashmere, of course, but only because that was what he had. He wore heavy rimmed glasses, his thick hair was pale brown, messy, and going gray. His only jewelry was a simple wedding band and an analog watch. The watch was expensive, but nowhere near what Tyrone Earl's had cost. He was who he was.

"Since Cole has essentially revealed that we don't have Paul Valenzuela, I'll simply ask you where he is."

"I'll simply ask why you care about Paul?"

"That isn't your business. I understood you'd been told that more than once."

"You order State Department men around all the time?"

"When they need it. Paul Valenzuela?"

"Your guess is as good as mine."

"Probably better, but that's beside the point. It isn't your guess we need, it's your knowledge. Are you hiding Paul Valenzuela? Is he hiding on his own, and if so, where? We can make it very much in your interest to tell me."

"Who's we, Mr. Dobson?"

Behind George Conrad's fine desk he sat back in the chair as he would in any office of his own. Relaxed, at ease, only his soft hands that moved back and forth on the chair arms, stroking the wood, to show he was tense, disturbed. "You know, you really don't have any idea what you're into, Fortune. Paul Valenzuela, you, the ladies here, are over your heads. There is far more involved than you realize. If you do know—"

"National security, the fate of the nation? The Major and Cole hammered that one into the ground."

"Possibly those things, yes, but very much more than that. You could all be badly hurt."

There was no menacing tone, no hint of an offer we couldn't refuse. He just said it, his blue eyes unchanged behind his glasses, his feet on the floor, his hands still on the arms of George Conrad's desk chair moving slowly but steadily back and forth. But it was a threat. Naked, heavy, definite and very certain.

"The Major already said that."

"I'm not the Major."

"Who are you?"

"If you weren't so ludicrous, Fortune, you'd be funny. The rugged individualist tilting at windmills and giants. The Don Quixote populist. The gnat."

"That's the last thing you are, isn't it, Dobson? Populist or individualist."

His eyes behind the heavy glasses were a shade less blue. His hands stopped their slow, inexorable stroking of the smooth wood of the chair arms. I'd reached some faint soft spot. A point of private, personal ego. He thought of himself as unique, the true free individual, a mind entirely his own, the ultimate libertarian. When you find a soft spot in the Dobsons, you push.

"Did you think I wouldn't know your name, recognize it? Know who you are?"

He was no Max Cole. He had been baited by the best, moved in a world where control was everything. Control and maneuver and facade, and in the end only power mattered. A facade as polished and impervious as granite. But I had hit him. He had not expected me to know his name and who he was. His hands began to move again on the arms of the desk chair, but his eyes had changed behind the heavy glasses.

"It made no difference if you did or didn't, Fortune."

He was saying it made a difference, but either way had its advantages. He would have preferred I didn't know who he was, maintain his advantage of secrecy. But if I did know, it might make me tell him more, back away faster, and couldn't hurt him in the long run. Advantage was what he lived by and for.

"How do you fit in with Paul Valenzuela and the Irishman, Dobson? A little private aid for your friends at State? Or are they helping you out?"

"The Irishman? You believe Paul Valenzuela is with O'Neill? It was O'Neill's thugs who attacked you? Is Valenzuela working for O'Neill? What is the connection?" He glanced toward Esther. "Family in Guatemala? Some involvement with the Indians down there? Is that Valenzuela's connection with Madrona?"

"Paul is an American," Esther said.

Dobson waved that away as irrelevant. He would wave a lot away as irrelevant. "I mean his roots. Is his family from Guatemala? Possibly Nicaragua?"

"His family is from Los Angeles," Esther said.

"Your husband's career is in jeopardy, Mrs. Valenzuela, if not far more." She was being obtuse, uncooperative. "It would do you well to cooperate, minimize the damage his at the least very stupid actions have done."

"The token Latino," I said. "That's one of the risks you take with minorities."

He looked at me with a raised eyebrow. I had said something that surprised him and even interested him. "What risk are you talking about?"

"When you bring outsiders into your power structure you may have to contend with their different views, *their* priorities, *their* standards."

"Is that your own experience, Fortune? Your own thinking?"

"I can even read," I said. "You have to be careful those new people from outside conform. They have to have the right views or you could be asking for trouble."

"How do we make sure they have those views?"

"By making sure before you bring them in that they're the right kind of minority or outsider."

"Yes, exactly." He nodded. "Exactly right. A matter of careful education and selection. I've told people that so very many times. Especially in Washington. It's criminal how few people listen, how so many fewer have the vision to implement obvious truths. You have a good mind, Fortune."

"But all the wrong attitudes. Me and Paul Valenzuela. It looks like someone made a mistake with Paul, didn't they? He slipped through. That has to be corrected. Paul has to be quickly neutralized."

From the eyes behind his glasses I saw him consider how soon I would have to be corrected, neutralized. It wasn't anything he would have to bother with himself. What he had to bother with he'd gotten. He was convinced that I thought Paul Valenzuela was with the Irishman, voluntarily or involuntarily, and that knowledge was what he had wanted. That, and maybe to get me to finally go away.

"Mistakes do have to be neutralized if they can't be corrected. You impress me, Fortune. Impress me more by showing the good judgment to go on about your own affairs. You found Paul Valenzuela, you've done your job. If Valenzuela is with the Irishman, they are undoubtedly in Guatemala by now. What more can you do? Let the Major and the CIA handle it."

He stood up, put the desk chair back neatly under George Conrad's desk, walked toward the side door. There was no need to wait for an answer, he'd already delivered his threat and would see no reason to repeat himself. The chauffeur opened the door.

I said, "Got all you needed from us?"

He glanced back. "Yes, I'd say so."

"You're sure?"

He sighed in the doorway. "It's sad how little ordinary people understand of what really counts, of what is really going on in the world. Where the real danger lies. What the enemy is really doing. Or even who the enemy is."

The chauffeur followed him out, closed the door.

In the silence of George Conrad's office we listened to the limousine start out on the elegant upper Eastside street. I wondered if Deputy Assistant Secretary of State Max Cole had been out there waiting the whole time. Did Martin Dobson allow Cole to ride with him in the limousine, or did he make him drive his State Department car a few paces behind?

"God," Kay said. "He gives orders to ranking State Department men? Why don't I know a man who can do that?"

"He's not in State," Esther said. "I've never seen him in Washington. I've never even heard of him. What has he got to do with Paul?"

"I don't know what he has to do with Paul, but he sure has some problem with the Irishman."

"But who is he, Dan?" Kay said.

"The invisible man. He keeps a low profile, in Washington and out."

"He's in the government?" Esther said.

"He was, maybe he still is. But, as he said, he's a lot more than that."

22

When his mother brings home the sullen black boy one cold winter night in 1952, Martin Dobson has his first power struggle. The boy's mother is in the hospital where Martin's mother is a nurse.

"She has no one to take care of Russell," Martin's mother tells Martin and his father. "They have no heat in their shack, the father couldn't get work, drank up their welfare, disappeared a year ago. The boy has nothing to eat at home since she came to the hospital. She gives him her food when he visits her."

"The father couldn't get work, or wouldn't get work?" Martin's father says.

"What does it matter, Frank? The boy needs help."

"It matters to us. We don't have a hell of a lot ourselves. The goddamned government will ruin us all with its handouts."

"We live on your veterans disability, Frank. People need to help each other. Martin won't mind sharing his room with Russell for a few days."

Martin, who has been watching the sullen black boy ever since his mother brought him home, minds very much sharing his room with Russell. Russell is dirty. Russell stinks. Russell has a mean smile when the adults aren't looking at him.

"I work and you work," Martin's father says as he walks out of the house to tend the chickens. "I can't help what happened in the war. I wish we didn't need the pension."

"Mrs. Greer can't help being ill, Frank. I'm not at all sure Russell's father could help what happened to him."

Martin hates Russell for taking his room away. He hates Russell's mother and father for being too poor to take care of Russell. Martin does not want to share his room, does not want to let Russell wear his shirts and pants and sweater. He does not want to share his favorite cereal at breakfast, his dessert any time. If it were the two of them he knows he could keep what is his. He is bigger than Russell. But it is not the two of them. It is his mother and Russell. He cannot beat his mother.

Russell sleeps in his room, wears his clothes, eats his cereal and dessert for five days. Then the mother gets better, Russell goes home. Martin has his room, his clothes and his favorite foods back. He vows to himself that the power struggle with Russell will be the last he loses to anyone.

Two years later his mother and father divorce. His mother spends too much time at the hospital, his father spends too much time working to raise, package and sell his chickens. They agree on little about the purpose and direction of life, have different aims. Martin stays with his father. The chicken farm does not do well. His father blames it largely on regulations and taxes, and dies suddenly three years after the divorce. By then Martin's mother has moved to an inner city hospital in another state, does not insist he live with her. He decides to live with his paternal grandparents on their fifteen-acre apple farm. His grandfather is a disciple of Ayn Rand. Her philosophy of individualism and self-interest appeals to young Martin.

"Government got no call mixing in people's lives, Martin." His grandfather explains to him. "Man wants to be a damn fool, that's his business, and no reason on earth other responsible, hard-working people got to save him from going under."

"My teacher says government got a responsibility to protect people, make rules, Grandpa. Like you can't let people go around spitting on the sidewalk any time they want to, or yellin' fire in a theater."

"Man spits on *my* sidewalk, he don't do it again. Any damn fool who panics because some nut yells fire without seein' there *is* a fire deserves what he gets."

"Doesn't the government have to make sure everyone has the

same chance, Grandpa? I mean, that nobody cheats or fixes the game or something?"

"You mean make it all equal, boy? Nothing's ever equal, and don't let them tell you it is or ought to be. Folks ain't born equal. Some are smarter, some have more talent, some have more guts, some work harder, some get a better start. A lot of people have to work harder to get less, but that's the way the world is. Some win, some lose, some break even. If I lose I don't expect anyone to take care of me."

When Martin graduates from high school there is no money to send him to the college he wants to attend. After his father's death the chicken farm had been sold to pay debts, his grandfather isn't a rich man. But his grandfather knows the local congressman, Martin discusses his problem with the sympathetic legislator. Together they find the Federal War Orphans Act. The Federal government pays his tuition and expenses for the four years. His grandfather laughs.

"You found an angle, boy. That's smart. Use everything you can to get what you want."

What Martin wants is to be a great scientist, to make new theories and discoveries that will shake the universe. At the university he majors in physics, with an emphasis on the subatomic particles that have always fascinated him. He does well, graduates near the top of his class.

"It must be grand to fulfill such a longtime dream, Martin," his grandmother tells him. "I know you'll be a fine scientist."

"I'm not going to be a scientist, Grandma," Martin says.

In his junior year, when he is investigating his future job prospects in the field of physics, Martin finds that there are few openings in government work for particle physicists. Most research is being done at the best universities, but there is something of a glut in the market. Applicants with a new Ph.D. are starting at not much more than five thousand a year, there will be an instructorship for at least five years, followed by a long, slow process of stair steps to a final full professorship. This prospect is not what Martin sees for himself.

That year the number-one field in pay and advancement for postdoctoral positions at universities is economics. He adds a course in basic economics to his senior year, finds the subject interesting enough, decides he will do his graduate work in this promising field. His three years of graduate studies are paid for by a National Defense Education Act fellowship.

"I realized I probably wasn't going to be Einstein, so it seemed that the practical move was to pick the field with the most future potential," he tells an interviewer years later when he is one of the youngest advisers to a newly elected president.

This dispassionate assessment of the marketplace proves as advantageous as his investigation of Federal aid opportunities seven years before. By the time he is thirty-one, Martin is a full professor of economics, but has also discovered economics is a practical science, a theory exciting only in the application. Academic research in economics theory does not move him.

"With theoretical research out, there was no way I could move to a better school, so there were only two real choices open. I could move up through administration, eventually become a university president, perhaps head of an entire state system. Or I could remain in teaching, branch out into private consulting and public policy work. Making money is the real name of the game in this country, especially for an economist, and the key word on the administration track was *eventually*. I decided to go into the marketplace, test my real knowledge of economics."

Dobson Associates gives Martin his first million, and the vehicle for him—educated entirely with public funds, a well-paid professor at a public university—to write, lecture and advise as a committed champion of less government interference, individualism, fiscal responsibility and free enterprise. With his second million he runs successfully for Congress on these same principles, becomes the friend and confidant of the movers and shakers of the corporate world.

"They were the men who really made free enterprise work, who benefited the whole country. They are the ones in the end who made us the richest nation on earth."

Congress does not hold Martin long. It will be another slow climb to true power and influence, and the pay is far from what he has come to expect for his efforts. After a second term he thanks the party for its trust and support, but tells its leaders to find another candidate. His businessmen friends are quick and eager to hire the bright and still comparatively young economic theorist in a consulting capacity, nominate him to sit on various corporate boards. Martin's true rise begins.

"I was financially comfortable, but it was past time to make my permanent contribution to the future. The nation and the world had been in the hands of big government and collectivist theory too long. Too much attention was being wasted on the have-nots, when it is only the haves who can save us all from worldwide bankruptcy. The basis of life is individual ambition. Someone had to stand up and point that out to the next generation."

Martin, with the backing of his corporate clients, becomes a fellow of a conservative think-tank supported by corporate funding. There he writes the books on the failure of the welfare and social security programs, the need for private control of all aspects of modern life from medicine to transportation, except, of course, where it is necessary for the government to protect our national interest, way of life, investment and free enterprise. It is these books that bring him to the attention of conservative presidential candidates, turn him finally into the powerful invisible man.

A man behind the scenes through three campaigns and two administrations. High on the campaign trail and in the kitchen cabinets. A man who makes presidents. The architect of self-reliance, of small government, of all people helping themselves.

If persons are capable of self-support they should not receive any money from others who work and pay taxes no matter what their age or position in society. The hardworking should not have to pay for the doctor bills or subway rides or child care of those who work less hard.

Advocate of tax reform and private investment in all aspects of modern society from urban renewal to prisons to environmental cleanup.

Private risk and capital is the only way to benefit everyone in the country and the world.

Martin serves administrations on the highest levels, until even conservative presidents fail him. They prove too weak to maintain commitment to the theory and practice of true freedom and total individual responsibility, too afraid to offend powerful and greedy minority groups and entrenched big government bureaucrats for fear of losing esteem and power. They want to please the crowd, the mob, and the crowd will never be pleased by the harsh truth.

He resigns, returns to the world of private enterprise where he vanishes from public view. It is known that he has joined the high echelons of certain corporations, forms a link between these corporations and the government. But exactly what he does and for whom, remains almost completely unknown outside the back-rooms and boardrooms and hidden rooms of political campaigns.

23

My shoulder throbbed and my head ached. Kay slept, her left hand on my chest. The second-floor bedroom of the Summerland house was dark. Outside, the late-night ocean air was clear and cool. The islands out at sea would be visible in the morning.

The man watching the house would be visible.

He had tailed us since we left Esther Valenzuela early in the afternoon, was across the street outside when we went to bed. Kay had not seen him, I had not told her.

Who scared me more? The Irishman or Martin Dobson?

What scared me most about Dobson was that he had let us know who he was. When the invisible become visible it is time to be worried.

After we left Esther Valenzuela I spent the rest of the day in the library trying to find out more about what Dobson was doing without an elected job, an administrative position or a presidential campaign to work for. I had found nothing. The effort tired me out, my shoulder kicked up and the ribs were sore so I went home.

Now, in bed and awake, I worried about Paul Valenzuela. Dobson, the Major, Max Cole and the CIA did not have him. The Irishman could have him, the three men who attacked me his men. Or no one could have him. The three who attacked me could have been the Irishman's men still looking. Paul Valenzuela could have his own reasons for vanishing. Everyone could be lying. The age of the big lie, the official line, propaganda. The definition of justice as whatever secured the desired social order, the one you favored.

The man outside in the cool night hoped I would lead him to Paul Valenzuela, or that Paul would come to me. There was no other reason to be out there in the sea wind. Unless he was there to make sure I wouldn't find Paul Valenzuela. Which might not be too hard, I didn't have much to go on.

The Sojourner is a reminder of the sixties' counterculture. The coffees are varied and good, and you can sit in a corner far from the door. Sergeant Chavalas likes the Sojourner and café au lait.

"You still can't even talk about Madrona, Claudia Nervo or the Valenzuelas in the office?"

Chavalas stirred his glass mug. "They've been given a story that sounds right and comes from people who work for Washington. The government's grateful for our cooperation. You messed up their efforts to rescue Paul Valenzuela, have a big imagination. The CIA is handling it, no more Major." He stirred his mug of coffee some more. "World Military Incorporated claims the Major is still in Mexico, never left at all. Our man must have been an imposter." He finally drank some of the good coffee. "We're cooperating. It's on hold, the CIA will keep us filled in. We stay out of their way. If something turns up locally, we'll handle it and pass it on."

Café au lait is one of the Sojourner's special coffees. I don't drink much coffee, switched to tea during the big coffee price war some years ago, but tea isn't a specialty of most American cafés.

"How do they explain Paul Valenzuela?"

"He never came in to us, his wife never filed a complaint. As far as we know there's no crime connected to him."

"He vanished from the motel where I had him stashed. Someone knifed me, chased me."

"He probably walked away on his own, is hiding out from his bosses. He could be involved in drugs, guns, politics. You were attacked by narcotics traffickers like Sylvestre Madrona. You can't identify them and they've probably left town. Which is pretty close to the truth, right?"

I had to agree. "What about Madrona? Anything new? Anything from Tyrone Earl?"

"Madrona's wife came up here from Guatemala to claim the body, ship it home."

"Tyrone Earl checked out maybe an hour before I went back for Paul Valenzuela. Who checks out of a hotel in the middle of the night when the room's already paid for?"

"A rich businessman who has to get somewhere else fast on business."

"Paul Valenzuela could have been the business."

"You want me to go to the captain with 'could have'?"

Sometimes I can feel a little for the law-and-order people. Proper procedure, constitutional rights and democratic rules can be a pain when you know the truth and other people won't cooperate.

Chavalas said, "You think Valenzuela's here in town?"

"I'm pretty sure he's not."

In the sixties' atmosphere the patrons of the Sojourner were primarily the beard-and-jeans health-food set, the humanity-and-environment subculture. Martin Dobson would not be popular here. Life as power struggle does not go down well with honey, brown rice and vegetarianism. Yet, in the end, the final power struggle for the planet would probably have to take place here. If it wasn't already too late. For them and maybe for Paul Valenzuela. Somehow, I sensed he was involved in the same struggle whether he knew it or not. A matter of attitude, feeling. Not thought out, not planned. Spontaneous, but just as dangerous.

"What do you have for Tyrone Earl? Home address?"

"Just the office on his card. Down in L.A. He never gave us the Mexico address. It didn't seem important then."

"You wouldn't have a man on me? Maybe I'm lying? Maybe I'll lead you to Paul Valenzuela?"

"You think you're being watched?"

"I know I am. Maybe the captain? The lieutenant?"

"They don't even want to talk about Paul Valenzuela." He finished his coffee. "You want me to scare him off?"

"I won't find out anything that way."

"You going after Tyrone Earl?"

"If I can find him. He's my only lead."

He drank his coffee. "We haven't gotten an answer at that office number since he left town. L.A. is a big city." He looked at someone who passed the windows. "That girl assistant of Madrona's, Dolores. She went back to L.A. after Earl showed up and we got her statement. She didn't have an address, Earl said he'd give it to us. He never did. But a day or so ago she called."

"Called?"

"A law-abiding person. She was in her new apartment, called to tell us where she was if we wanted her." He wrote down the address in Hollywood. "I'll keep my eyes and ears open, but I'm pretty sure the action's moved."

My tail was across the street playing the tourist game when we came out of the café. He was fascinated by the reconstructed Presidio chapel and the stacks of adobe bricks to be used to recreate more of the old Spanish fort for the glory of history and the tourist dollar.

Chavalas eyed him. "Sure you don't want me to at least find out who he is?"

"If he's State or CIA I might need him later, if he's not he might lead me to Paul Valenzuela."

Chavalas continued to watch the chunky man in a neat blue suit no tourist would have worn in Southern California even in spring. "My guess is CIA."

"The drug barons hire better dressed guns every day."

He walked away up Santa Barbara Street toward his office a block away. CIA was my guess too, but I wouldn't have bet my pension on it. If I had a pension.

The black car, a Ford, parked on the cross street, its nose far enough out for the driver to see me as I took the walk to Esther Valenzuela's parents' house. George Conrad's eyes were confused, his manner distracted. Not much of the normal routine was working in the Conrad house. He nodded toward his office at the rear, wandered away. He and his wife had no experience living with the kind of pressure that had been on them the last weeks. Few middle-class Americans did.

Esther Valenzuela wasn't in the office. The side door into the garden was open. She sat on a white-painted wrought-iron bench under a twisted old native oak. They are scraggly trees with their crooked limbs and constant scattering of dead brown leaves among the dusty green, but they have an endurance that has survived drought, fire, pollution and the development of man. Esther sat with her eyes closed, her head against the old tree, something of its strength on her face.

"You've heard nothing?"

"No."

"Would you tell me if you had?"

"Probably. Unless Paul told me not to."

"If someone else told you not to?"

She opened her eyes to look at me. "I'd have to decide what was best for Paul."

"You want me to go on?"

"I can't help him. Someone has to find him." She looked slowly around the lush and well-tended garden of her parents. "They've stopped coming to the house. The Major, Max Cole, those CIA men. Ever since that Dobson was here. I don't know where they are or what they're doing. I don't know where Paul is, what he's doing."

"I'll have to go to Los Angeles."

"You think Paul's there?"

"That's what I think."

"That Irishman has him?"

"I think he's with the Irishman."

"He's not involved in drugs, Mr. Fortune."

"How about guns? The rebels?"

She said nothing. Then, "It would be new. After I left less than a month ago."

"I'll call you when I can."

"I'll be here.

Outside the black Ford was gone from the corner. At the Anacapa Street light I thought I saw it four cars back, but it didn't really matter. I was going home to Summerland. He knew where to find me. My shoulder had started to hurt from the activity, my head had begun its dull ache. Tomorrow I would go to Los Angeles and the glitter and smog, today and tonight I would spend with Kay. I hadn't had a real chance to welcome her home in or out of bed. Lunch, a bottle of wine, a quiet dinner. Those small things are important too.

At the house I waited in bed for her to finish her morning's work. Before I had undressed, eased my jacket and shirt over the thick bandage, I had looked out our bedroom window. The Ford was there. The CIA, or one of the Irishman's guns, didn't make a lot of difference. I was caught in the middle. Esther Valenzuela was caught in the middle. The whole world was caught in the middle. That was the trouble with self-interest. There was always more than one self and one interest. The wars are between the ins and the haves, with the outs and have-nots ground in the middle.

24

Los Angeles meets you at the top of the Conejo Grade. Back and down, the broad coastal plain from Camarillo to Ventura lies a thousand feet lower and ten degrees cooler. Above the grade the heat of the valley welcomes you with the promise of much worse to come once you have driven on through Thousand Oaks and Westlake Village, Agoura and Calabassas.

The city itself welcomes you with a squeeze from four down to three lanes and an instant traffic jam. Maybe the good city fathers knew what they were doing. You're forced to slow down, but with any luck and the right time of day or week or year you get moving again once the flow adjustment has been made. At least you can usually move with some speed as far as the first backup for the 405 interchange, which can be anywhere from the city line to the Sepulveda Flood Basin depending on the time of day, week or year.

On a relatively cool weekday morning after ten A.M., I got almost all the way to the basin before the slowdown for the San Diego started, reached the address for Mayan Imports Inc. before eleven. The address was a new yellow-brick-and-balconies office building near the dry concrete chasm of the Los Angeles River in Studio City. The directory showed Mayan Imports, Inc., on the fourth floor. A building of many small offices without a big-name corporation. At least it had an elevator.

I hadn't spotted the black Ford all the way down from Santa Barbara, but he was there somewhere.

The name was on the door, but no sound was inside when I pushed it open. No sound and no furniture. Or rugs or file cabinets or people. The inner office was equally empty, only a telephone on the bare floor. A two-room office that had been cleaned out. There wasn't even a phone number written on the walls, or an overlooked business card on the floor.

Building management had its office on the ground floor. A pleasant young Latino woman smiled from behind a typewriter at one of the three desks in the office. Mayan Imports had moved five days ago. She knew nothing about Mr. Tyrone Earl, had never met him. She sent me in to the manager himself. He had never met Earl either, a gang of men had moved Mayan Imports' entire offices in half an hour. Paid by mail, no forwarding address. No address on the envelope, not even a postmark. Delivered by messenger. There was a warehouse. He had the address somewhere, did I want it? I wanted it.

The warehouse was in Sylmar. A flat one-story building in an industrial park in a developing area on the northern edge of Los Angeles. Police cars from at least five different city departments and the federal government were parked in front and back.

Uniformed LAPD men stood all around the building, had the whole block cordoned off. SWAT team sharpshooters in full assault gear were on all the roofs. It looked like an invasion force on alert and ready to repel an expected counterattack. Brass in gold braid and civilian suits streamed in and out of the warehouse. There isn't much outside a riot that can bring out so many cops, so much brass and so much cooperation.

It had to be a drug bust, and from the number of cops, the SWAT team on the roofs and the size and excitement of the brass contingent, it was a big one. That meant the Feds were from Drug Enforcement Administration and maybe the FBI. There was no way I was going to get any closer without being run in as a suspect. They'd be waiting to pounce on everyone who showed up with any interest in the warehouse or the people who had leased it. What was my connection to the warehouse? What was I doing around the warehouse? What did I know about the owners of the contents? Where were the owners?

I considered the advisability of even staying where I was. They'd notice me sooner or later, and this was not a place to be noticed. Then I thought about the possibility of trying to talk to the nearby businesses in the hope of getting another lead to Tyrone Earl. I settled for watching as long as I thought I could remain unnoticed on the chance someone from Mayan Imports might come around. It was a long shot, but it was all I had besides Dolores Rios-Shay.

It was hot in the valley, hotter inside the Tempo, got even hotter as the sun beat down on the smog and the inversion pinned it between the sea and the San Gabriel Mountains. The police continued to mill around, all except the SWAT team posted on the roofs and probably other vantage points out of sight. A lot of flashbulbs were popping inside the warehouse. DEA agents carried out cardboard boxes and black gymnasium bags and loaded them into cars. When they had three cars full, they drove off armed to the teeth with LAPD helicopters overhead. They hadn't brought out enough for it to be coke or horse. Probably money. After the DEA convoy had gone, the brass climbed into their chauffeured cars and drove away one by one.

The SWAT team went after another hour or two. Then the detectives, until there was only a small force of the uniformed to keep out trespassers and thrill seekers. I waited in the Tempo until it was almost dark, but no one who could have been from Mayan Imports or any other drug ring appeared.

The law of cities says that some areas will rise and some fall from era to era. Hollywood's name still stands for the glitter and glamor of the movie business, but in the last decades of the twentieth century much of the once-golden neighborhood has turned into a blighted and dying area of hookers and hustlers, pimps and tricks, derelicts and deviates. On any given night along the two miles of Hollywood, Sunset and Santa Monica boulevards from La Brea to Western they are there to claw for any way to survive.

They were already on the streets as I drove looking for Dolores Rios's new apartment. The young and the desperate, the unlucky and untalented, who have come to Hollywood in search of fame and fortune in the movies. There is little work now for beginners, so they find their way here. The vice squad sweeps the area from time to time, but the police can't stop the tide. Police and governments can never stop what people have to do to exist except by killing them.

Dolores Rios's address was a bungalow court on a rundown side street off Santa Monica. It was in better shape than the street. The grass was mowed, the flower beds around the front steps of the attached bungalows were well-tended and full of color. Dolores's unit was toward the rear, bright and bold Guatemalan curtains at the windows. There was no answer to my rings. I tried knocking. Nothing happened. It was after six. I sat on the steps to wait. She hadn't had time to learn to type yet, and cleaning women work late, ride slow buses home.

"Señor Fortune! You are come for me?"

She carried a plastic shopping bag, wore the white uniform of a maid. Some people want a lot for their eight dollars an hour. She beamed, glad to see me. How many people did she know in the U.S.? My angry inner voice said that Tyrone Earl could have done better for her. My more logical voice said that Mr. Earl, or whatever his real name was, had done well. If he was who I thought, he could have put her to cutting and packing cocaine. He could have put her in a better job she couldn't handle with her lack of language and lack of skills. Better to do what she was comfortable doing until she learned the language and gained confidence in a strange land.

"You will come in?"

Earl had done more than find her cleaning work and an apartment. She was back to her authentic self. The silver blonde hair was again its natural rich black. Her soft face had begun to fill out, she looked better in the simple white uniform than in the silver backless and high-heeled pumps. The velvet brown skin no longer resembled an Acapulco tan. It could not have happened overnight without help.

"You will sit?"

Even her English was better. The young and eager learn fast.

"You will eat?"

Proud but nervous. The polite *campesina* in her home, but with little to offer a guest. I shook my head, smiled at her, sat on a nice green-and-blue patterned couch. There were two armchairs to match, a fake mahogany coffee table, corner tables, two table lamps, a large color television set, the works. The furniture was better than the room with its worn carpet and grimy paint. Not the kind of furniture I would have expected her to pick out, too North American plastic.

"You know where the Irishman is, Dolores?"

She sat on a wooden kitchen chair someone had left in the living room in front of the television. In the maid's uniform, the plastic bag on the floor beside her with her hand still holding it, almost bursting with the joy of having such a fine home.

"Ireeshman—? I don' know Ireeshman."

"El Irlandés? Tyrone Earl?"

"Mister Earl? *Si*, Mister Earl he is give me this *casa*." She waved her free hand to sweep the whole magnificent little room. "He is good man, Mister Earl." She touched her long black hair, giggled. "He take to *beauty parlor*, yes?"

"Where—?"

The woman who came out of the bedroom was Dolores Rios forty years older in her native Guatemala. Small, dark, thick and broad-hipped with sagging breasts in a bright native *huipile*. Her hair was as black as the girl's, her face was the face of an old woman. An angry face and violent Spanish mixed with words I didn't even recognize. Like a broken dam, the words spilled in their anger as she perched on the edge of an armchair and glared at me. Somehow, I was the cause of her anger.

"Dolores? What is she saying? Who is she?"

The old woman glared at me, and then at Dolores, launched into another stream of half Spanish. She had realized I didn't understand her. Dolores looked at both of us.

"She say she know El Irlandés. She say . . . she . . ." Dolores searched her mind for the words in the strange language, "*mucho . . . mucho grande*. She . . . she . . ." She gave up and sat there helpless, literally wringing her hands at her inability to translate.

I said, "Is there anyone around here who could translate, Dolores? Maybe a neighbor?" In Los Angeles that is not as fanciful an idea as it might sound. Especially not in a poor and rundown neighborhood.

"*Ayyy, si. Si!*" She jumped up and ran out the front door. She still carried the plastic shopping bag.

The old woman and I sat there and watched each other. I smiled. She glared. Silence hung like a tent over the small room. A chasm lay between us. The helplessness and distrust and ignorance our mutual inability to communicate condemned us to. She was angry and suspicious and I had no idea why. She knew I had asked about the Irishman, but had no idea why. All we could do was sit and watch each other warily and hope for someone to help us understand each other.

"I have friend!" Dolores Rios hustled in a slim blonde woman with Indian features. "American, talk Spanish *muy bueno!*"

The blonde wore jeans, a Tecate beer T-shirt and basketball shoes. She smiled to me.

"Sandra Guzman. I speak English a lot better than Spanish now, but I was born in Costa Rica. Dolores doesn't talk it so bad for someone been up here only a couple of weeks. She's a nice kid. Reminds me of myself when I first come up here. 'Course, I was always blonde. No Indian, right? Well, not much anyway."

She grinned, and sat down on the couch beside me. Dolores beamed at both of us. She had two friends. The old woman only glared at me. Sandra Guzman ignored her, winked, glanced around at the various tables.

"So where is it? What you want translated?"

Dolores told her in Spanish what we wanted. She stared at the old woman, and then at me. Doubtful.

"You mean you want me to tell you what she's saying when she says it?"

"Take your time, Dolores can help. Maybe all I need is the sense of it, okay?"

Dolores spoke gently in Spanish to the old woman, who turned her eyes and anger to Sandra Guzman and rattled out a stream.

"Whoa! Slow down. That's some dialect."

Dolores spoke to the old woman who looked at all of us with suspicion but when the words came again they were slower.

"She says the Irishman took her husband away and killed him. Hey, what is this? You—"

"I'm an investigator looking for this Irishman, Sandra. Ask her where the Irishman is now."

Sandra asked the old woman. "She doesn't know and doesn't care. He is in Guatemala. He is in hell. Something like that. She uses words I don't know, probably Indian."

"Who was her husband?" I could guess now, but I wanted to hear it.

Dolores said, "Don Sylvestre, Mr. Fortune. I don' know he is married."

"What's she doing here?"

Dolores spoke in Spanish to Sandra Guzman. Three-way translation isn't the fastest way to go, but it was all I had.

Sandra Guzman said, "Dolores says the old one's name is Gabriela Madrona, she was married to Don Sylvestre over twenty years, had a lot of kids. Then Don Sylvestre went away with the Irishman and she never saw him again. When he got killed in Santa Barbara the police asked the Guatemalan government who was next of kin and they sent her up here to claim the body."

I said, "Ask her how she knows the Irishman killed her husband?"

Gabriela Madrona stared at Sandra Guzman as the Americanized Costa Rican told her what I'd said. Then she turned her eyes to me, sat suddenly immobile as she talked.

"She says her husband was a good man. They lived in a fine village. The Irishman came and made him grow something bad. I don't know what, it's not a Spanish word she's using. Anyway, the Irishman paid her husband a lot of money for whatever it was. Her husband acted like the landowner. Then he left the village with the Irishman. He never came back. The Irishman took him away and got him killed. The Irishman led him into an evil world and killed his soul and then his body. The Irishman is a bad man who doesn't pray." Sandra Guzman looked away from the old woman who was still talking. "What she's saying is the Irishman killed the guy by leading him astray, taking him out of his village and into the wicked world. Like that. She doesn't mean he really killed the guy."

"Why is she here with Dolores? What happened to Madrona's body? Did the Irishman send her here?"

Sandra translated, Dolores answered. "She got no money. Body go to Guatemala, she stay. Mr. Earl he say we be friends, she stay with me. We like, *si, Señora*?" The last to the old woman with a smile.

Gabriela Madrona smiled at Dolores, waved her arms at me as Sandra Guzman struggled again to translate. "Her husband was no husband. Dolores is a fine girl, like she was when she married

Madrona. She was a girl when she married him, she's an old woman now and she doesn't have a husband. All the years he never sent money for her or his kids. Loosely translated, he never gave her dog shit from all his money, never gave the village dog shit of help. Good riddance to evil. Let his mother and his brothers bury him, not that he ever gave them shit either. She couldn't care less. Let the Irishman bury him. They would probably use his body for their evil work anyway, whatever that means. She likes Dolores, Madrona treated Dolores like dog shit too. She sure likes that word. Mr. Earl is a good man who helps them. They will help each other."

The old woman finished, and suddenly smiled an almost toothless smile. I realized Gabriela Madrona was no more than in her early forties. It was only her life that had made her look like an old woman. She smiled at Dolores, at me, at Sandra Guzman. Together, she and Dolores would support each other. Especially with a helpful neighbor like Sandra Guzman. People help people.

"She said the Irishman was a bad man. Now she says he's a good man. Ask her what changed her mind."

Sandra asked. Gabriela Madrona almost spat on the floor, stopped herself at the last moment. "The Irishman is an evil man, he turned her husband into the devil."

I was confused. "Dolores?"

"I not know El Irlandés."

"Tyrone Earl is—"

"Mister Earl very good."

I looked at both of them. Neither of them knew Tyrone Earl and the Irishman were the same. Or was I wrong? Were they two different men after all?

"Has Señora Madrona ever met Tyrone Earl?"

Dolores shook her head. "He tell me she come to here. He send man bring her to here."

Gabriela Madrona knew the Irishman, but had never met Tyrone Earl. Dolores knew Earl, but nothing about the Irishman and the drug trade.

"Do you know where Mr. Earl is?"

She nodded. "You want?"

Lack of communication is the cause of a great many problems in this world.

25

To go from the streetwalkers, decay and desperation of a faded Hollywood, to the catered parking, obscene spending and power of Beverly Hills, is to go from the bottom of our world to the top. From the hopeless to those who don't need to hope. From the used to the users. From those who want and will never get, to those who have and will always keep.

I did not drive fast, aware all the way from Hollywood of what I was doing. It could not be so simple. If Tyrone Earl were the Irishman, and there was really no *if* in the picture after the raid on Mayan Imports' warehouse in Sylmar, he would not trust his real address unguarded to Dolores Rios. My CIA watchdog somewhere behind was a measure of security, but not much. When you walk into the jungle you belong to the jungle. If it wants you, it can take you. This jungle was as green and lush as any Amazon, but the houses were bigger, the lights brighter, and it was far more dangerous if you had come to take anything from it. It would be a lot safer to take gold from the Amazon.

The house was a large one high at the head of a canyon that looked down at the rest of the world. You don't get a lot of land in Beverly Hills, and other houses are always in your view. Maybe that's why they build walls around their entrances, pools and patios, have so much hedge and bush and tree they almost block their own view. They've paid so much to live here they want to believe there isn't anyone else. The lights were already on all across the hills and through the trees and hedges, but there was no light in Tyrone Earl's house.

I parked up the deserted street where I could see the driveway entrance. The empty street is one of the problems of trying to watch a house in Beverly Hills. The other is the police. The real job of any police department is to serve and protect the people who pay for it, which means the taxpayers and politicians of the city it works for. But the Beverly Hills Police Department is one that carries its duties to an extreme. They patrol and watch and answer calls from citizens who worry about a car parked on their empty street. They would be around, and I could only park maybe a half an hour before they found me. Then I'd have to move, find a spot on the cross block for another half an hour. Move again, find another . . .

It wasn't the police who found me.

"Keep the hands high when you get out."

There were two of them. The one on the right side of the car had his gun low against his leg. The one on the left leaned in the open window and did the talking. Where he had his gun I didn't know, but he had a large square bandage of gauze and tape above his temple where his hair had been shaved. I had a pretty good idea I'd found the shadow that had knifed me behind Cabrillo Boulevard. Maybe he didn't have a gun, only his knife. If he recognized me, he didn't show anything on his lean face.

I hadn't been waiting even five minutes. They had to have picked me up at Dolores Rios's bungalow, followed me or sent word on ahead. It wasn't a big surprise.

"I'm not carrying," I said, got out with my hand high.

The silent one with the visible gun came around the car, showed no reaction to my solitary arm, patted me up and down anyway. He was Latino, maybe thirty, said nothing. The other didn't look especially Latin, had no accent.

"The driveway and up."

I didn't ask which driveway. The big house at the end of it was still dark.

"Around the house."

The concrete path led around the house to a brick patio that bordered the large pool in the dusk.

"Through the hedge."

A darker opening led through the hedge at the edge of the slope behind the house. On the other side a path wound through thick brush to a set of stone steps down to the rear of a smaller house on the street below. A drug king doesn't survive outside his home territory by being careless or stupid.

"Back door."

Inside, two more Latinos sat with cans of beer and talked in Spanish. They were both armed, didn't even look at us. Gunmen, *sicarios.* The house opened into a large sunken living room with the patio through a wall of glass. Along a small side hallway we turned into a TV room. Tyrone Earl worked at a table. Another Latino sat against the wall behind Earl where he could watch all the windows, had an assault rifle across his knees. Earl looked up, smiled.

"Sit down, Dan."

The silent gunman had dropped off along the way. The spokesman with the bandage on his head indicated an armchair that faced the desk. He took his seat on a replica of a side chair from Regency England between the windows behind me. Earl, or whatever his real name was, acted like a man with individual taste, but nothing in the room fitted the flamboyant personality of the owner of the Koenig customized Ferrari. A rented house.

"So," Earl pushed back his chair at the desk, smiled that big smile. "You tracked me the hell down."

He still wore his jeans and flight jacket, was comfortable in them like a man who has worn them for a long time. But his tanned, craggy face with the heavy nose and brow was drawn with tension. The gold medallion of the rearing horse with the green emerald eyes hung as usual in his chest hair at the open collar.

"It sort of looks like you found me."

He shrugged. "You had to know I'd have Dolores's place watched."

"It occurred to me."

"You must have a hell of a big reason for finding me."

"It's big enough to my client. She wants her husband back."

The wooden chair under the man behind me creaked. Behind Earl the *sicario* with the assault rifle uncrossed his legs, set his feet flat on the floor.

"Husband?"

"Paul Valenzuela. I told you in Santa Barbara that's what I was working on."

"Why would I know anything about Paul Valenzuela?"

I glanced at the *sicarios*, then back at Earl who watched me without a smile, without any expression. Blank and bland and neutral. He was telling me it was possible that if I backed away now, pushed no farther, there might be no real risk. I hadn't come this far to back off.

"I've talked to Paul, know about the tape of the telephone call to the ambassador."

"How much do you know about the call?"

"Most of it."

"And you could guess a lot of what you don't know, right?"

The two gunmen moved again, restless. Earl took a cigarette from a carved and brightly painted wooden box that looked like something he would own himself.

"You think I have Paul Valenzuela somewhere? Why would I want him? Or a tape of my own phone call, Dan?"

"I don't know for sure, but . . . What do I call you? Earl? O'Neill? Or just the Irishman?"

"Take your choice."

"Tyrone Earl is cute, by the way. You like playing games."

He gave the big, loud laugh. "Spotted that, did you? Not one out of a goddamn thousand would. Not even in Ireland. You must read history. What the hell else is there except playing our games? That's all anything really the hell is. One fucking big game." The laugh became the grin. "Hugh O'Neill, Earl of Tyrone courtesy of Queen Elizabeth who wanted to co-opt him and sure as hell did. When'd you spot it?"

"When Paul Valenzuela told me about the phone call. The name O'Neill."

"Hugh John O'Neill." He listened to the sound of the name out of his own mouth. "I wonder if that is my real name? Or just plain Jack O'Neill. The Irishman. That has a ring to it. Rodriguez Gacha the Mexican, Hugh John O'Neill the Irishman. That poor dumb son of a bitch Gonzalo. The risk you take, right? No one stays bought when someone else offers more." The anger under his tired voice, in his gray-blue eyes, denied the hard cynicism. "My real name? I'm not so damned sure I know anymore. What the hell does it matter? The Irishman's about as good as anything." The anger turned on me. "What would I want with my own phone call? Some dumb *barrio* kid in a two-bit banana republic embassy who thinks the world ought to be clean, honest and fair?"

"You seem to know a lot about a man you don't know."

"Hell, Valenzuela isn't exactly a kraut name, is it? It's not a hard guess that a Valenzuela came out of some *barrio*."

"Hard to guess his views of the world."

The Irishman said nothing, only sat behind the desk and focused his anger on something not even in the room.

I said, "You're pretty sure of what you have, and you don't want Paul Valenzuela showing the tape to anyone before you make your deal. Or maybe you like Paul as an extra threat, don't want the Major and the CIA to stop him and destroy the tape. He's an insurance policy, another bargaining chip. Maybe you already made your deal, want to help the Major eliminate an unexpected complication."

"Hell, then I'd just blow the kid away, right?"

"If you have Valenzuela and the tape you can hold it over them. A kind of guarantee of good behavior in the future."

He leaned back in the chair and clasped his hands behind the long graying blond hair. "That's an interesting mind you've got, you know? Downright nasty. We could use you, Dan. I mean it."

"I don't do well in large organizations, and I don't deal in drugs. Coke, horse or anything else. I don't work for people who destroy other people."

"You pay taxes, don't you? You buy products of companies that rape the Third World. You drive a car from companies that pollute the world." As restless as his silent gunmen against each wall, he stood and paced. "We don't make the conditions that drive people to drugs, Dan. We give the Third World some hope and make the misery a little easier in your world. What the hell, life stinks for most people."

"Drugs don't make it better."

"Who says so? Drugs make the world a hell of a lot more tolerable for a lot of people. In Latin American villages they can barely subsist the way things are. The *campesinos* aren't fucking dummies, they know the big market and big bucks are in growing dope for the good old U.S.A. Why the hell should they starve because regular crops don't earn them peanuts, any more than your tobacco farmers give up the weed for crops that don't make ten percent as much?"

He turned to look at me, waited for an answer. I didn't have one. If I lived in some village where there was never enough to eat, where my family had no chance for more than bare subsistence, and someone offered me a way to eat good and help my family, I'd grow coca or opium or damn near anything.

"There isn't a drug problem in the world?"

He shook his head in both disagreement and wonder. "There's a goddamn addiction problem, all right. Substance abuse, that's the technical term, right? It's one hell of a killer all over the world. They figure over five hundred thousand people die from substance abuse every damn year in the U.S. alone. Maybe three hundred thousand from tobacco, up to two hundred thousand from alcohol. Even a few thousand from illegal dope. In nineteen eighty-five around thirty-five hundred died from all illegal drugs combined. *Three* thousand. Hey, that has to be stopped, right?" He paced the room under the silent eyes of his gunmen. "Ninety-nine percent of deaths from substance abuse come from tobacco and alcohol. So your administration declares a big war against the other one fucking percent."

"One percent of unnecessary misery is too much."

He shook his head as if unable to believe how anyone could get away with fooling people so easily. "Maybe sixty million Americans have smoked pot. You know how many died so far? None! Not one goddamn reefer death. Dope means big violence, right? How about this: no illegal drug is as strongly associated with violence as alcohol. We're not even talking about drunk driving. The goddamn health cost of grass, coke and horse combined come to a lousy fraction of those from tobacco and alcohol, the real killer opiates. We're not one iota worse than the tobacco and booze tycoons. Washington sure hasn't declared war on them."

I leaned toward him. "I don't like what they do either, O'Neill. The Irishman, right? That has a real romantic ring, swashbuckling, the freebooter. But you get rich on human weakness, failure, desperation, hope, sickness and poverty the same as the tobacco and booze companies do, the gamblers and pimps."

Behind me the lean *sicario*, the one with the head wound, swore, "Shit, Irish—"

"Hold it, Oscar." The Irishman held up his hand. "Never hide your goddamned head, you know? Don't be afraid to talk about what you do. You ashamed of us, Oscar? We do make a living on other people. That's called free enterprise, the free market. The backbone of democracy. Individual entrepreneurs, Oscar, heroes of the free world. Right, Dan?"

"The government doesn't seem to see it that way."

"We take money out of corporate pockets, that's all."

"You want people to think of you as Robin Hood?"

"Hell, that's not a bad idea." He sat down at the table again. "Maybe that's what we are. Robin Hoods."

"All you are is a drug dealer hanging on to an empire that's falling apart. I've been to your warehouse in Sylmar. There had to be a tip-off to bust a cache that big. I've seen your partner dead on a warehouse floor. I've talked to his widow who hates what he did to her and his kids and his village so much she doesn't even want to bury him. She couldn't care less. Let El Irlandés bury him."

I sensed the eyes of the two *sicarios* like weights on me. The Irishman rocked in the chair behind the desk. He seemed about to answer me when another of his *sicarios* came into the TV room. The new man came in fast, bent to whisper to Oscar, the gunman with the bandage on his head where I'd hit him. Oscar stood up, went to the Irishman. The Irishman listened, nodded. Oscar left with the new *sicario*. The second gunman against the wall who watched the windows did nothing. It was full night now out in Beverly Hills.

The Irishman said, "So you talked to Sylvestre's wife. She doesn't see me or Sylvestre as Robin Hood, does she?"

"She sees her husband as a man who treated everyone like dog shit."

"I expect she does." He listened in the quiet of the Beverly Hills night outside the house. "Sylvestre was no Robin Hood. I had all the advantages, the easy life, the luxury of wanting to be Robin Hood. Not Sylvestre. He never had the chance to be anything except what he had to be."

26

The village lies between the mountains and the jungle. No one in the village knows why the village is here or who built it. It has always been here. The people have always been here. The land has always been here, and the landowners. Everything has always been done in the same way.

Most of the people work on the large *fincas* where the landowners grow coffee, cotton, sugar cane and even some bananas. The bananas were brought from the eastern coast where the great foreign plantations used to be, although the villagers do not know this. These crops are all for export, mostly to the United States. The wealth of the nation comes from these export crops. They are the source of everything the country builds and does, the income of the government and the middle class, the pay and power of the military.

The villagers have no choice but to work on the *fincas* to plant and tend and harvest these export crops. There is no other way to earn the money they must have to support their families and the village. There is no way to earn extra money to leave the village and find better work in other places. There is no way to raise and sell crops of their own that might give them enough money not to work on the *fincas*, to leave and look for better work. No way to do more than subsist in the months when the *fincas* do not need them to work.

A circle of perpetual toil for perpetual poverty. The men work all day on the *fincas* to earn enough to survive the months when there is no work, come home and forage for extra food, cut wood in the forest for heat and cooking and, perhaps, to sell in the market town, tend to the few animals. The women bear the endless children, raise them, watch most of them die from lack of the food children must have to grow. The women tend the small plots where the few vegetables are grown, make the clothes, wash the clothes, mend the clothes, weave and make baskets to sell in the market town for a few extra coins.

No matter how hard or long they work they do not have the food to sustain this endless work on the *fincas* of the landowners and in their own small village. Most can barely rise each new morning to go to work, live day in and day out in lethargy, exhaustion and mental depression. The children who somehow live do not have enough protein to allow their minds and bodies to develop fully, will never do more than work on the *fincas*, cut wood in the steep forests, weave blankets to sell for nothing to American tourists.

In the village between the mountain slopes and the jungle, Sylvestre Madrona is one of the stronger children who survive. He can work harder than most, is angrier than most.

"He is the lucky one," Madrona tells his wife when their first child dies. "The child is better off, Gabriela. He will not live as we live. We will have a fiesta to celebrate!"

The men get drunk and chase the women through the village. The younger women laugh and scream and hide but not too well. They all dance in the night after they bury the child.

In his young days, before and after the death of his firstborn son, Sylvestre does not drink much. He can and does work harder than most men in the village, has more food in his garden for the other children that will come each year, is noticed by the local manager on the *finca* where he works. It is the largest *finca*, over fifteen thousand acres, is only one of many owned in the nation by the great Alvarado family so pure in its European blood and ways that an Alvarado is insulted if called *ladino*.

"You work well, boy. What is your name?"

"Sylvestre Madrona, *Jefe*."

"Do you think you can boss a field crew?"

"I do not know."

"Well, I say you will do this well and I know what I say."

"Yes, *Jefe*."

"I will speak to the *padrone*."

Sylvestre becomes the straw boss of all the men from his village, is expected to encourage the men to work harder and pick more. He tells the villagers that if they all work together they will all make more money. They do earn more money, but Sylvestre earns the most, and soon Gabriela is in tears when he comes home. Exhausted he lies on their mat and listens to her tell of all the women who will not speak to her when they wash their clothes in the river. The men who insult her and come at night to bleed her goats and trample her garden. The children who steal food from their children.

The village men will no longer drink with Sylvestre. At fiestas he is alone, in the religious processions he is given no part. In the fields they will not eat with him, in the village they walk away when he comes near.

"You do not understand," Sylvestre tells them. "I have a plan for the money we all will have. We will all save our money and we will grow corn like the *ladinos*. We will clear a field and make a place to grow our own corn to sell in the market town. Then we will have money to grow more corn and even cotton to weave into the blankets and sell more. It will be slow, but it is the only way we will ever have our own money and not have to work on the *fincas*."

The villagers are skeptical, wary, reluctant. They have always failed at whatever new they tried, have always failed at any risk they took. The smallest triumph has always turned into nothing. Sylvestre persists. He cajoles, persuades, encourages. He contributes the most money, borrows the tools from under the nose of the *finca* manager without permission, organizes, works the hardest to begin the clearing of the field. It is hard to do the backbreaking work after a long day on the *fincas*, but the field is at last planted.

The corn sprouts and grows tall and each night the whole village goes to stand and look at it. Then the rains do not come. On the *fincas* the landowners irrigate. In the village the men watch the corn die. On the *finca* where Sylvestre works the manager discovers that he borrowed the tools without permission and makes another man foreman. In the village the men get drunk.

Sylvestre joins them. There is no use trying to change their lives. The way it has always been is the way it will always be. God Himself does not want the village to change, wants them to work forever for the landowners on the *fincas.*

Sylvestre drinks more, works less, sinks into the lethargy of the village. Gabriela grows fatter, his children die or do not die. He works on the *finca*, cuts wood to sell so he can buy *aguardiente* to get drunk at festivals, sleeps in a stupor many nights. He and the village are barely aware when a new *padrone* arrives at the largest *finca*. One landowner is the same as another. The work will always be long and hard, the pay always not enough. Why would the village care who is *padrone*? It is over a year before Sylvestre and the village become aware that this new *padrone* is not the same.

A giant golden-haired man, he speaks bad Spanish with the accent of a *norteamericano*. The manager, who has ruled the *finca* longer than all but the oldest men of the village can remember, is no longer manager. All the old *padrone*'s staff is gone. The men of the new *padrone* do not know about coffee and cotton and sugar cane or even bananas, walk with guns, ask many questions when anyone goes on the land of the *finca*. These new men stand on the roof of the *finca* and watch all day. Large cars arrive at the *finca* with generals in magnificent uniforms and well-dressed *padrones* and almost-naked ladies who laugh and lie on long chairs beside a pond the new *padrone* builds in the ground.

The new *padrone* also builds in a remote part of the *finca* a wide road of black that goes nowhere. Great birds fly down from the sky to the wide road and fly away once more at night. A smaller square of black is built near the house itself where the birds with windmills come. This is all strange to the village, but strangest of all is the greater money the new *padrone* pays for work, and the name of the new *padrone*: El Irlandés.

"What name is this?" the oldest villagers ask.

"It is a place far away across the eastern sea," a younger man who has been once to the capital city says.

"This *padrone* is not from across a sea," another says. "He is a *norteamericano*, a *yanqui*." This man spits in the dirt.

Sylvestre says, "What does it matter who or what he is? His money is from paradise."

The others are not sure. They are wary again, suspicious. Nothing can change, nothing can be better. Sylvestre himself is not sure, but there is something about this Irishman, this *yanqui padrone*, that reaches inside Sylvestre even when he lies drunk on his mat in his shack at night. He sees in this strange man an alien world of which he understands he knows nothing. A world far even from that of the old *padrones* who have always owned the *fincas*, the generals in their resplendent uniforms who sometimes came to the old *padrones* and who now come to this new *padrone*. Somehow, he is aware that it is the world of the great silver birds that fly high in the sky over the village, that come from where Sylvestre does not know, and go to where he does not know.

"This *padrone* is not as the others," Sylvestre tells the men. "This *padrone* is not as always."

When the new *padrone* comes to the village with a crop he will pay the villagers to plant in fields they will clear from the mountain forest above, Sylvestre is the only man to listen. The others are afraid, see evil magic in what they have never done, a crop that cannot be eaten or drunk or made into clothing. When Sylvestre hears how much money the *yanqui padrone* will pay for the villagers to plant and harvest the new crop, he too is afraid. What could be worth so much money?

"Poppies," the Irishman tells him. "A flower that makes medicine that *norteamericanos* who want beautiful dreams will pay very much money for. I will buy all you grow, make the medicine myself. All you have to do is clear the fields under the trees and plant the flowers."

"I am afraid," Sylvestre tells El Irlandés.

"That's what they want you to be, the generals and the landowners."

"I do not understand what it is you tell me."

"They do not want you to understand, Sylvestre. The landowners and the generals. They want you to be an ignorant man as well as a poor man. They don't want you to know why your village has always been the same and always will be. They want you to think it's God's plan, a force of nature, the way the world is made, but it isn't."

As he listens to the Irishman, the big, powerful, golden-haired giant who has taken the largest *finca* from the landowner who always owned it, Sylvestre is more afraid than he has ever been. Inside he is shaking, because somehow he knows what the Irishman is telling him, and knows that it is true.

"The truth, Sylvestre, is that you and all the villages must be ignorant and poor to make your country work. You have to be kept always ignorant and poor or the generals and *padrones* could not survive, keep what they have. They need you to be poor and ignorant because without an unlimited supply of cheap labor no country that depends on a few crops for export could exist."

Sylvestre does not understand all the words the big *yanqui padrone* uses, but he understands what he is saying. The *padrones* could not live in the *fincas* if they did not have him and the other men of the village to plant and pick the coffee and cotton and sugar cane and bananas for not enough money to live. For not enough money to feed their children. For not enough money to ever leave the village.

"All you are is a cheap back, a pair of hands and an animal that breeds more cheap backs and hands. Your country is built on keeping you poor and weak, and my country helps the rulers of your country keep you poor and ignorant because we want cheap coffee and cotton and sugar cane and bananas. Your children die, Sylvestre, because Americans don't want to pay too much for a banana with their breakfast, so the companies that sell bananas must buy them very cheap or they will not make enough profit."

Sylvestre understands enough. Deep inside all the years he lay on his mat and listened to the night of the village he has known that something was not right.

"I will plant the flowers, *padrone*."

"I'm not a goddamn *padrone*, Sylvestre. I'm the Irishman."

The other villagers are too afraid to plant the Irishman's flowers, do not dare to do what they have never done. Sylvestre must take Gabriela and the older children and they clear a small field, plant the poppies. He takes care of them, nurses them, harvests the raw opium. Sylvestre earns more money than he has ever had, talks much with the Irishman.

When Sylvestre is growing his third field of the miracle flowers, the soldiers come. The villagers all hide, but the soldiers find many who tell them that it is Sylvestre who grows the strange flowers. The *commandante* of the soldiers arrests Sylvestre, is going to burn the field and his shack and take him away when the Irishman arrives from the *finca* with his men. The Irishman talks to the *commandante*, gives the *commandante* a fine cigar.

They drive in the Irishman's big vehicle to the *finca*. Soon the soldiers go away. They do not take Sylvestre, they do not burn the field.

The Irishman laughs. "Everyone needs more money, even that *commandante*'s general, and one field is no threat, right? Cut the general in for enough, slip the *commandante* a taste, and they couldn't care less if everyone else goes down the tubes."

Sylvestre listens and learns. He knows now that the flowers that are worth so much money are also illegal. This frightens Gabriela and worries the villagers. It does not frighten or worry him. He clears more fields, grows more poppies, the Irishman pays him more. He tells the Irishman to grow no more coffee or cotton or sugar cane so the village men must work in Sylvestre's and the Irishman's poppy fields to earn any money. The villagers begin to envy him again as in the days when he was the boss of their *finca* crew, and he begins to despise them. Gabriela does not despise them, wants him to stop growing the evil flowers. She wants all to be as it was. She does not want him to be the boss of the village and be hated. The villagers want to tear him down, keep him as poor and ignorant as they are.

Sylvestre comes to hate the villagers more than they hate him. He wants to live as the Irishman lives. He wants to learn about the world, learn all he has never been allowed to know. He wants to go away from the village. He asks the Irishman to take him with him to where the Irishman is always going.

"What about the village?"

"It will never change. They will never listen to me."

"You wife? Your family?"

"They are as bad as the village."

The Irishman smiles. "I think you'll do very well with me. I think we can do good work together."

Sylvestre goes away with the Irishman. He learns a great deal. He meets younger women. He lives in fine houses. He never returns to the village or even to the *finca* the Irishman still owns. He buys a *finca* of his own in the country far from his old village. When the Irishman sends guns and money to the rebel guerrillas who have grown stronger, Sylvestre does not. They are villagers like the others, they threaten his new *finca*. He wants no part of them.

27

The Irishman listened to the night, to the end of his own story, or maybe to something outside. For an instant I thought I heard a sound in the night, distant and gone, as the Irishman went on talking in the small room.

"What else could he become? He had his own interests to defend like everyone else once he got to the top, right? Didn't want any part of helping the *campesinos*, his old village or any kind of rebels."

"Not like you."

"I didn't start poor and ignorant. Just dumb and ignorant. I had all the chances."

"So you have a different lifestyle. Austere. No silver blondes."

"I live high on the old hog. Why not? What else do I do with my millions? Silver blondes are out, though. My wife wouldn't like that. Not out in the open."

"She doesn't travel with you?"

"She prefers Mexico. Cabo. Acapulco. The dinner parties. She doesn't like the way I travel."

"But you send her money."

"She has money."

"Not like Madrona's wife and kids and village."

Mito, the cook and bodyguard who'd been with the Irishman at San Ysidro Ranch, appeared soundlessly in the study, spoke softly in his part-Spanish, part-Indian dialect. The *sicario* behind the Irishman with the assault gun across his legs got up and left the room. Mito took his place, seemed to go to sleep instantly. He still had no visible weapon.

"The money and power went to his head. It does to most of our heads. I tried to talk to him at the start, but he was damn angry. They'd all tried to stop him, keep him poor and ignorant like them. He swore he'd never help them, never go back."

There was movement out in the night around the house. Heavy movement. Feet running and brush breaking. The feet seemed to shake the ground up the slope behind the house toward the decoy house at the top of the higher street. Mito sat unmoving. The Irishman listened. I stood up.

"Stay in your chair, Dan."

Mito opened his eyes, watched me until I sat down again. The sounds continued outside.

"Has the money and power gone to your head?"

"I suppose so. At the beginning. Not now. I've been around too goddamn long to take it all so seriously."

"But you send aid to guerrillas? You help peasant rebels down in Guatemala, El Salvador, Colombia?"

"You sound like you find that hard to believe."

"The others in your cartel are like Madrona, shoot rebels on sight now that they're rich."

He smiled, but his blue-gray eyes weren't all that amused. "Give an Irishman a horse and he'll vote Tory. They all started even worse than Sylvestre, scrounged in the gutters of Medellin or lower before they were six, never had an education. Now they're all landowners, have a stake in the system. Law and order, property rights over human rights. All they really want to be is good capitalists, free enterprisers, self-made tycoons."

"But not you?" I listened to the running, the heavy breaking of brush, the pounding of many feet out in the night. The Major and the CIA? Police? A rival gang? The Irishman watched me listen to the sounds, took a slim cigar case from his flight jacket pocket.

"Of course me. Get mine, live high. That's why I had this made." He pulled the medallion of the rearing horse with the gold mane and emerald green eyes from his open shirt. "The

Irishman's horse, right? So I don't get too fucking set up with myself. No goddamn different from anyone else. Horse makes life sweet for this Irishman, but not always Tory. Maybe because I never had to beg, scrounge or steal to stay alive. Because I had a nice white middle-class upbringing. High school, university, ROTC, the whole bundle."

"You're right, I find it hard to believe."

The Irishman drew a pair of long, thin cigars from the case he'd taken out of his jacket pocket, offered me one. I shook my head. He put the second back into his pocket, lit his, watched the smoke rise in the room. An edge to his voice, bitter.

"Because drug lords can't help the people, Dan? Can't see the desperation of the poor and want to do something about it? Drug lords can't see colonialism and the goddamn banana republic governments it subsidizes and keeps in power?"

I heard the single gunshot. Or was it a loud backfire? Out in the Beverly Hills night. I know a gunshot, even in Beverly Hills. Close in the night, echoing against a wall to sound like a backfire. Behind the Irishman, Mito opened his eyes, turned his head to listen. I stood again.

"Sit down, Dan."

"Someone's shooting out there. Someone who doesn't like what you do or are."

"It's being taken care of."

I sat. The Irishman smoked, looked at his elegant cigar that was probably real Cuban. "I wish I could give it up. The smoking. You don't smoke, do you?"

"Not any more."

"No stress? No tension?"

"I manage."

"You must be happy in your work."

We all sat and listened. The room as tense and alert as a jungle animal. He let the smoke of the fine cigar fill his mouth, drift out. Looked at the tip of the cigar to check the ash crown as cigar smokers do.

"Would you believe I help out both sides to keep the pot boiling? Keep everything in a nice fat chaos so no one has time to go after me? That sound better to you, Dan? A better theory for the evil drug lord?"

"It's easier to believe. You didn't get into selling drugs because you wanted to help your fellow man."

"No, you're right, I didn't. You'd never believe how I did get into it the first time. The second time . . ." He shrugged again. "Well, you don't really want to hear that story. And I don't think you really give a fuck in the wind about Sylvestre. Except maybe to know who killed him."

"Who did?"

The next two gunshots echoed in the night from the left. The running and brush breaking. The unmistakable burst of an automatic rifle. Mito was at the room windows. He had a weapon. A small PPK that seemed to be part of his hand. The Irishman leaned forward on his elbows on the desk, the cigar in his mouth, his hands clasped to support his chin.

"I don't know, not for sure. Only that it wasn't me."

"What did happen that night? What was Madrona doing in that warehouse?"

He watched Mito at the window. "I got a call at my ranch down in Guatemala. It was our contact at the embassy. He knew about my call to that asshole ambassador, told me it had been taped, which I figured it would be, and that this kid had stolen the tape, which I hadn't figured on. I wouldn't want that tape to get into the wrong hands until I've got a solid understanding with Washington, so I sent some men to get it from the kid. They tailed him to Dulles, but something spooked him, he slipped them."

"He spotted the Major at the airport, knew him."

"So did my people. Our old buddy the Major. They lost the kid, but they didn't lose the Major. He led them out to Santa Barbara, they contacted me and Sylvestre. We had to know who was after that tape, who didn't want it out besides us. The Major's a field man, so Sylvestre went up to spot who was behind him."

"Did he?"

Two people ran close to the house, trampled the bushes of the patio. Heavier feet ran. A scream in the night. The low, choked, guttural scream of a man. It didn't come again.

The Irishman smoked. Got up suddenly and began to walk the room. "I don't know. He spotted the CIA and Max Cole from State. It's possible only State and Langley are worried about what I can tell. I've given cash to people both of them wanted to help out, done work and favors for both of them."

"But you don't think so."

I listened for another scream, a shot, anything. There was only silence.

"Sylvestre wouldn't have been caught flat in that warehouse unless it was goddamned important. Important enough to take a big risk."

"Like the Major meeting someone?"

Mito came away from the window. Sat down behind the Irishman. Closed his eyes once more. The PPK had disappeared.

"Who didn't want us to know who he was. There was no goddamn reason to blow Sylvestre away otherwise. We know the Major, he knows us."

"Someone Sylvestre would recognize. Or you would if Madrona got back to you. An unknown face wouldn't have meant much."

The Irishman sat back in his chair. "Sylvestre could have hoped to hear them say enough to tell him who it was."

"It would have to be someone you worked with who really doesn't want that known."

"That could be a lot of people."

"What do you think Claudia Nervo really wanted up here?"

"That Guatemalan agent? That's an easy guess. You can bet the Guatemalan military have a man inside the American embassy too. Her boss general is probably afraid I've got a song to sing about him. He wants me, the tape, and no deals. The CIA did me a favor on that one."

There were no more sounds in the night beyond the windows and the house. The question was, should I tell him what I knew about the other man in the warehouse that night? "How much is that Sylmar bust going to hurt you? From the look of it the cops made a hell of a haul."

"About twenty tons of the best Colombian snow. It'll hurt the street most. The supply's going down for a while, the price up. A lot of needy people are going to have to tough it out. We can replace the coke pretty easy, that's not much problem. It's the cash they grabbed. This is a cash business, I'll have to go back down and float some more hard money to meet our payroll." The slim cigar was down to a few inches. "You've got a pretty damn good idea who tipped the Sylmar bust, don't you, Dan? Who was in that warehouse with the Major?"

"Maybe," I said. "Where's Paul Valenzuela?"

"Safe. He's safer with us than he'd be out on the street. We only need to hold him a while until the deal goes down. I don't think the Major and his people would be so gentle."

"How long is a while?"

"As long as it takes. If I knew who else wanted the tape, maybe it'd go faster."

You have to judge the chances, weigh the possibilities, make a decision. There was no sound now in or out of the big Beverly Hills house. I took the chance.

"You know a Martin Dobson?"

Car doors opened close outside. Footsteps walked heavily on what sounded like the enclosed patio. A great many footsteps and the sound of dragging. Heavy dragging.

"I know Martin Dobson," the Irishman said.

I told him of Dobson hurrying from the warehouse the first night. How Dobson had come to me and Esther Valenzuela to question us, dismiss Max Cole. "He's been hovering around from the start. He wants Paul Valenzuela an awful lot."

"I'll bet he does." He had stopped listening to the night outside, or watching me, or even smoking. "You talked to Dobson in person? He showed himself to you? In the open?"

"He didn't seem to like how Max Cole was handing it. Or the Major, for that matter."

"No." He laid the remnant of his elegant cigar in a heavy ceramic ashtray on the table. "I should have guessed."

The tall *sicario* I'd hit, Oscar, appeared. Another gunman in better clothes, a silk suit that had gotten dirty, was with him. They had their guns. The Irishman listened as they spoke low to him. He nodded, stood up. He didn't look happy. No smile now, and a hollowness in his eyes.

"I've got to hold you, Dan. They tailed you here. Dobson and his people have more ways to get at someone than it takes to skin a cat. I can't let them talk to you."

"Paul Valenzuela?"

He shrugged, motioned toward a door out of the room. There wasn't much point in trying to resist. I never carry my gun in Los Angeles, too much risk from the police. Maybe the police would have been better. The *sicarios* fell in behind me as we left the dining room. Mito led us through the dark living room toward glass doors out into the patio, across it and out through the high hedge to the hidden driveway and garage. Two white delivery vans stood in the driveway. Both had been newly painted, the Mayan Imports, Inc., logo faintly visible under the fresh coat.

The two bodies lay behind the vans in pools of blood on the concrete in the light from the open door of the garage. One was the chunky CIA man in the black Ford who'd tailed me yesterday. The other was Walter Enz. Their throats were cut wide open, bullet holes and knife gashes in their blood-soaked suits. The *sicarios* opened the rear doors on one van, tossed the bloody and limp bodies inside.

"They were coming down from the other house. What a goddamn waste." The Irishman watched his gunmen throw the bodies into the van. "They killed Sylvestre and the Nervo woman, tried to kill you. They came here to kill me, kill all of us. The chance they took."

I wanted to sit down. Hold my head in my hand. Get into my car and drive. They weren't going to let me do any of that.

Two *sicarios* came from the garage with buckets and heavy brushes, began to scrub the blood on the driveway. A dangerous way to live, and a nasty way to die.

The Irishman watched the van doors close. "Most of my men started out in the squatters' slums in half the cities of Latin America where kids drown in open sewers every day while the rich oil their beautiful bodies on Copacabana Beach protected by the police. They don't value other people's lives much. No one ever gave them any reason to think life had any value."

Oscar behind me prodded me up into the second van.

28

We had been parked for hours. Close to some freeway. Even under the freeway. In the dark van inside the night it was impossible to be sure. It's impossible, really, to be sure of anything. That's a cliché, we say it all the time. Most of us don't really believe it. I believe it.

Not to risk is not to live. That's a cliché too. It's also true. It was Captain Scott, the Englishman who died with all his companions on their way back from the South Pole, who wrote in the journal found with his frozen corpse, "We took risks, we knew we took them . . . therefore we have no cause for complaint."

There was nothing else I could have done. The two dead CIA men proved that, if I'd needed proof. I'd had no choice but to find Paul Valenzuela the only way I could. Things had come out against me. My car and the bodies of the two CIA men would be found far from the house, far from Beverly Hills. The Major and Martin Dobson had been given a message they would know but would never prove.

The lean *sicario*, Oscar, sat in the back of the van with me. He held an automatic half hidden by his crossed arms in a fatigue camouflage shirt, had his knife in a sheath at his back, never took his eyes from me. My shoulder had stiffened under the bandages, my broken rib was sore, my head ached. I wasn't going anywhere. Parked, we sat silent and looked at each other for two and a half hours by my watch before the van lurched into motion once more. We drove. I dozed.

I woke up to voices and the rear doors open. Moonlight. The vague outline of a dark house among thick, high bushes. Tall palms against the sky, the odor of eucalyptus. A glow high in the sky that had to be L.A., but which part of the vast sprawl of fifty cities and two counties that is Los Angeles? Shadows that moved across the moonlight against the distant glow and the trees and bushes motionless in the warm night. A figure flanked by two others rose to climb into the van, stumbled under the low top to sit against the other wall. I had found Paul Valenzuela.

"Mr. Fortune?"

"Where are we, Paul?"

"Somewhere in L.A., Burbank, Pasadena. Up near the mountains. Is Esther all right? How did they get you?"

I told him how Esther was and how they had gotten me. He sat across the van hunched against the outer wall, knees up, arms around his knees. In the Dodgers' windbreaker, chino trousers, and high basketball shoes he'd worn in the cabin off Paradise Road a week ago. The doors slammed, locked on the two of us. The van started. A second motor was close behind as we moved out once more.

"I'm sorry they got you, Mr. Fortune."

"What happened at the motel?"

"They just walked in through the connecting door to the next unit. Two of them with guns. In those camouflage fatigues. I thought they were soldiers working with the Major. I thought you'd turned me in. Until I found out who they were. Four more came in when they opened the door. These were different, flashily dressed, laughing. Three were. The other was the Irishman. He said he was sorry but they had to take the tape, hold me for a while . . ."

The Irishman had tailed us from Figueroa, seen where Paul was, sent his men to pick the easy lock on a connecting door. So much for caution and a secret knock. He had been sorry. So very sorry he had to hold Paul, take the tape. A gentleman who didn't blink at two men with their throats slashed. The necessary was necessary. A good companion, and ruthless. The world we live in.

After the illusion of enlightenment and the triumph of the mind came the twentieth century.

". . . They took me in the van to that house, held me in an upstairs room. They gave me a TV, and when there were a lot of the flashy dressers in the house they let me go downstairs to eat. They talked to me about their women, their cars, their jewelry, their money. I tried to talk about the poverty in Latin America, in the L.A. *barrio*, how Latin people must work together. They laughed at me. They sneer at the Africans of Brazil, the Indians of Peru and Bolivia and Ecuador. They're all part Indian or black, but act as if they were superior. They are Europeans. They live like the gangs in the *barrio*. They all carry guns, feel close to nothing and no one except their home village and their family. Nothing else exists."

"That's the world of most people," I said.

"It's not my world, Mr. Fortune."

The van was on a freeway and moving fast, the other car probably close behind, not that it made any difference at this speed. We could break the doors open, but where would we go? What chance of survival for someone who jumped out of a moving van at seventy miles an hour on a crowded night freeway? The odds had to be higher on a chance somewhere ahead.

"What made you take the tape, Paul? Why not give it to the ambassador or the CIA man? That's the key. What no one could have foreseen. The kind of insignificant little event that starts wars, revolutions. Not what ninety-nine percent of young men in your job would have done. Was there something the Irishman said? Something the ambassador said?"

He sat as he had since he'd entered the van at the house among the palms and eucalyptus. Knees up, arms wrapped around the knees hiding his face. "I fell in love with Guatemala, the people. Their survival, endurance, bravery. Such a savage kind of strength to even get up each morning with the life they have, the despair of every single day. I rode all over the country and the cities, read everything we have at the embassy. Guatemala has the most natural resources in all of Central America. It has eight million people. Six million of them live in poverty. The cost of basic foods is out of the reach of those six million. They're hungry, homeless and sick each day of their lives. The ruling five percent get sixty percent of the national income. From export crops grown by the cheap labor of the six million."

"Is that what you heard in that phone call? About Americans being part of keeping the people poor?"

On the freeway the traffic had thinned. A less-traveled freeway. Through the lower noise of the lighter traffic I heard a car that remained close behind, made no attempt to pass with the rest of the traffic flow. The sound outside the van took on a new tone. The solid echo of a city of close buildings was gone. Each car as it passed was isolated as its noise faded across the night without an echo. Open country, the freeway outside the city.

"Democracy is a myth in Guatemala. A joke. A word to hide exploitation and repression. The country has more human rights violations against its own people than any other country in Latin America. One third of all *disappearances*, a worse record than Haiti, El Salvador or Chile. Civilian or military *presidente* makes no difference. The same leaders crush any opposition. If they don't, the five percent that run the country might lose their comfortable way of life. So U.S. officers trained in Vietnam advise the army on how to keep control. We always have, all over Latin America."

The van slowed, curved, slowed further, came to a stop. A freeway exit. Sat in the night, the freeway traffic passing on above. Turned right, drove on through silence in the night, began to bounce and buck over an unpaved road. I listened to the night, the motor of the second car behind. If we broke open the doors, jumped, we had a chance to land unhurt. The night was dark. There should be trees and thick brush. Or desert ravines. Only the car behind would see. It would depend on how far behind, how much it bounced on the rough road, how fast it could stop.

"Way back in nineteen twenty-seven there was a State Department memo saying, 'We do control the destinies of Central America . . . national interest absolutely dictates such a course. Governments which we recognize and support stay in power, those which we do not fall.' In nineteen seventy Henry Kissinger said, 'I don't see why we need to stand by and watch a country go communist due to the irresponsibility of its own people.' We gave a puppet power in Panama, took it away from him when he didn't do what we told him to do."

I listened to the motor behind us drop back, come closer again, drop back. There was a pattern. When the van struck a level stretch of the poor road the motor behind faded. When the van bounced and yawed so much I had to hold to the floor to keep from being knocked over, the car behind closed in.

"What I heard in that phone call was an arrogant American who had done things for our government he knew they wouldn't want known. I'd read about the drug kings aiding our support of the ruling classes. This Irishman could perhaps even prove how the governments down there use the anti-drug campaign to hide their repression in Guatemala, to cover attacking the *campesinos* and the rebels the way I'd seen it happen. I took the tape, called Mr. Cole. I hoped—"

It was a matter of close timing, of quick action. Of being able to break open the van doors from inside fast enough that the driver and the guard in the cab had no time to react.

"Paul. We can break out the next time the van has to slow. Sit on the floor, brace yourself, put both feet against the door. When I say go, kick as hard as you can. Then jump and run."

He looked up. Stared at me. I felt the van surge ahead, speed up. A smooth, straight patch of road. The motor behind faded away. I was up, bent under the low top.

"Paul! The door!"

I braced my back half against the side wall, feet up on the door. I felt the van slowing again. Paul crawled and braced himself against the opposite wall. The second car was still far back. The van slowed, began to buck and bump and sway.

"Now."

We kicked as hard as we could. The locked double doors burst open, slammed back, swung open again. The van bucked and heaved and yawed over the rough road. Behind, the lights of the second car, still on the smoother section, moved rapidly closer through a pitch-black night.

"Jump!"

I hit on both feet, rolled, tried to come up using my arm. The impact was too much for my bandaged shoulder and one arm. I sprawled on the rocky road. The lights of the trailing car swept across me. Paul Valenzuela had landed well, rolled up quickly, came to help me.

"Run, for Christ's sake! Make them chase us in two directions!"

He pulled me up. "Ravine!"

We plunged into the narrow arroyo. There were no buildings, no trees, no bushes. In the east a faint line of light showed the dawn coming over the empty land as we stumbled ahead. If we could be deep enough into the desert before the dawn . . .

They stood above the ravine. Two on each rim. Two ahead, two behind.

One of the flashy dressers said, "That was pretty stupid."

Oscar fired over our heads.

"That's enough."

The Irishman stood at the edge of the small arroyo. "You had to try. Let's get the hell back on the road."

Two jumped down into the arroyo, pushed us ahead of them back to the van and trailing car. Paul Valenzuela sat again in the rear of the van, back against the side wall, knees up.

"We almost made it."

It was no longer as dark inside the van with the first light of dawn through the doors that hung broken and open. Outside the sweep of the barren desert from sky to sky with nowhere to hide.

"Almost," I said. Sure.

A broad layer of light edged the eastern sky along the rim of the wide desert when the van stopped again.

"Out."

The *sicarios* pushed us toward two dilapidated aircraft hangars the color of the desert. From the emptiness and arid alkali of the ring of far mountains, with the light picking out their tops above the still dark desert, we were closer to Indio than to Palm Springs. Inside the hangar two big trailer truck rigs were parked side by side. Both were clean and trim and newly painted the same as the vans. After the big Sylmar bust, every border guard, highway patrolman and sheriff between L.A. and the border from San Diego to El Paso would be looking for trucks marked "Mayan Imports, Inc."

"Up."

They herded us through an opening in the rear wall into a compartment fifteen feet long inside the sixty-foot trailer. A steel panel slid over the hole, bolts screwed in place. Two canteens of water and a paper bag of sandwiches lay on the floor under the light from a single small bulb high in the real back wall of the semi-trailer. One of those pale green portable chemical toilets complete with door you see at construction sites stood in one corner. Vents gave plenty of air.

"I hope you don't have claustrophobia, Paul."

"They didn't build this for us, did they?"

"The last bounce on the Trampoline. The drug pipeline to ship the coke and horse north to that warehouse in L.A. A little people-smuggling too. Cocaine and H don't need a toilet."

"Wouldn't the border people see that the interior of the trailer is too short, Mr. Fortune?"

"At most crossing points there are so many rigs they can't inspect more than a small percentage. Fifteen feet out of sixty loaded with legitimate imports? They're not going to measure unless they have a strong reason to suspect dope. When the truck is carrying dope it'll mostly go overland, cross at a remote spot, pick up the interstate on the U.S. side. The compartment's really for protection against spot inspection in the U.S. That doesn't happen often."

"How do we ever stop any of it?"

"A tip, mostly. Or a piece of knowledge we pick up and use before they know we have it. Like the name Mayan Imports, Inc."

He looked around the silent cubicle at the portable john, the bag of sandwiches, the canteens. Walked to the back wall, sat down with his back against the steel and his knees up again.

"I'm sorry, Mr. Fortune. I didn't mean all this to happen."

"What did you mean to happen?"

"I wanted to help."

"Help who? How?"

"Guatemala. The people. What we should really be doing in Guatemala, everywhere in Latin America, instead of what we've been doing."

"Did you think they'd slap you on the back? See the light and reform? They won't. No more than your Guatemalan generals will see the light. It's power, advantage, money. A whole lot of money. On all sides."

The truck engine started, gears ground, the big rig lurched forward and swung in a wide turn. A long, slow turn that finally straightened. Gears ground again, brakes let off air, the rig swayed and settled in a medium gear as it bounced down the rutted dirt road we had come in on. Wherever we were going, we were on our way. It did not make me feel free and happy.

"They can't drive us all the way to Guatemala."

I knew what he had on his mind. I had it on mine too, and had since I'd looked down at the two CIA men with their cut throats gaping up at me like the gutted bellies of small animals. He was staring at it. Death. It fills the mind, death. When you stare at it, it leaves no room for anything else. You can't think too much about it or you can curl up and die instantly.

"They can't drive cocaine all the way from Colombia. They fly it up, they can fly us down."

I didn't believe for a second the Irishman was holding Paul Valenzuela only to keep the Major from getting to him. That was one reason, maybe, and for today. But there was another reason, more positive, and for tomorrow. Something he wanted from Paul. Some advantage to him.

Neither of us had slept all night. Even fear can't keep you awake forever. By the time the big rig began to roll on a good road, Paul Valenzuela was slumped against the pale green portable john. The last I remembered was the sharp exhale of air brakes as the truck slowed, turned. The increase of speed. Flying with only the sound of rushing wind.

La Trampolina. A 3,500-mile route of cocaine from Medellin and Cali in Colombia to the hungry markets of the U.S. That doesn't even count the thousand-mile trip of the coca paste from the poor *campesinos* of Peru and Ecuador to the refinery laboratories of Colombia. Why the desperate farmers grew the leaf was easy to answer. Why so many people in the richest nation on earth had so desperate a need for the comfort and escape from reality of mind-killing drugs was another matter. There were answers, but not many who cared to listen, or cared at all.

When I opened my eyes the bright sun glared through the air vents. My shoulder was tight and throbbing, but not as much as yesterday, my ribs were sore but there was no headache. I ate a ham and cheese from the bag, washed it down with water. There was still only the rush of wind, the whine of the tires against the road, but I had a sense of vast open land and a narrower highway.

"Where are we?"

Paul Valenzuela stretched his back, twisted his neck, awake but heavy-eyed, unrested. I told him what I had decided about the land and the highway. He ate as he walked from side to side to work the kinks and stiffness from his body.

The truck flew on.

We used the toilet.

It grew hotter in the hidden compartment. I took off my corduroy jacket, he put his windbreaker behind his head. We sat through the long, hot day, ate another sandwich at some point, drank water, talked. Paul knew nothing of Martin Dobson.

"I never heard of him, Mr. Fortune."

Darkness came when the rig turned off the two-lane into a rougher road with the sound of gravel under the tires. A road that twisted, undulated, needed the heavy breathing of the air brakes to maneuver the big semi. An odor of brush and aridity through the vents.

All night.

We slept again.

Dawn and the better road arrived together. Another two-lane highway, blacktop, but not as good as the earlier road.

"You think we're over the border, Mr. Fortune?"

It was my guess. Arizona into Mexico. The wide emptiness of northern Mexico. Where no questions were asked and a lawman would have to act like a lizard or rock to have any hope of not being seen. A desert with airstrips anywhere and everywhere. The sunlight had faded to a pale yellow again outside the vents before we found our airstrip. The air brakes pumped, the trailer curled in a long circle and came to a stop. The great, empty silence of an uninhabited planet lost somewhere in the endless universe.

The cab doors opened, feet jumped down. Voices were small and lost in insignificance. The tailgate doors clanked open. Bolts unscrewed and the steel panel of our cell slid away. The cook/guard, Mito, poked his head in.

"*Pronto.*"

In the evening sunlight, as far as I could see on all sides, there was nothing. No houses, no movement. No birds, not even a vulture. The single dirt track road with nothing but the tire marks of our single semi rig in the dust. A horizon so unbroken it seemed to curve like the photographs of the surface of the moon. The northern Mexican desert.

Only a crude airstrip, a mound of plastic-wrapped pallets, two twin-turbo aircraft, many men already loading the semi with the pallets, more with ready assault rifles who watched all points of a 360-degree compass, and the Irishman apart with two other men who searched the sky and looked at their watches. The next bounce along *La Trampolina*.

The Irishman nodded to us. "Sorry about the ride." His smile widened into his big grin. "No try for a breakout this time, Dan?"

"I can be as crazy as the next man, but I'm not stupid."

"Then climb aboard that plane."

Mito walked behind us to the turboprop. Inside the plane he and the lean Oscar took seats behind us. The Irishman sat with the pilot. Five more men clambered into the cargo bay. The engines turned over, the pilot aimed us down the empty airstrip. To the right the enormous circle of the sun rested on the rim of the world.

As we lifted I looked across the desert. No matter how high we went, there was nothing.

29

With the first line of dawn across the great green jungle to the east, the turboprop swept in a long circle over the Guatemalan highlands. The volcano peaks of Fuego and Pacaya rose above the clouds beyond wide Lake Atitlan to the south, mountains vanished in high mists to the north. Out of sight beyond the volcanoes, Guatemala City sprawled its millions across its ravines in the *tierra templada*. On the other side of the mountains to the north lay Mexico where we had flown most of the night, stopped only once to refuel at another bounce down *La Trampolina*.

At the end of the long circle the plane descended straight along the spine of the Sierra Madre until a dark highland valley opened between the wooded slopes of the cloud forest. Thick trees rushed past, the twin-engined plane settled down on a lighted blacktop airstrip hidden close against the mountain wall where the dawn had yet to reach. A camouflaged truck and two jeeps waited at the end of the strip, headlights on. Mito and Oscar hustled us to one of the jeeps. Mito joined the Irishman in the lead jeep, the rest of his men piled into the truck.

The dirt road curved down through the dark trees in a series of tortuous switchbacks, entered a mountain village as the dawn reached the valley. Dark-skinned people in dazzling colors crowded the edge of the road between the small, bare, widely spaced houses. They all smiled and waved as the Irishman passed, called to him in their Indian-Spanish. The town elders and officials in high hats, *ladino* suit jackets and orange striped trousers of the region, stood together and bowed. The Irishman waved back, called out what sounded like "Fiesta!" The villagers cheered. A group of young men who stood apart with pistols and automatic rifles and ragtag uniforms waved their weapons.

Two miles beyond and below, among towering slopes of coffee trees, the *finca* stood half a mile off the road. Guardposts were visible on both sides of the road as it came up from below. Armed men stood on the roof of the sprawling house. A squad came out to circle the jeeps in the rear parking area in front of the garages, the truck drove off to somewhere beyond the house. A burly military type in camouflage, who looked as *norteamericano* as the Irishman and I, huddled in serious conference with the Irishman, as Oscar and two of the welcoming squad escorted Paul Valenzuela and me into the house from the rear.

Separate rooms on the second floor. Largesse from the lord of the manor? Or a precaution against us making a coordinated break again? Towels were laid out in the private bathroom, covers were turned back, a robe and changes of clothes hung in the closets. But the door was locked, and there was no key inside. A pleasant prison until time for whatever need of us he had. The windows were barred with Spanish colonial-style decorative wrought-iron bars, the windows themselves locked, the room air-conditioned. There were no electric lines coming into the remote *finca*. It would be self-contained: bottled gas, electrical generator, garbage incinerator, its own fuel supplies.

Have you ever been so bone-weary, so grimy inside and out, that a bath and bed are all you can think of if you risk death for it? On the buckets I sailed in during that long-ago war, after a hurricane, twenty-four-hour watch, wolfpack alert, air attack, the end of most voyages were like that. Too tired to think, locked in, undoubtedly guarded outside the door as well as on the roof and road, there was little choice if I could have made one. With my bandaged shoulder I used the elegant sunken bathtub, the expensive soap, the soft towels that could have been in a five-star hotel. I didn't shave. Went to bed.

* * *

The gunfire was a heavy .50-caliber machine gun. A long burst. Another. Awake before I knew I was, I lay alert and looked all around the room that was a bright gold with soft yellow light.

At the window the fierce sun was low in the west down the long valley. Another burst from somewhere across the lawn of the huge ranch house. They were hidden in the forest of trees that surrounded the *finca*. Machine guns dug in all across the front of the *finca* that faced the narrow road up from below. Always there to protect the drug shipments and transshipments, the testing only routine? The way we had tested our guns on the buckets every time we entered the war zone? I stood at the window until the sun was gone. Not down, but behind the mountains, a yellow glow still over the forested peaks and ridges like a halo. I watched the *sicarios* deploy among the trees and the guardposts under the direction of the burly *norteamericano* or European.

"Señor?" A knock and a voice. "*El padrone* is to tell dinner one half hour. I come back."

I ignored the clean clothes neat in the closet, dressed again in my wrinkled jeans, work shirt and old corduroy jacket. When the voice returned, I was ready. Two guards and Paul Valenzuela were in the hall, we all walked behind the skinny houseboy in his white jacket down to a formal dining room. A massive chandelier hung over the carved oak table that would have seated ten even without being opened up. Federalist-period sideboards and china cabinets, finely patterned wallpaper, silver candelabra, bone china and good crystal, sterling, and cloth napkins in silver rings. The Irishman sat at one end of the long table, indicated seats on either side of him.

"Paul, Dan, sit down over here."

He hadn't changed his clothes either, still wore the jeans and flight jacket. Oscar the *sicario* was at the table. Maybe he was Sylvestre Madrona's replacement. The burly drill sergeant was there too, still in his fatigues. They sat together at the other end of the long table from the Irishman, spoke only to each other. The military type had an accent I recognized, and his presence made immediate sense. Israeli. Trainers of the world's mercenaries. No questions asked.

"Rooms okay?"

The candelabra, china, crystal, sterling, and napkin rings all had the crest of the gold horse with the green eyes. Bottles of white wine stood at each end of the table. Montrachet Marquis Laguiche. Mito and four white-coated Indians came in with the first course. A salmon mousse. The cook-bodyguard still wore his jeans, but his handwoven shirt was white and decorated with flowers this time. Dressed for a formal dinner.

Paul Valenzuela said, "The rooms are very nice. The rooms are wonderful. Not like the shacks of the villagers."

The Irishman poured wine. "If I changed the village the government would be on me like a tiger. I do what I can."

I said, "They love you in that village."

"I bring money into the area. Lots of work, high pay."

"Opium poppies?"

"Not here. Picking, gardening, repairing, fence building, all kinds of work at top dollar. I remember their birthdays. A fiesta three or four times a year. *Viva la fiesta! Viva El Irlandés!* They love me as long as I give them plenty of cash."

"Some of them looked like guerrillas."

"From EGP, Guerrilla Army of the Poor. One of four groups in the rebel coalition, URNG. I told you I worked with them."

He drank the great wine, looked at the glass as if not all that happy to be with such a wonderful wine. Not where he had once seen himself being. He swirled the pale golden liquid to catch the light from the silver candelabra. "They're the oldest insurgency in Central America, and the least known up in the States. Guatemala's the most important banana republic to the U.S. The most business investment. United Fruit is dead, long live United Fruit. It's Del Monte now, still ships two billion bananas a year. Great for potassium, cheapest fruit the U.S. housewife can buy. Coffee for gourmets. Washington doesn't want the consumer reading about death squads and U.S. advisers, Indian guerrillas and dope dealers, down here. Real bad for business."

Paul Valenzuela said, "Is violence the only way for the Indians? All the poor? Does violence really help anything?"

The Irishman continued to swirl the beautiful wine. "You ever notice how it's always the rich people in power who tell the poor who have no power that violence is never the right way to change things? It's always the secure old-family U.S. president who tells the leader of the blacks of South Africa who just got out of twenty-seven years in prison he has to renounce violence."

I said, "If all that military preparation out there isn't for the guerrillas, who are you worried about?"

"Who says we're worried about anything?"

"All those machine guns in the trees."

"Routine drill. As a matter of fact, I may not have to hold you two much longer. Looks like I've got my deal. That makes this a party, fiesta!" Laughed the big laugh. "The Major's on his way down to talk."

"You trust him?"

"Of course I don't trust the son of a bitch. The Major'll act for the Major and whoever the hell's paying him. It's up to me to act for me."

"Dog eat dog."

"I'll drink to that."

"The machine guns and alert are for the Major."

"Be prepared. I was a Boy Scout back in Iowa."

Paul Valenzuela said, "Now you sell drugs, get rich from the despair of poor people."

"Shit!" So loud Oscar and the Israeli broke their talk at the other end of the table to look at him. "I'm not the one who made millions of people need drugs to live through a day! It's a shitty world, Valenzuela. What the hell does it matter how the poor bastards die? Drugs, booze, nicotine, starvation, pay so low they never get a chance to live, despair or suicide."

He drank the great wine as if it were beer. "Hell, the U.S. had a drug problem ever since World War Two. There hasn't been any real change in addiction and crime. But the president says the drug war's important. TV, newspapers and magazines whoop it up. The public is convinced. An old Secretary of State, Dean Acheson, said, 'Control of the population has always required that external threats be presented in a manner that is clearer than truth.' It distracts the voters from real problems."

I said, "You mean the U.S. is making the poor drug kings look worse than they are to scare the public?"

"Okay, a joke, but if people start thinking about why life isn't so good in most of the world they just might figure they've been given the short end of the stick. Hell, the real cause of the growth in drugs is Washington itself. In the U.S. they war on the poor to help the rich. Down here they keep anything from changing.

What do you think I've been doing for State and the CIA all these years?"

"What have you been doing?" Paul said.

"Putting out money, air fields, planes, couriers, supply routes to help Washington keep everything the way it's always been here. As long as we helped against the insurgents, they looked the other way even in the States. Just say no. Revive the family. Back to basics. But they didn't do a damn thing except go after small-time dealers. Hot air and cops."

Mito and the four white-coated Guatemalans appeared with the main course, bottles of Chateau Ausone to go with the rack of lamb. The Irishman abandoned the wonderful white, hunched at the table over the red that had cost a month's wages for an entire village of *campesino* coffee pickers.

"Eighty percent of the chemicals to process our stuff comes from U.S. corporations." He laughed his big laugh. "Tankers run from Texas across the Gulf to Cartegena with a million pounds of methyl ethyl ketone. You know what methyl ethyl ketone is used to make? Rubber cement. You know how much rubber cement is made in Colombia? None. Zero. You know what else methyl ethyl ketone is used to make? Bingo!"

"Is that why they took you into the cartel?" I said. "To deal with Americans? Why would they trust an American?"

"Hell, I was experienced in drugs, smuggling, supply routes, payoffs, coercion. They were smaller then, starting out on an international scale. I had the connections. I was already an international strongarm man, that's what the CIA is. It was my biggest asset. If I'd been DEA, they'd have cut my throat. But CIA? Open arms."

"You were in the CIA?"

"A lot of years."

Paul Valenzuela said, "That's how you know Carl Foster."

The Irishman nodded. "We go back a long way, Carl and me."

30

Carl Foster, the Irishman, and Rear Admiral Jonas Hardee, U.S. Navy, Ret., meet in the quiet bar of the Arizona Inn in Tucson. Urbane, expensive, discreet. The reserved dark wood front desk so unobtrusive you don't know at first it is a hotel open to the public, the long corridors so cool in the heat of the southwest summer day. Real antiques of the Old West in the public rooms, the high-ceilinged dining room that seems like a miniature of the Harvard Club in New York but looks out onto a Spanish colonial courtyard colored and shaded with Southwest vegetation. The bar itself spacious and airy yet private, sheltered by plants.

"What will you have, Hugh?" The Admiral has called the meeting.

"Beer," the Irishman says. "Beck's if they have it."

"Carl?"

"Scotch, hold the water," Carl Foster says. There is an edge to his voice. Belligerent and a shade nervous.

Rear Admiral Hardee orders only mineral water for himself. The Admiral is the regional director of the Central Intelligence Agency for Latin America. Carl Foster and Hugh John O'Neill are agents under his jurisdiction. When Carl Foster called with the problem, Hardee was resting at his Tucson home. The matter was urgent, Hardee arranged to have his two agents fly up from their assignments to meet him here. A bantam rooster of a man with a fringe of gray hair around a severe, clean-shaven, patrician face, Hardee gets to the point without much waste of time.

"Carl tells me you've been spending perhaps too much time with the wrong people, Hugh. He questions their value to us. At least, their value to justify such close association."

Even resting at home the ex-admiral wears a vested gray suit, white shirt, school tie, gray silk socks with garters, well-shined black shoes. He looks like some old photograph of a Confederate general, Joseph E. Johnston perhaps, as he sits erect. Elite, confident, firmly in and for the power structure.

"He questions their value to whom, Admiral?"

"To us," Carl Foster snaps. "The Company. The country. What we're paid to do."

The Irishman grins. "How can you say that, Carl? They know more about what's going on in Colombia than the *presidente*. More money and a better organization."

"They're goddamn gangsters."

"When the hell didn't we deal with gangsters, murderers, liars, rapists, racketeers and pirates?"

"When they can't do us any fucking good!"

Hardee says, "All right, Carl. Remember where you are." The ex-admiral watches the Irishman. "This Rodriguez Gacha, this Escobar. As I understand it they sell drugs, smuggle gemstones, engage in various other criminal and strongarm actions. Are men like that consistent with your ideals, Hugh?"

"I wouldn't know," the Irishman says. "I seem to have lost those a long time ago."

Vietnam is heating up when he graduates from Iowa with full ROTC training and his pilot's license. He goes into the service, is sent to school for intelligence training. Before he really knows what has happened he has been recruited to fly for the military supply airline operated by the Central Intelligence Agency, Air America. A vital tool to work with the various irregular rebels against Hanoi and Uncle Ho, to take supplies into the tribal guerrillas who support our effort to bring democracy to Southeast Asia, independence and self-determination to Laos and Cambodia, the Meo tribesmen and mountain Hmong enslaved by the Vietnamese communists and their quislings in the south, the Viet Cong.

It surprises him to find that the war of the Meo tribesmen against the Vietnamese Communists in Laos does not exist. Air America does not exist. He and his fellow pilots, agents, cargo handlers and military advisers to the Meo do not exist. The CIA is not in Laos because the U.S. is not in Laos. The U.S. is not in Laos because the Vietnamese are not in Laos. The Meo war is against Laotian Communists, is an internal matter. There is even a royal Laotian prince at the head of the local Communists, and the U.S. does not interfere in internal affairs of independent nations. So he and Air America are not there, which is unnerving but doesn't make any difference to their runs to bring supplies and guns and advisers to the Meo.

A larger surprise awaits him. It takes time, but he finally realizes that the cargo he and his fellow pilots and cargo crew bring back from the Meo in Laos is their opium crop. Once he realizes this, it also becomes clear what happens to the opium the CIA has brought out of Laos for their secret allies in the non-existent war. It moves on through the Company's various pipelines into the U.S. itself where it is processed into heroin and brings a nice price which is duly returned to the helpful tribesmen to maintain their economy. The CIA takes care of those who help it accomplish its mission no matter who they are.

When the extent of this aid operation for their allies, and, incidentally, a substantial aid to their own operations budget since the grateful Meo have no objection to a small cut for the carrier, becomes common knowledge in Southeast Asia, Air America is soon dubbed Air Opium by barracks comics throughout the war zone. When this brings a certain critical attention, and some questions from their own personnel, such as himself, the entire matter is quickly cloaked under the blanket of "in the interest of national security." Or, don't ask. It doesn't exist anymore than the CIA presence in Laos, and what are a few thousand more American addicts compared to saving Laos from Communism?

He says, "Opium, Agent Orange, the overthrow of Diem, the bombing and invasion of Cambodia, none of which happened at the time, or if it did *we* certainly had nothing to do with it, kind of made any ideals sort of amusing."

"Shit," Carl Foster says, "Laos didn't go Communist until we got kicked out and the Vietnam Commies moved in. If it had all been run by the Company we'd have won that damned war. What we did *worked*, goddamn it."

Admiral Hardee says, "Everywhere in the world deserves to have freedom and democracy, Hugh. If we had a fair, open, level playing field everywhere, that would be fine. We would never have to interfere. But as long as that isn't the case, we have to fight fire with fire and that means sometimes doing what we would not ordinarily want to do."

"You mean like helping out that old anti-Communist Chinese Nationalist General still up on the Chinese border in Burma with his private army after over forty years? The one that sells most of the opium in the world? The one I flew missions to sometimes to get info out of China?"

"Burma is still a democracy, Hugh, and China comes closer all the time. I don't condone the opium trade, but—"

"But democracy is worth a few million addicts?"

The older man's ramrod back stiffens even more, his eyes are firm. "Democracy and freedom are worth anything."

With the U.S. pullout from Vietnam, the Irishman is reassigned first to fly clandestine agents and money into Bolivia where the Torres government is not acting the way Washington wants. It is time for another change in Bolivia. The situation has gone downhill for U.S. purposes since '67 when the Company provided training and leadership for the Bolivian counterinsurgency forces hunting the guerrillas led by Che Guevara. That effort had been one of their greatest triumphs when Che himself was captured and executed. (For the squeamish American public the well-known leader's death had to be reported as occurring during the melee of the fight, his identity unknown until later.) But while they are working on the Bolivian coup, selecting the proper man to lead it and take over at the head of a more tractable, pro-U.S. government, a far more dangerous situation develops farther south. Salvador Allende, an avowed Marxist, is freely elected president of the more advanced and democratic nation of Chile. This sends off panic alarms in Washington, is going to present a major challenge for the entire foreign policy apparatus of the U.S. government. A Marxist in Chile, even a democratically elected, popular and populist Marxist like Allende, is unacceptable. There can be no question of that in Washington. The problem is, with the Marxist duly elected in an election at least as fair as the U.S.'s own, there isn't a great deal that can be done in the open. Enter the CIA.

Operation Centaur swings into action. The Irishman is given the job of collecting the contributions and coordinating the slush funds of the U.S. companies that do business in Chile, and putting these millions to work in Chile where they will do the most good. It is a rush operation, State doesn't want Allende to have any chance to look good to the world or the people of Chile.

"Not one day, you all understand? Not one minute of peace to put in any programs, change anything."

His second assignment is to fly in the millions of forged Chilean banknotes to deluge the country with the phony money and fuel a big inflation. That is pretty easy. Much harder is the third job—to go in and locate groups the Company can rally to give any kind of popular support to stabilize the situation after the coup. That there has to be a coup is clear from the start. There simply isn't time to wear the Marxists down with embargoes and other economic pressure, to starve them out. There is no organized support for the coup we can exploit and supply for a grassroots counterinsurgency. In fact, the people seem to want Allende and his Marxists.

"We're not going to stand by and watch U.S. interests go down the fucking drain just because Chilean voters are stupid."

It has to be a coup, and bring in the military.

"Generalissimo Pinochet and sixteen years of the iron fist, but, hey, a hell of a lot better than a popular Marxist, right?"

"What the hell's all that got to do with scumbags like Gacha and Escobar? Pinochet's probably the only general down there didn't deal drugs," Carl Foster says. "See what I mean, Chief?"

Hardee isn't listening to Carl Foster. "You wanted another Cuba, Hugh?"

"I wanted my country to back the decision of the people, what I know as democracy. But I was naive, wasn't I? Marxism isn't democracy by definition. Not even if the people elect it."

Carl Foster swears, "What in hell has that got to do with our job? If it's bad for the U.S., then it's up to us—"

Hardee says, "If the election is really democratic, Hugh, fair and honest, we will always support—"

The waiter brings a third beer. The admiral is still sipping his first mineral water, still impeccable in manner and appearance and habit, the patrician. Carl Foster finally orders a second whiskey. He won't drink too much in front of the boss.

The Irishman drinks, laughs and shakes his head. "The smoke screen even for me, Admiral? Hey, I'm with the Company, I know what we mean when we talk about democracy in other countries."

"What do we mean, Hugh?"

"Rule by elites—landowners, businessmen, the military, the ones who've always ruled—that favor U.S. interests in their countries, keep conditions right for us with token elections carefully controlled so only the right people vote. I mean, Nicaragua's not a democracy, so we have to go in and restore it, right? But El Salvador, South Korea, Indonesia, South Africa, and our good pal Colombia are real democracies so they're okay."

Carl Foster says, "Who the hell's side are you on, O'Neill?"

"Maybe that's what I'm trying to figure out."

"Christ!"

"Whose side are you on, Carl?"

"*Our* side, goddamn it! The country's."

"Which country, Carl, the two percent or the ninety-eight percent? The two percent that owns ninety percent of our wealth, or the rest of us? Hey, those figures are just about the same as in El Salvador or Guatemala. Shazzam!"

Carl Foster drinks his fresh whiskey, glances at Hardee, not sure of the turn the talk has taken. The dignified older man has been silent in the hushed elegance of the bar for some time. He sips his mineral water, clears his throat.

"What has all this got to do with your sudden association with two common thugs such as Rodriguez Gacha and Escobar?"

The Irishman is silent as the other patrons of the elite bar talk and laugh in hushed tones. "I read in a magazine that the CIA really didn't want Allende killed, some rogue elements down there got out of hand. That there was no popular support for Arbenz in Guatemala when we sent in our invasion to overthrow him. How we've just 'discovered' a Honduran truck driver who swears he took arms from the Sandinistas to the rebels in El Salvador." He drinks his beer. Good imported beer. He likes good things. "I'm not sure I want to be in an organization that routinely lies to and hoodwinks its own citizens. Are we all just another banana republic? El Salvador at home?"

There is an edge to Hardee's voice. "People could think you were ashamed of your country, Hugh. I'm sure—"

"I've been ashamed of my country for a long time, Admiral."

Hardee continues to study the Irishman. "What do you want from your country, Hugh?"

"What did I, you mean? Before I worked for the Company? I wanted respect for other people and their rights. Live up to our words: life, liberty, pursuit of happiness for everyone. Help out the huddled masses, not use them to make profits. Some socialist ideals tossed in: freedom from hunger, power to the people, equality, brotherhood. All the bleeding-heart crap."

"Jesus," Carl Foster says, "this is worse than I thought."

Hardee ignores Foster. "Foreign gangsters, thugs? Crude, uneducated, brutal, and stupid. The Company must be better than that, Hugh, even though we may not meet your youthful ideals."

The Irishman finishes his third beer, glances around at the elegant bar. "I don't like what I'm doing or who I work for. And I don't much like myself, either, or anything else I see. The world I want isn't going to happen. Capitalist, socialist, fascist or anarchist, it's all materialism and self-interest. Human feelings washed away by swimming pools and champagne."

He raises his glass, sees it is empty. "All the years in our good CIA have taught me one thing, Admiral. The world I want isn't going to come by evolution or revolution. If it ever does come, the only way is by the evolution of the human species into something better. It's a lot more likely we'll destroy ourselves before then, and good riddance."

He waves for another beer, looks at Hardee and Carl Foster. "So I've decided if you can't beat 'em, join 'em. Get mine. Live the high life. You know the poet Rimbaud, Admiral?"

Hardee's voice is stiff. "I've heard of him."

"He decided the whole fucking world was hopeless. People were horrors. So he quit poetry, became a man of action, never wrote another line. You're looking at a man of action."

Carl Foster says, "If you try anything illegal in the U.S. we'll step on you, O'Neill. Don't think you'll get favors."

"Hell, Carl, you'll realize how I can be used. For Company and country. I'll be a real useful man." The Irishman's loud laugh echoes through the quiet, discreet room.

31

Oscar and the Israeli had gone. The Irishman went on talking. He seemed to want Paul, or me, or both of us, to understand him. Or he was talking to himself and didn't care what we knew. Not worried about anything we knew.

In the lavish dining room there were two of us to one of him. I didn't think for an instant we were alone. The *sicarios* would be somewhere. He might or might not be telling the truth about releasing us, be talking to us for a reason, but with a mountain forest outside the *finca,* the villagers and guerrillas on his side in an unknown country, we needed more advantage.

"How long before the CIA started using you?"

"As soon as they realized our connections to the generals. It got heavier when they wanted to start the *contra* war going in Nicaragua, needed to set up all the old Somoza guardsmen with a believable army. We had long-time associations with the Somoza people, right? When funding got tougher, we got a lot cozier."

"How much cozier?" I said.

He listened to the night through the high hacienda windows. There was the sudden sound of activity out there, movement in the darkness. "Cozy enough for them to leak secret stuff to the U.S. newspapers and blow a big DEA undercover operation against us. Then there was this Honduran general, Bueso. Mega-ambitious, mega-*contra* backer, and mega-drug player because he needed mega bucks to take out his civilian *presidente* boss in a coup. When he got himself indicted on drugs up in the States everyone from the White House on down went to bat for him, got him off with a little time in a stateside country club."

Mito and his silent team in the white jackets had brought in the cheese and French bread while the Irishman told his story. We ate the good Jarlsberg and fine ripe Stilton, finished the great Ausone. The Irishman held his glass suspended as he again listened to the voices and movement out in the mountain night.

"Word went out that if we had a military or intelligence relationship with the U.S. they'd look the other way. And if the U.S. laid off, everyone laid off. A free hand."

"Now the deal's over, the war's on."

"They needed a new war, we're it. Gacha's dead, Escobar's on the run, but I'm alive and I'm not running."

Mito and his white-coated team cleared off the cheese. They brought tarts and fruit, a great Vin Santo and a not-quite-great Chateau D'Yquem. Coffee and a cognac so old I couldn't guess at its cost. The Irishman was drinking the best he had tonight. He opened the Vin Santo, poured the heavy amber wine.

"Why did you take that tape, Valenzuela? Why didn't you turn it over to Carl Foster? Hand it to the ambassador?"

"I wanted to help," Paul said. "Help the people here."

The Irishman drank, laughed in the room with the movement outside in the *finca* night. "Hell, all most people would do with your help is build an empire for themselves. They don't want freedom and justice, they want security and safety. Most of them'd rather have a rich life for themselves than a decent life for everyone. Ready, willing and able to live high and wide on the suffering of other people."

"So you decided to be the same," Paul said. "You never thought about trying to change that?"

"Change? Hell, you're me twenty years ago." He was drinking like a man on leave from the front who would go back tomorrow. "I thought about it. But when everything is measured only in cash, money in the bank, the message to everyone is that nothing matters except making money. Not how you make it, or when, or where, or from who, or for what. Just make it." He shook his head. "Out on the barricades nowadays, Valenzuela, you're going to be mighty goddamn lonely."

The movement on the *finca* grounds had stopped, the mountain night as silent and motionless as a mountain night ever is. Wind in the thick trees around the big house, out among the coffee trees thick on the slopes. Animal cries I couldn't recognize. The movement of the earth itself.

I poured a glass of D'Yquem for myself. "But you're going to fight on your own barricades, tell the world what's been going on down here. The Don Quixote of the drug peddlers."

"Something like that, Dan. I've been on both sides, there isn't a hell of a lot of difference. Maybe I'm tired of the whole game, but I won't go down alone."

"Most of what you've said tonight anyone can read in U.S. newspapers and magazines. Some newspapers and magazines anyway."

"They can read it slanted and shaped. Most don't want to hear, don't believe it, or don't give a damn. From me they'd have to listen. I've got the details." He set his empty glass almost delicately on the table with the tall candles burned down to stubs in the silver candelabra. "The names and places that don't get in the newspapers."

"What names?" I said. "What places?"

He leaned back against the carved chair that was like all the regal chairs used by a thousand *hidalgos* over the centuries from Spain to the mountains of Guatemala. Closed his eyes, sat in silence. When he opened his eyes again they were fixed toward Valenzuela. "Small names, like La Penca in Nicaragua where that bomb blew away nine people at a press conference. A CIA operation all the way. Big names, like Martin Dobson."

"What about Dobson?" I said.

"Try a company named International Inter-Trade Corporation."

Paul Valenzuela said, "Dobson and that company have large investments and business interests in Guatemala?"

"By the ton. It was Dobson who set it all up in Guatemala. Arranged the network of generals, drug lords, CIA and State to keep everything the same down here, the people in line by murder, repression, low pay, hunger. But he made a big mistake. I was ex-CIA, he talked to me. I have the tapes, videos, documents."

State had made a mistake with Paul Valenzuela, got an independent instead of an Uncle José. Dobson had made another, found a maverick where he'd expected only an old CIA man out for himself. That was what scared them about the tape. Government can only go so far in breaking its own rules in the open. Then it has to hide what it does, the details people will believe. The Irishman had the details. He was the horse's mouth, authentic. One person who might be believed, could reach the public, the newspapers, even the courts. Americans believe the man who was there, the one in the know.

"Who is Dobson?" Paul said. "I mean, what position does he have in the government?"

"He's a big corporation man. Who the hell do you think your government works for?" The Irishman's violent gestures in the light of the burned-down candles painted black shapes across the walls and the high windows. "For fifteen years in the military and CIA I was a high-class hit man for the corporations, the banks, Wall Street. I made the world safe for the corporations, protected profits. That's the purpose of capitalist government. Once you realize that, it all makes sense."

Paul said, "It's the government looking out for business, especially big business."

"Hell, Valenzuela, the government *is* big business. Why did we go into Chile so fast? Because the people wanted us to? No, because ITT and the U.S. copper companies were scared of losing their hold. It's *change* the corporations don't like. A country that wants to own its own resources, use its own land. Nationalization and agrarian reform. No more cheap labor and raw materials. That's when the generals send troops to restore 'order,' when Washington goes in to restore 'democracy.' "

Paul Valenzuela's dark eyes were fixed on the gesticulating figure of the Irishman as he talked in the guttering light of the dying candles.

"Right here in Guatemala the U.S. overthrew the first and last elected president who cared shit about the people. Not because Arbenz had bought eastern bloc weapons, but because he talked about a forced buyout of United Fruit Company's unused land for the use of local farmers. United Fruit whistled, the CIA sent troops from Honduras. Bingo, a general in power in Guatemala City and no land for the *campesinos*. How about asking yourself how come after Nixon promised, and I quote, 'energy independence by 1980,' the U.S. dependence on foreign oil has gone up not down? Hey, the oil companies?"

He stood, walked to the high window that overlooked the invisible front lawn of the *finca*. He watched something move across the unseen lawn. "In the CIA I was told I was a freedom fighter. I *was* a freedom fighter. For the Fifth Freedom of business—the freedom to exploit. The right to make a buck no matter who it hurts or cheats or kills. Like Nestlé and its baby formula that's lethal to infants in backward countries. Free trade in a free market. Like growing and selling the coca and the poppy instead of food if that's what the market wants."

He walked back toward the long table with its bottles of wine that reflected the weak light of the burned down candles, poured cognac. Drank. Threw the glass against the wall.

"Mito!"

The cook-bodyguard came in with his team to clean up. The Irishman pinched out the stubs of the candles himself.

"But Dobson and Washington don't like the drugs their free market says get produced and sold. Free enterprise is bad this time. Wrong result. And with Panama and Nicaragua back in line, order restored in Central America, they don't need me anymore."

He called out in the Spanish I still couldn't decipher. Three of the *sicarios* in camouflage came in. "Only this evil drug dealer isn't going to roll over, run and hide like the Mexican and Escobar. There's maybe a little resistance in the banana world. They're so mad in Costa Rica the legislature has banned everyone connected to supplying the *contras* and the death squads. Maybe they'll ban the CIA next. Maybe other banana republics will give up growing bananas for U.S. Wheaties. Maybe if I give 'em a fight I can beat Martin Dobson. Make the U.S. public mad as hell at how the corporations manipulate everything for their own good. How about that idea?"

He gave us the grin. It looked more like the grin of a wolf, of a skeleton, of a dead man.

"The Major isn't coming down here," Paul said. "You don't have a deal with Washington."

The Irishman looked at me. "I want to talk to Valenzuela alone, Dan."

He nodded to his *sicarios*. They took me out.

32

A universe of light.

Shadows and the light.

Light across my face. Light that flashed, probed around the strange room. Shadows that moved behind it. A room I struggled to remember. Then remembered.

"Quick, American." The voice of the Israeli instructor.

My clothes held out from behind the flashlight in the dark room with the sharp black chill before a mountain dawn. A pair of hiking boots dropped at my feet at the edge of the bed. They had velcro fastenings. The flashlight picked out my hand as I struggled to put them on.

"Come."

Mito led us, the Israeli came behind us. Into the dark hall and down the stairs with no light anywhere in the hacienda. Only the flashlight bobbing and probing ahead. No sound beyond our booted footfalls on the polished wood and stone floors loud in the wide corridors and high rooms. The Irishman still sat in the dining room, alone at the long table, another bottle of the great Ausone and a half-full glass in front of him. The only light was an electric lantern, the drapes drawn. He wore the camouflage fatigues like the *sicarios* and a holstered pistol, an AK-47 with full banana clip against the table beside him.

"The Major coming?" I sat at the long table.

He smiled. No laugh, no grin, only a tight smile. "Just a little ahead of schedule."

"Not alone."

"Not alone." He drank the fine wine. "Name of the game, Danny boy, right?"

"And not unexpected."

Now he laughed the loud, ebullient laugh. "Christ, no, not unexpected. People who lie to millions every day, blow up their own journalists, hoodwink their allies and sucker their friends, don't have a word that's exactly good as gold."

"Why didn't you get out?"

He looked into the rich red wine. "We talked about it. We don't figure it makes much difference. None of us wants to rot in a Guatemalan or Colombian or even a U.S. prison. If we got that far alive." He drank. "Hell, maybe we'll beat 'em off."

"How many?"

"The villagers are down counting what noses they can now." He shook his head. "That's the part I hate. They'll take it out on the village. Especially if it's *kaibiles*."

"The Guatemalan army? Not the police and CIA?"

"The war on drugs, right? Army, special forces, the works. No need for death squads or the Company. I'm a drug lord."

"You've got the villagers, the guerrillas."

"The villagers have enough trouble, the guerrillas have to fight a real war." He poured another glass, enjoyed the play of the lantern light on the red stream. "Hell, maybe my run's just over. I think I knew it up in Beverly Hills. When you said it was Dobson. Those two CIA men. I can't blame my men, they never had a chance to be different any more than Sylvestre. I can blame myself. I did have the chance."

He drank. "I saw the world was a dog-eat-dog power struggle. The three secret words: Fuck you, Jack. I was different. Robin Hood, Captain Blood. The noble outlaw, the free pirate. But I'm just the same. Me, Dobson, the Major, the Medellin boys. We're all the same. You can't play with the devil without becoming the devil. The Irishman's horse. I watched the villagers grow the coca, my opium. They deserve a better chance. For life, not death. I can't go on. I can't go back. So it's time to go somewhere else."

He set his empty glass on the long table. "I was wrong. You're wrong. You know but you don't do. Valenzuela's right. He didn't know what he was doing, but he followed his gut. I've given him what I've got on Dobson and the rest. Names, places, papers, tapes, even home movies. Video of him and me. No need for you to know any of it. You don't carry weight, no one would listen, and it's safer that way."

"He carries weight?"

"He works for State at the embassy down here. It gives him credentials. It's something."

It wasn't much, but I didn't say that. Maybe it was enough. Maybe someone would listen.

"The guerrillas are moving out, they'll take Valenzuela, you and Aaron with them. The Israelis wouldn't want him found here."

"The guerrillas are running?"

"There aren't enough to make any difference, and the army'd hang 'em by their balls if they caught them. We're drug dealers, they'll be nicer to us." He looked at his empty glass. "They're good kids, they wanted to stay. I'm a hero around here. I like to think it's not all opium bucks. The Mexican border's two days away. The guerrillas have contacts with the Mayan refugees over the border. They'll get you on to Oaxaca. Then it's up to you."

"We can handle that."

The Irishman stood. A faint light ringed the rim of the mountains outside the window. He was a man who'd seen all the bad and changed into maybe not good but different. It might not even be too late. He held out an envelope.

"American money. You'll need it. You won't have guns. If you get caught you can claim to be prisoners. It might even help. Depends on who catches you."

Out on the dark lawn Paul Valenzuela and the Israeli Aaron stood with ten small men in ragged wool ponchos over grimy farm clothes. Paul and the Israeli both wore the same ponchos. Someone gave me one against the chill of the mountain morning. The small men were no more than boys, but all carried assault rifles. The Irishman shook hands with the oldest guerrilla.

"Rigoberto here speaks good Spanish, Valenzuela and Aaron can talk to him. Do what he tells you." He looked at Paul. "You have the stuff?"

Paul nodded. He was carrying nothing. Whatever the Irishman had given him would be hidden somewhere under his clothes.

The Irishman grinned. "Remember, anything you hear about tonight will probably be a lie. Hell, it *will* be a lie."

He laughed that big, open laugh and vanished into the predawn darkness.

We moved across the lawn and around the big house in the pitch black with the rim of dawn high on the peaks and ridges. Past the swimming pool and the garages and up through the slopes of coffee trees. The dawn lightened as we went up to meet it. The guerrillas watched the sky as we grew more and more visible. It was close to an hour before we topped the first high mountain shoulder above the coffee terraces. The thick forest stretched beyond, the dawn touched the valley below and the *finca*.

They came up the road, through the trees on both sides of the road, and down from the sky. Heavily armed, fully equipped, motorized. In wide-brimmed fatigue hats, berets, hat badges, shoulder patches, combat boots, blackened faces, ammo belts and light machine guns. The Guatemalan army.

"*Kaibiles.*" The Israeli had binoculars, pointed. "In the berets with the ammunition belts."

The helicopters came in from the valley floor below, half hidden against the mountain slopes on the far side of the *finca*. A ground-to-air missile from the *finca* exploded one chopper in a ball of fire brighter than the sun that was not yet up above the peaks and ridges. The other choppers banked away, landed on the coffee slopes between us and the hacienda as the Irishmen's invisible defenders opened fire and drove the army attackers to ground. I held out my hand for Aaron's field glasses.

Kaibiles jumped from the choppers, spread through the coffee to cut off escape up the slopes. The pilots climbed out, armed and alert but not moving from their aircraft. Two removed their flight helmets. Pale faces and tall, light hair and American flight gear.

"American pilots," I said, focused on a figure who climbed rom a smaller one that landed last. "It could be the Major."

Paul took the glasses. "We have to go back, Mr. Fortune, talk to them."

"We're the last people they want to talk to. They won't want any American witnesses."

The guerrillas were anxious. We were standing too long on the mountain, looking back. Aaron swept the valley below once more with his binoculars. "Your Irishman will need a great deal of luck to escape."

Below all signs of battle had vanished, the attackers under cover. The only war in sight was the burning helicopter, some trucks on the road, and the choppers below us with their pilot advisers leaning on them. To the north and above the *finca* where the road climbed on upward toward the hidden air strip, smoke and flame rose against the dawn sky. The village was burning.

"In most parts of the world you need some luck just to stay alive," I said.

The oldest guerrilla, Rigoberto, said, "We will go."

We went down through the forest into the next narrow valley and up again through the trees to the next high shoulder. Up and down, always among the tall forests, along narrow trails I could not have seen if the guerrillas hadn't been there to lead us. The mists rested on distant high peaks, the sun filtered through the thick forest cover the whole long day. Low to the east, high overhead, low to the west. We carried no food, but were given some in villages perched along the ridges. Food and some rest and information. There were no soldiers in the hills where we moved.

"You worked with the Irishman before?" Aaron the Israeli asked as we climbed and descended, walked and rested.

"We don't work with him at all."

"So? Emissaries, perhaps?"

"You might say."

"For me a job. Now I go home."

"No commitments?"

He shrugged. "I am the expert. I commit to my trade. To Israel, perhaps." His laugh was a bark. "Of course, to money for me, yes?"

The web of narrow trails. The mountain plots of corn and beans hacked from the forest. The silent villagers with food for us from their small supplies. The empty villages. So many empty villages. The villages of refugees across the border in camps, and of those relocated in new "model" villages "protected" by the army from the subversive guerrillas.

"The Irishman has given your friend papers of importance?"

"I don't know what the Irishman gave him."

We moved until we could move no farther, slept that night in an empty house in one of the abandoned villages. My shoulder throbbed, my ribs hurt, but they were both getting better. Moved on as the second dawn filtered through the trees. Up and down, the second day longer than the first, and then night again. Night and the border. A warning from Rigoberto that we were now in Mexico, the modern world, and must be careful of our safety and our money. A pistol for each of us. Handshakes. Thanks. The boy guerrillas turned back to the south. The three of us went on to the north with even more silent Indians. To sleep that night inside a barren refugee camp crowded with lost Mayans whose faces have not changed in a thousand years.

"This Major. He works for your State Department?"

"Indirectly."

In the morning there was a Mexican with an old pickup truck headed for Oaxaca. He had lived in Los Angeles, he knew *gringos* when he saw them, knew the lack of proper papers, had his duty to report us to the authorities. He also knew the value of guns and money, *gringo* money, and the fucking authorities could do their own fucking work, hey? In Mexico, guns and money will get you most things. Oaxaca, *Señores*? Hey, no fucking problem. Climb into my beautiful truck, *Señores.* Perhaps a little money now, the rest in Oaxaca, *si*? We were back in civilization.

By mid-afternoon we were in Oaxaca.

"I think we do not remain here," Aaron suggested. "The truck driver is not to be trusted."

An American charter pilot saw our money and guns and before the end of the third day we were in Mexico City and in a hotel which, while no improvement over the Irishman's *finca,* was a lot better than the forest or the human stench of the refugee camp. It did have one advantage over the *finca.* It had a telephone we could use. We agreed to say nothing of substance that could be picked up on a wire tap. Aaron didn't need the telephone, had gone straight to the Israeli embassy. Kay picked up on the first ring.

"Dan! Where are you? Are you all right? They found your car in Santa Monica. I've been worried sick. What were you doing in Santa Monica? How is your shoulder? Are you—"

I smiled in the distant hotel room. There is a thrill to being worried about. I told her what I could.

"Mexico City? What are you—?"

"I'll explain when we get home. What I want—"

"We?"

"Paul Valenzuela's with me, has been for a few days. Kay, listen, we want to get home as soon as we can. Wire money to the hotel. I love you, I'll call from the airport when we get in."

"Sergeant Chavalas called here yesterday. He's been worried too, said he has something important to tell you about Madrona."

"We'll be home tomorrow."

Paul called Esther. He spoke low, short, to the point. Maybe she'd been worried so long the pressure had left her too tight to react to joy. Or maybe joy had a different meaning now, between two different people in a different world.

"Meet us at the airport."

He hung up, said nothing about the call.

We ate, went to bed, my body battered but a lot better.

The Israeli, Aaron, did not reappear.

33

Esther Valenzuela stood apart from the crowd that waited behind the low wall for the passengers to come down the stairs that had been rolled out to meet the American Airlines flight from Dallas-Fort Worth. She had been there most of the day.

"I didn't want you to call the house. They could have the telephone tapped again."

She kissed him, shook hands with me, asked no questions. Even her clothes were different. Loose men's beige cavalry twill pants, blue work shirt like one of mine, running shoes. Her pale blonde hair tied back in a ponytail. The biggest difference was on her face. Her eyes no longer wide and nervous. I thought I saw the beginnings of creases around them, of lines from the corners of her mouth.

"No one followed you?"

"I don't think so. I haven't seen anyone since I've been here. I walked around while I waited."

"I'll go home with you to be sure," I said.

I called Kay. "I should be home in half an hour. Anything going on there?"

"No, Dan. Hurry, but be careful."

Esther drove the green Subaru, watched the rearview mirror. Paul told her most of what had happened on the way. He didn't tell her about what the Irishman had given him. She told us no one had been near the house since the day I left almost a week ago. She didn't know if Deputy Assistant Secretary of State Max Cole was even still in California. If any of them were.

"The policeman, Sergeant Chavalas, called a few times. That was all."

"We'll call him from the house," Paul said.

"Maybe we should go straight to him," I said.

"I want to go home first."

He didn't elaborate and I didn't push it. I told Esther about the two dead CIA men, the attack, and the trip back. Her face hardened. She was making the same mental trip the Irishman had. I hoped it wouldn't take the same long and tortured route. No one followed us from the airport or intercepted us on the way to the upper Eastside. No one waited on the street in front of the Conrads' house or in the driveway. They were waiting inside. The two in the dark suits with guns were in the entrance hall.

"They just walked in," her father said when he opened the door. His voice confused and a little stunned.

The Major leaned against the bookshelves in the study at the rear of the house. He was back in his civilian resort wear. Tall and lean in the navy blazer with the faint bulge where his Beretta was holstered under it. Pale gray slacks this time, a dark blue shirt. Proper Montecito uniform. Max Cole wasn't there. Martin Dobson sat again behind George Conrad's desk.

"You've had quite an adventure," Dobson said.

Paul walked to the desk. "Where's Secretary Cole?"

"We won't need him anymore."

"I work for him."

"You work for your country."

"Who do you work for, Mr. Dobson? It is Dobson, isn't it?"

"All of us work for the same country, Paul. My name is Dobson, yes."

"Or do we all work for you, Mr. Dobson? Does the country work for you?"

Dobson leaned back in the desk chair. He still wore his dark brown cashmere suit, guards tie, polished oxfords. The tie was skewed this time, but nothing else had changed. Either he had twenty of the same suits, ties and shoes, to save the bother of boring decisions every day, or he cared so little about such trivialities as clothes that we'd happened to catch him twice in the same outfit. He didn't notice me watching him. Not worried about me at all. Only about Paul Valenzuela.

"Are you actually going to believe an international drug dealer, Valenzuela? Can you really accept his story of what is going on? His twisted version of the world?"

I said, "How do you know what the Irishman's version of the world is, Dobson?"

He still didn't look at me. "I've had a number of dealings with him by now, Fortune. I know very well how he thinks."

"Whose version of the world should we listen to?"

The Major said, "The real one, Dan. What we all know."

"What we all know," I said, "is what we've all been taught."

Dobson waved the Major silent, looked from me to Paul. He didn't seem to have even seen Esther. "You listen to what is self-evident. To history, reason and experience. To the world itself. To what everyone agrees is true."

"You mean to the movers and shakers. The official line. In other words, to you."

Behind the heavy-rimmed glasses the eyes he turned on me were annoyed, impatient. The unexpected action of an unimportant young man had blown up out of all proportion. He needed to bring it to a close, remove the threat to his world, return the young man to the fold if that were at all possible. It occurred to him at this moment that the Irishman might not be his only opponent for Paul Valenzuela's soul.

"Who do you listen to, Fortune?"

It was a good question. We all listen to someone. "I guess I listen to the voice that rings true to what I see, answers my questions."

"And what do you see?"

"I see that you view government's job as protecting and maintaining property rights at home and abroad. The freedom to help the rich and your corporations to get richer."

"Party politics." He was more than annoyed, he was angry.

"All anyone has to do is look at who gets the real welfare in this country, who the government rescues when they go belly-up. Not mom and pop but Chrysler, right? I read a newspaper piece that put it in an interesting perspective. A worker getting minimum wage for forty hours a week since the birth of Christ wouldn't have earned as much as Lee Iacocca did in two years at Chrysler.

And those were bad years when Chrysler lost market share, profits went down, workers got laid off."

The Major said, "So Iacocca's smart."

"And the rest of us are dumb. I'll agree on that, Major."

Dobson glanced at his watch, looked toward the door into the back hall. He was waiting for something. "You don't believe in freedom, Fortune? You don't believe this is a free country?"

"It's free for you and your corporations. It's free for the government to create wars to scare the voters, distract them from what's really going on."

The Major said, "Drug dealers don't scare you, Dan?"

"Dobson scares me a lot more."

"He scares me," Esther Valenzuela said. Her female voice was like the sudden breaking of a sound barrier in the study. Everyone looked at her. Martin Dobson stared with the eyes of someone who saw her for the first time. Paul reached to hold her hand.

The Major said, "The Irishman and Madrona were *drug* kings. Drug sellers are despicable. What more do you need to know?"

"Were?" I asked. "Were drug dealers?"

The Major reached inside his jacket, gave me a folded page from inside the first section of yesterday's Los Angeles *Times.* The story appeared on an unimportant inside page.

MAJOR FIGURE IN DRUG CARTEL SLAIN

Guatemala: *American-born leader of the ruthless Medellin cartel was in charge of expanded heroin production coming from Central America.*

GUATEMALA CITY—Second in command to the slain Gonzalo Rodriguez Gacha, Jack O'Neill, known as the Irishman, has himself been slain in a successful operation against his stronghold in the Guatemalan mountains. According to government spokesmen, anti-narcotics units of the army guided by loyal Mayan villagers surprised the drug lord in a swift dawn raid.

The lightning attack overcame O'Neill's army of *sicarios*, and strong units of the Communist-led guerrillas working with the drug cartel to increase the opium poppy cultivation in the mountains. O'Neill himself was shot to death when he attempted to escape by helicopter soon after the

> raid began. The army suffered minor casualties, but the local village was burned by the guerrilla units to cover their escape across the mountains.
>
> O'Neill's American citizenship has raised some questions that were posed to Carl Foster, an aide at the U.S. Embassy in Guatemala City. Mr. Foster reserved comment pending an investigation.

There was a news photo that showed four bodies laid in a row on the ground like a catch of fish. What wounds I could see were all in the chest. Behind the bodies and the grimy, bandaged and tired soldiers, the *finca* had burned almost to the ground. The wrecks of two helicopters were visible. There had been a hell of a fight, and the picture had not been taken early. I recognized only one body: Mito the cook. The others could have been anyone.

Martin Dobson said, "Perhaps you should be afraid of me."

I handed the page back to the Major. "That Israeli must have contacted you from Mexico City. The only way you could have been here waiting."

"An intelligent man with experience in the real world. He recognized valuable information when he heard it."

The study door opened. One of the two men in suits came in. He closed the door, leaned against it, looked at the Major and shook his head. The Major looked at Dobson. Dobson turned to Paul Valenzuela. It was what he'd been waiting for.

"The Irishman gave you documents, tapes. They're not in your wife's car, at the airport or in this house. You must still be carrying them. We want them."

Esther's voice said, "Do you always get what you want?"

"Don't be as ridiculous as Fortune, Mrs. Valenzuela. May I have them now, please, Valenzuela."

"No."

The Major stepped away from the wall of books. Dobson held up his hand, studied Paul Valenzuela.

"Are you still going to believe the lies and ravings of a drug dealer and murderer? Or a bleeding-heart private detective who knows nothing of the realities and dangers of the world?"

"I don't judge what I believe by who says it, Mr. Dobson."

"Then how do you know what to believe?"

"Like Fortune, I believe what explains the facts, answers the questions. What I've seen down in Guatemala fits with everything the Irishman and Fortune said."

Dobson nodded to the Major. "Search them. All three."

I looked at the man who leaned on the door. He had his gun in his hand. So did the Major.

"I'm sorry, Mrs. Valenzuela, but we don't have time for the niceties, and your husband leaves me no choice. Unless he wants to give me the material now and save a great deal of fuss."

Paul said, "I don't have it with me, Mr. Dobson. I'm not that stupid."

"I hope you are that stupid," Dobson said. "Anything else could be a great deal more stupid. Major, Purvis."

They searched Paul first, then me. We stripped, leaned against the wall while the Major and the CIA did a complete search. Smugglers hide contraband anywhere they can. As far as they knew the Irishman's information could be on microfilm.

"Nothing." the Major said.

Esther Valenzuela stepped toward the Major. She stood in front of him without expression, removed her twill trousers, her blue work shirt. Her bikini underwear would not have hidden a page. The Major patted her down, stepped back.

"Everywhere, Major," Dobson said.

"The underwear," the Major said. "Lean against the wall and spread your legs."

The Major completed his search. Shook his head to Dobson. Esther Valenzuela dressed without expression. Paul and I were already dressed again. Dobson looked at each of us in turn the way a professor looks at a stupid class.

"I really hoped you wouldn't make it necessary for me to—"

The new voice came from outside the study. "I hope you two have permits for those guns. Because if you don't, you're both under arrest right now."

The outside door into the garden was open, Gus Chavalas stood in the opening. Both the Major and the CIA man turned their guns on him.

"I know you two aren't that stupid," Chavalas said.

Uniformed policemen stood outside each window, pushed in through the door from the back hall behind the CIA man.

34

Chavalas came into the room. The Major and the CIA man lowered their guns.

"Smart move. Now hand them to the officer who will pass among you. We've already collected the other guy outside. Pick 'em up, Jack."

"We have permits," the Major said. "Purvis is CIA, your captain—"

"Then there's nothing to worry about. But we'll just check. Wouldn't want any more guns disappearing."

Martin Dobson said, "This is not your business. I—"

"Go ahead, Jack," Chavalas said, watched as the patrolman walked to the Major. "Any of you going to say we don't have the right or the authority?"

They said nothing. Chavalas nodded. "You okay, Dan? Mr. and Mrs. Valenzuela?"

Dobson said, "They're perfectly all right. We've already spoken to your captain, he has agreed to cooperate fully, I—"

"Things have changed," Chavalas said. "Who the hell are you?"

"Who I am is none of your business. I think—"

I said, "His name's Martin Dobson. He's more or less behind this whole thing." I told Chavalas about the State-CIA-drug king network in Latin America, the Dobson part of it in Guatemala.

Everything the Irishman had told us and what had happened to him.

Dobson said, "Everything Fortune has told you is a complete fabrication, as are the slanders of the dead drug dealer." He did not move from Mr. Conrad's desk, sat as comfortably as he would have at his own desk. "What we're here about is a matter of national security as I explained to your captain. Major Hill is on special assignment for the State Department, Mr. Purvis is with the Central Intelligence Agency. As you see—"

Chavalas said, "You know, I'll bet you've got a connection to International Inter-Trade Corporation. An officer, maybe? On the board?"

I said, "What makes you think Dobson is with International Inter-Trade Corporation, Sergeant? Who are they?"

"They're a big conglomerate," Chavalas said. "Headquarters in New York, Dallas, London, Caracas, and, make a note, Guatemala City. Plants, ships, warehouses. In food products, chemicals, mining, textiles, shipping. You name it, they own it."

"What food products?"

"Coffee, sugar, bananas, for starters. Then all kinds of manufactured products all over the world. Just happens to have food processing plants in Guatemala. Mines in Guatemala. Is building a big pesticide plant in Guatemala. Its plants, mines, ships, farm holdings are in the names of its subsidiaries and divisions. Inter-Trade itself seems to be a holding company. That's why the public never hears about it."

"The public never hears about most corporations," I said.

Dobson said, "What has all this got to do with us, or with you, Sergeant? It is Sergeant?"

"Sergeant Chavalas. What it's got to do with me, and maybe with you, is that we traced the warehouse out in Goleta where Sylvestre Madrona was killed to Inter-Trade Corporation. The Ohio trucker is a subsidiary of a subsidiary."

"What warehouse, Sergeant?" Dobson said.

"The one Fortune saw you and Major Hill come out of. The one the Major and the CIA men carried Madrona's body from to dump at our bird refuge."

"Fortune is a liar and an associate of a known international drug lord. He barely escaped the attack in Guatemala that killed his gangster boss."

"His story against yours, that what you mean?"

"More or less."

"And you with the best lawyers money can buy. No contest, right?" Chavalas shook his head. "But that's not what I came about. We found some other stuff about the Madrona killing, I came to pick up Major Hill there."

The Major folded his arms where he stood in front of the books. The CIA man looked shocked, almost said something. Paul and Esther had a gleam in their eyes.

Dobson said, "Exactly what does 'pick up' mean?"

"Take in. Hold and talk to. Bring in for questioning. Whatever."

"You mean not quite arrest. On what charge, Sergeant?"

"Well, assuming they do have permits for those guns, the way they were using them to threaten and intimidate peaceful citizens is pretty close to assault. But let's just settle on suspicion of murder."

Dobson's voice was icy. "I've told you Major Hill is on a special assignment for the State Department. It is government business, damn it. Now—"

I said, "The government doesn't have the right to go around shooting anyone it wants even if it'd like to have that right."

"Let me handle it, Dan," Chavalas said. "But he's right, you know? Even we cops have to face a hearing every time we shoot someone."

The Major was angry. "We aren't any two-bit local police!"

Chavalas said. "When you can be placed at the scene of a murder in my jurisdiction, have a motive for the shooting, and participated in a coverup to obstruct a police investigation, you're going to have to answer questions. Especially when you denied even being in town at the time. That's going to really worry a jury."

Dobson's voice was still ice. "Major Hill was under direct orders from Washington to do whatever he did. He is a soldier, he follows orders. In the national interest."

"You know, I'm getting tired of that phrase," Chavalas said. "I don't care whose interest a crime is committed in. I arrest people who commit crimes. Other guys sort it all out."

The Major said, "It's Fortune's word against my company and the State Department that I was even here."

"Oh, you were here, Major. We finally found some prints in the warehouse and on Madrona when we dug deep. We matched them to your Army records, so let's go down to my office and talk."

"My prints? Where?"

Chavalas smiled. "All I have to do is read you your rights, give you a call to your lawyer, and let the D.A.'s people take it from there. Jack, read the guy at the door his rights too, we'll take him in, check out that weapon and his papers." He turned to Paul and Esther. "I want you two to come along. I already got Dan's story, but I'd like you to give me your stories where they concern Madrona and the Major."

Dobson still sat behind the desk. "You don't really think anything will come of this, do you, Sergeant?"

Chavalas looked at Dobson while his men read the Major and the CIA man their rights, then escorted them to the side door. Paul and Esther followed the police out.

"As I said, Mr. Dobson, that's not my job. You private government types have lost a few trials recently. We'll maybe keep the Major and the CIA out of Valenzuela's hair for a while. We're still looking into your connection to the warehouse. I could be back."

"I'll alert our lawyers."

Chavalas followed his men and the Valenzuelas out and across the yard. In the study, Martin Dobson sat at the desk and stared at the closed side door. I sat in the leather chair that faced the desk. Dobson finally sighed.

"Such stupidity. No wonder we never get anywhere anymore. Too many petty obstructions."

"Is everyone and everything only a cog in your corporate wheel, Dobson? What happened to the great quest for democracy?"

His face said he was becoming tired of me. "What has Valenzuela done with what the Irishman gave him, Fortune?"

"I don't even know the Irishman gave him anything."

He raised his glasses to rub his eyes with a thumb and forefinger. "Fortune, please, don't be so stupid."

"You know, Dobson, for a smart man you don't think. I said I don't *know* that the Irishman—"

"For God's sake, Aaron told us—"

"Aaron doesn't *know* the Irishman gave Paul anything either. He never saw anything, I never saw anything. The Irishman said he gave Paul proof of your dealings, but we don't know he did."

He thought about it. "How do I know that's the truth?"

"You don't."

"That's a problem, isn't it?"

"Whom can you trust?"

He continued to analyze his problem even as he talked. One part of his mind distant, the other part in the study with me.

"Those who depend on us, who have something to gain."

"Self-interest," I said. "That's how you make people believe what isn't true. The same way Hitler made the Germans believe what wasn't true. Most people are either afraid or indifferent. They care only about their own interest, actively or passively. The Irishman said it pretty well: the three secret words: Fuck you, Jack."

"Self-interest is our essence, Fortune. It has accounted for all progress."

"Too much self-interest is the *problem*. Unless we can beat it, we're all not going to make it. Hell, if the Major has to think of his self-interest, *you* may not make it."

He pushed the chair back from George Conrad's desk, stood up. Whatever decision he'd had to make, he'd made.

"The State Department has very good lawyers too, Fortune. The Major is in no jeopardy."

"What's the law for, Dobson? To keep the rest of us in line?"

"The law is to keep peace and order."

"And if the law blocks what you want?"

"The government changes the law."

"In whatever country?"

He came around the desk, headed for the side door. "In whatever country."

He went out through the house, probably to thank George and Ethel Conrad for their hospitality. He paid attention to form, mended fences, maintained his power base.

I called Kay. "It's going to be a little longer."

"How much longer? I'm only human."

"Keep thinking about that. Get someone to drop my car off at police headquarters, okay?"

"I'll bring it down."

"Stay and work. It could be all day."

35

The Major lounged in Chavalas's office. He was in a hard chair but he didn't look uncomfortable, smiled at me. An assistant D.A. did look uncomfortable. He scowled at his watch as I came in. Then he stood and left. The Valenzuelas weren't there.

"Down the hall dictating their statements," Chavalas said. "Our good Major refuses to answer any questions without advice of counsel, has done absolutely nothing illegal, and anyway anything he did was under government orders and in the national interest. That about sum it up, Major?"

The Major looked at his watch.

Chavalas said, "A representative from the State Department is on his way up from L.A., should be here any minute to post bond, spirit the Major away."

"In a murder case?"

"The captain and the D.A. don't feel we have enough to make a charge. We're calling him a material witness. There've been a lot of phone calls."

"I'll bet," I said. "The CIA men?"

"Checked them out, let them go."

The Major said, "I'm surprised you people had that much intelligence."

I said, "You show him what you have yet?"

"Not until we have to."

"Can I see it?"

Chavalas picked up a manila file folder, handed it across his desk. My statements were first after the status sheet, all three of them: the night of the warehouse; the shooting at my house when Claudia Nervo died; the night of Paul's disappearance from the motel and the attack on me. Last were the reports on the warehouse investigation, the physical evidence from Madrona's body and the warehouse. The warehouse trace showed the Omaha trucking company that leased the warehouse was a subsidiary of an Omaha food distribution corporation owned by a subsidiary of International Inter-Trade Corporation. There was no indication that Inter-Trade officials had any knowledge of the day-to-day operations of the food distribution firm much less the trucking company. The physical evidence against the Major consisted of two poor fingerprints of his left hand taken from a plastic envelope that held the shipping invoice on a crate inside the warehouse, and a single thumbprint on the glass crystal of Madrona's watch.

"You've been working," I said.

The Major said, "He's been wasting his time. Why don't you go out and catch criminals, Sergeant? You know about criminals? Gangsters, thieves, drug addicts, muggers, perverts?"

"Not murderers, Major?" Chavalas said.

"If I did shoot Madrona, and I don't say I did, he was a drug dealer, I was working for State and the CIA to stop his illegal activities. Fortune didn't see me shoot anyone. You don't have the gun or any motive except duty. I'm a soldier."

The prints in the warehouse backed my story of what I saw, but what had I seen? Maybe the Major had gone to the warehouse later, I had made a mistake about who I saw. The print on the watch proved the Major had known Madrona. The Major would admit he had known Madrona, could have touched his watch anytime. Long before or even after Madrona had been killed by someone else.

The Major said, "You know about the Classified Information Procedures Act? The Attorney General can refuse to let even a court see sensitive data. Classified data on our intelligence operations all through Latin America is in this all the way. A judge would have to dismiss. I couldn't get a fair trial."

"That's for the lawyers," Chavalas said. "I just arrest people when I have reasonable evidence to think they committed a crime in Santa Barbara."

I said, "I know you shot Madrona. You know I know. You and the CIA tried to kill me. You set up the Irishman."

He leaned toward me in the hard chair. "Tell me about Walt Enz and the other CIA guy. Your Irishman killed them. You were there. In a war people get killed."

"He wasn't my Irishman. He was as wrong as you are. Almost as wrong as Dobson."

"Who's right, Fortune? You?"

"I don't know who's right or who's wrong. I know it's not a law of nature or God that there should be luxuries for some and not necessities for all. I know that neither nature nor God says the generals live in the *fincas* and the peasants in the huts. You remember Che Guevara? He went down to a Latin American country to give it a government his country wanted it to have. You, State and the CIA go down into Latin American countries to give them the governments your country wants. Martin Dobson went down to make sure a Latin country kept the government his corporation wants. What's the difference between you, Che and Dobson?"

"He's dead and I'm alive," the Major said. "That's one difference. The other is I'm for *us*, and he was for *them*."

"He was for his *us*. That's no difference at all."

"We're right and they're wrong! That's the difference."

"Yeah, that's the difference." I stood. "I'll drive Paul and Esther home when they're finished here, Sergeant."

Martin Dobson stood in the corridor with the uncomfortable assistant D.A. and three manicured men in three-piece suits. They didn't notice me. Paul and Esther Valenzuela came out of a room along the corridor. As we passed Chavalas's office, Dobson, the corporation lawyers and the assistant D.A. had been joined by two more men in dark business suits. One of the newcomers was Max Cole. They were all gesturing at Chavalas and the assistant D.A. while the Major looked on. We left them to their legal dance, went down to find my Tempo.

It was parked half a block up toward Garden Street. There was no limousine outside, no one followed us up the quiet streets of the upper Eastside. Mr. and Mrs. Conrad opened the front door before we were out of the car. They were substantial people who had always seen the rightness of the world they lived in. The last weeks had been hard on them.

"We were worried," Ethel Conrad said.

"Is everything all right?" George asked.

Esther said, "Everything is all right."

"We're fine, Mr. Conrad," Paul smiled.

Inside we sat in the large, comfortable living room that seemed like a room I'd first seen a hundred years ago. Ethel Conrad went to get coffee and cookies. George sat and watched his daughter and son-in-law. He looked from one to the other like a man who had never seen either of them before. They held hands on the couch.

I said, "Where is the stuff you got from the Irishman?"

"It's safe," Paul said. "I expected someone would try to get it. I took care of that when we were on our way home."

"Is it in Santa Barbara?"

He shook his head. "I think they're convinced you don't know anything about it, and it's safer to keep it that way. Even Esther doesn't know where it is."

"What are you going to do with it?"

He clasped his hands between his knees, sat forward, his face serious. "It exposes names, dates, details of the way Dobson and his corporations, the government and military down there, and our government, control Guatemala. Some people think that's our government's job."

Ethel Conrad returned with the coffee and a large plate of home-baked cookies. She poured while George Conrad passed the plate. He had listened as we talked, total incomprehension on his face. Questions about the government's job had never occurred to him. Everyone knew the government's job.

"It's a blend of Guatemalan and Nicaraguan coffees," Ethel Conrad said proudly. "I have it blended specially."

Paul looked at Esther, squeezed her hand. She smiled at him. The smile of a woman who had not existed a month ago. She had found the adult woman inside her, the woman who knew what she was going to do with the rest of her life.

Paul said, "I went into the foreign service to try to help my fellow Latinos if I could. That's what I'm going to do by exposing the Irishman's details. I know it's a bigger fight, but one man can only do one battle at a time."

"They won't let you stay in the foreign service. They won't listen to you.

Esther said, "If his superiors won't listen we'll go elsewhere, Mr. Fortune. The newspapers, magazines, television."

"You'd better get some help, some powerful organizations to back you."

Paul nodded. "It's what we plan to do first. Make contact with some government watchdog groups."

Esther said, "The first thing we do is leave Santa Barbara. Go somewhere no one knows us."

I finished my coffee, stood. "Keep in touch when you can."

I thanked the Conrads for the coffee. Paul and Esther walked me to the door. She held out a check.

"This will cover everything," she said, "except all our thanks. I don't think I'd have Paul back without you."

"I know you wouldn't," Paul said. "We'll try to write you. I suppose we'll have to come back for the trial."

"There won't be a trial," I said.

I went out to my Tempo, drove to the end of the block, made a U-turn, headed back past the Conrad's big house toward Mission Street and the freeway. Paul waved from the path to the front steps. The Conrads watched from the open door of the house. I turned on Mission for the freeway and they disappeared behind the cars and delivery trucks parked on the quiet block.

You always wonder at the end of a case. I had a strong hunch Paul and Esther would do exactly what they said they would. They might even make someone listen, make a difference. It was nice to think about as I turned onto the freeway at Mission to head home to Summerland and Kay.

I pulled off the freeway at Carillo.

When I'd driven out of the upper Eastside street there had been only one delivery truck. A brown United Parcel Service truck.

Flames still licked the torn and shattered Subaru when I turned the corner. Sirens sounded across the distance. On the street the only sound in the vacuum after the explosion was the screaming of Ethel Conrad down on the smoldering lawn.

I had seen the smoke to the east when I left the freeway, but I hadn't heard the explosion. Only in my head as I turned into the street where the pillar of black smoke rose from the burning metal and paint and oil that had been a green Subaru.

George Conrad tried to get close to the burning wreck in the driveway of his house. His face was blackened, his hands burned, but the fierce heat kept him away. He looked at me with eyes that had not yet begun to understand what had happened. A short circuit in his brain that only allowed reaction to the immediate command—get them out, save them, drag them to safety. I saw it many times on the old buckets during the war after an air attack, the instant action without thought or comprehension.

"Are they—?"

Conrad searched for a way closer, brushed smoke from his face, sucked at his burned hands. His suit coat was already burned, caught fire again as he went in too close. I had to pull him away, beat out the flames on his sleeve. He hadn't been a young man before, and now he was an old man. He looked at me with pain blinding his eyes.

"The package came. Paul got their bags. Esther had packed this morning. They wouldn't call, they would write. Paul waved. The car exploded."

He dropped to the lawn, his legs splayed like a baby's. His burned hands clung to the grass as he stared at the flames. Ethel Conrad had stopped screaming, moaned ten yards away across the lawn. The fire engines sirened into the street. Paramedics and police behind them. Gus Chavalas's unmarked car was last. The firemen had the flames out within minutes, moved closer in on the smoldering hulk. The police kept the curious back. The paramedics ran to Mr. and Mrs. Conrad while they waited. Chavalas stood beside me.

"They were in there?"

"I didn't know they were going to leave so soon. There was a package. It had to be what the Irishman gave him. From Mexico City, I'd guess. Not an original idea, easy to figure out."

"Ignition bomb?"

"Maybe, but I don't think so. They wanted those papers, must have been watching."

"Remote control?"

"You pick your time."

The paramedics continued to work on George Conrad's burns,

Ethel Conrad's shock. One of them went to call from their truck. The fire captain talked to the senior patrol policeman who came over to Chavalas.

"No chance, Sarge. Captain says he can't even tell how many were in there. They'll have to scrape—"

"The parents are over there, Jack."

The patrolman walked away. The paramedics packed up their equipment and went back to their truck as a car drove up and a gray-haired man with a white coat over his suit trousers hurried to the Conrads. Their family doctor called by the paramedics. There was nothing more to do but send the people home and clean up the debris. I walked with Chavalas to his car.

"We'll trace the bomb," he said.

"It won't do any good." I looked back across the lawn. The firemen were carefully pulling the blackened metal of the car apart. "They couldn't let Paul come out with solid evidence. Someone might have believed even a low-level State Department man, started an investigation, asked real questions. The bomber saw the package, saw them getting away. A two-bit hired hand."

Chavalas looked back too. "We'll find him, Dan. The captain will back me this time."

"It won't solve a damn thing."

We both watched the firemen pick something from the charred hulk. Something skeletal. Part of a suitcase maybe, or of a human body. Chavalas got into his car.

"You better be careful, Dan."

"What could I do to them, make a speech? A two-bit private eye they'll discredit without working up a sweat? No documents, no concrete evidence, no proof of anything? Write a book? Who would listen, Sergeant? The Irishman said it himself—we don't really want to know who runs our lives or how they do it. We want to have a ball, get ours."

Chavalas drove away without saying anything more. I went to my Tempo. The doctor and two of the firemen were helping George and Ethel Conrad into their fine old house. I wondered how they would explain the murders of their children to themselves.

I went home to Kay.